I0657407

In The Available Light

By Grayson Scott

Published by The Storyteller Society LLC (USA)
REGISTERED TRADEMARK - MARCA REGISTRADA

COPYRIGHT 2023 BY THE STORY TELLER SOCIETY
All Rights Reserved

ISBN #: 979-8-218-17648-8

PUBLISHERS NOTE:

This book is a work of fiction. Names, characters, places, and incidents are the product of the author's imagination or are used factiously, and any resemblance to actual persons, living or dead, business establishments, events, or locals is entirely coincidental.

Without limiting the rights under the copyright above, no part of this publication may be reproduced, stored in, or intended into a retrieval system or transmitted in any form or by any means (electronic, mechanical, photocopying, recording, or otherwise) without the prior written permission of both the copyright owner and the above publisher of this book.

The scanning, uploading, and distribution of this book via the internet or other means without the publisher's permission is illegal and punishable by law. Please purchase only authorized electronic editions, and do not participate in or encourage electronic piracy of copyrighted materials. Your support of authors and artists everywhere is appreciated.

A VERY SPECIAL THANK YOU

The older I get, the more I realize that stories (like all of *us*) need inspiration and guidance beyond the limited boundaries of their upbringing. So, dear reader, if you would afford me just a few moments to tell you the story of *this* story and to thank those that helped bring it to life:

I first outlined what would become "In The Available Light" in the late 90s as a script for a film that died, as many scripts do, long before seeing the light of day. Yet the story stayed with me through the years, even though it was buried deep within my ever-growing bucket list.

I picked it up several years later and wrote the first draft of the book. During those days, as I was fumbling around in the dark, Danene Yokeum was tremendously helpful in getting the first several chapters into shape. As the story transitioned from script to book, the biggest change was moving the location from Monterey, California, to Colorado Springs, Colorado. In the meantime, a few other writing opportunities appeared on the horizon, so, once again, this 'pet project' of mine was shelved.

A few years later, I happened to stumble upon it again, backed up on an old hard drive that I was clearing out. Surprisingly, I found the story of much more value than I had remembered. This time, I finished the book, and with the help of an old friend, Kelley Ryan, I finally had a finished manuscript of which I was incredibly proud.

Yet no one would read it. No one. Not my family, not even my agent at the time. The manuscript sat on a shelf in my house for years, gathering dust, and every time I saw it, I got depressed. I saved the file one last time and walked away from it, and writing completely discouraged.

Ten years later, as I was on the metro going into Washington D.C., desperately looking for something to read, I discovered it again. I had been through every book on my iPad two or three times when I stumbled across this story, abandoned to the nether regions of my iBook bookshelf. In fact, I had completely forgotten that I had turned it into an eBook at all. For lack of anything better to read, I opened it up and secretly hoped it would be terrible, thereby validating my reasoning for no longer being able to write.

Please don't think it is purely ego when I say: I loved it, which was a problem.

It had been so long that it was like reading a story by someone else that seemed to know my every thought. A few days later (I am only slightly embarrassed), I sat in my room, crying at the ending.

Soon after, I showed it to Kristin Yates, whom I worked with at the time, who just happened to be a fantastic editor. I asked if she would look at it and give me some feedback. Remember that I fully expected her to smile and say 'sure' and never hear back from her again on the subject. To my surprise, the very next day, she returned and said she loved it as much as I had. The fact that someone had FINALLY taken the time to read it was more encouraging than I can possibly express.

After a few weeks of working through some of the remaining kinks with Kristin, we assembled the book you now hold in your hands. Let me just say that without Kristin's incredible talent for encouragement, it may have been *another* ten years before I (or anyone else) discovered this story again. So if you hate the story, blame me; if you love it, thank her.

Ultimately, I am finally publishing this book for no reason other than my love for the story. I hope you enjoy it as much as I have.

This book is dedicated to my
beautiful daughters, Ciera and Ti'ana.
I love you both more than you will ever know.
Well… at least until you have children of your own.

"I've tried so hard to tell myself that you're gone/
But though you're still with me, I've been alone all along."
- "My Immortal" by Evanescence
From the album *Fallen* (2003)

"I want to look at life in the available light."
- "Available Light" by RUSH
From the album *Presto* (1989)

There is something about hospital hallways in the dark early morning when the

only light and sound come from the humming white fluorescent lights that can drain hope from a person. Motion sensors placed strategically throughout the deep catacombs of hospitals provide sterile light only where needed and create the illusion of being trapped between two black silent caves as people wait silently for the news that their lives will never be the same.

Mark Soderlind sat on one of the few small benches in the hallway in an isolated part of the hospital with his seven-year-old son, Alan, asleep in his lap. The boy was dressed in his pajamas, with no shoes or socks, because Mark hadn't had time to dress him after the paramedics had arrived. A nurse had given them a blue blanket an hour earlier, and Mark had used it to keep Alan warm, even though Mark was now sweating between the child's heat and the blanket.

Mark could not feel anything inside his own mind. He simply held onto Alan, finding comfort in his soft heartbeat and the steady pace of his lungs expanding and contracting as he slept.

Other than the boy, everything was a fog. He did not know what was happening or what shape his life would take once this night was over, and he couldn't bear to think about it. Mark simply stared at the bulletin board across the hallway from him, reading over the random hospital announcements. There was a red-trimmed piece of paper on the bottom right of the bulletin board that his eye was drawn to. It simply said, "Palmer Hospital welcomes gestational diabetes speaker, Dr. Mary Arnold," with a pleasant-looking woman smiling back at him from a headshot in the lower half of the paper. Mark guessed she was in her late forties. She had dark brown hair pulled back tightly and wore the standard white lab coat with her name embroidered in blue cursive letters on the front. She looked confident and secure in herself, someone that could be trusted. She looked happy.

Mark wondered if the woman was anything like the photo or if the split second it took for the film to capture the image had wiped away years of sorrow, anger, and heartbreak. Were there really people in the world that were ever as happy as they appeared in their photos? Are the snapshots left behind long after we're gone nothing but manufactured lies? A grand farce proclaims to future generations a joy not experienced in real life, thereby setting up another generation to believe there was a chance for something more than what really existed.

Maybe the older photos, from a century ago in black and white, where everyone was more somber and honest. Those sepia-toned images told a much different story than modern ones. They spoke plainly and honestly that life is hard and, as humans, we must work against all odds to gain even a little semblance of peace. That was the truth of life, Mark thought. Even when we gain a little of what we consider to be precious, like the boy who slept so peacefully in his lap, you had to fight for it to keep it. Peace or joy did not come without a fight, and the peace his son would now have had come at a terrible price that Mark had been willing to pay.

His thoughts were interrupted by footsteps in the distance coming toward him. The lights at the opposite end of the long hallway came to life as a doctor approached Mark and Alan. There had been other places in the hospital he could have waited for the news, but he did not want to be around other people tonight, not while he sat in the middle of this storm that raged around him.

Mark stood slowly and laid Alan on the padded bench, repeatedly covering him with the blanket. The boy stirred but did not wake up.

For a brief moment, Mark marveled at how fragile and unprotected his son was, as all children are, and how completely dependent the boy was on him. This sad realization was the only time during the evening that Mark felt he would lose himself and give in to the emotions building up, so he rose from the chair, pinching at his nose and eyes to stop the tears from flowing again.

He pushed the emotions back down and walked away from Alan, meeting the doctor several feet away.

The doctor spoke in hushed tones, so the conversation remained private even in the tiled hallways. The surgery was over, and the doctor explained what had occurred behind closed doors for the last hour and a half. Mark tried to listen and comprehend, but the doctor rattled off so many words that Mark did not understand that he quickly lost track of what was being said.

Mark looked back towards Alan and saw him sitting up, rubbing his eyes, and yawning as large as his small mouth would allow. The boy looked over at his father, still in the embrace of sleep, then laid back down on the bench again, knowing his father was close and that he was safe.

Mark turned back to face the doctor and was introduced to the police officers patiently waiting.

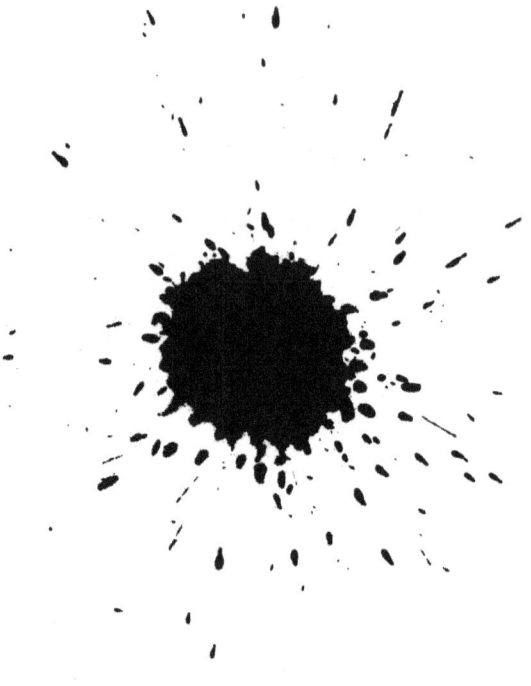

⁓ CHAPTER ONE ⁓

Mark woke up knowing that something was wrong. Sitting straight up in bed, fully awake and breathing shallowly, he opened his eyes wide and listened for any movement in the house. The early morning silence was just as it should be, but he could not shake the feeling that something was wrong. Reaching the chair next to the bed, Mark grabbed the t-shirt he had taken off the night before and quickly pulled it over his head as he stood up. Walking around the end of the bed in his boxers, Mark moved quickly into the hallway toward Alan's room.

The shirt still stunk from the restaurant: a combination of discarded food, bleach, and sweat that Mark smelled of every day after his shift. He had worked at the restaurant for fifteen years, and the smell was still as repugnant as the first day.

He threw open the door to Alan's room, expecting to see the boy asleep, tangled up in his bed sheets. The bed was empty, and the house remained silent.

"Alan?" Mark yelled back into the hallway.

Moving quicker, he went to the bathroom one door down from Alan's room and found that it, too, was empty. Looking in the laundry basket, Mark saw that Alan's bed clothes were nowhere to be found.

"Alan!" Mark yelled, this time louder than before, while he looked down the stairs to the bottom floor of the house. The living room was as silent as the rest of the house, unchanged from last night, except for the bright morning sunlight from the front picture window.

Mark ran back into the bedroom and put on his pants while looking outside and into the backyard, which revealed a fresh, crisp layer of undisturbed snow at least two inches thick.

Looking down at the clock on his bedside table, Mark saw that it was 7:34. They would have to leave for school in the next ten minutes to make it on time. Looking over at the bed, Mark could see where Shannon had made her half of the bed neatly before she had left.

"Alan! Where are you?" Mark yelled again, not able to hide the concern that was beginning to grow in his voice and the pit of his stomach.

Going down the stairs, Mark checked the front door and found it locked. Opening it, he felt the biting Colorado winter air forcing its way into the warm house.

"ALAN!" Mark yelled out the front door as he fumbled with his boots, noticing that Alan's small boots were still next to his by the front door.

"What, Dad?" A voice said behind him.

Mark turned around with his coat half on, wearing one boot, to see Alan still in his pajamas in the kitchen with a single headphone pulled away from his ear, eating a bowl of cereal at the kitchen island counter.

Wordlessly, Mark felt the pressure inside of him release, and for the first time that morning, he could breathe. Taking off his jacket and single boot, Mark joined Alan in the kitchen, where they ate silently until it was time to leave.

* * *

Fillmore Hill in Colorado Springs easily rivaled any of the famous hills in San Francisco, except drivers dealt with the seasonal bonus of ice and snow in winter. Because of the incline, most of the city trucks that dumped sand and salt on the road to provide traction waited until the rest of the city was taken care of before trying to tackle the monster hill. Until the city got around to it, (if they got around to it at all), it was nothing more than an ice rink on a steep grade.

Mark and Alan walked down Fillmore Hill every morning and then back up at night. Walking down the hill was a problem only when the snow was too deep for Alan; Mark would carry him on his back while he carefully picked his steps. At night, the process was the same. Mark would carry the small boy up the hill, often to find Alan asleep, resting quietly on his shoulder when they reached the top.

Alan's school was only a few blocks south of the hill, and Mark's restaurant was a few blocks north. With some cosmic luck, their schedules lined up most days, enabling Mark and Alan to spend the morning and early evening walking up and down a hill that many others in town felt nervous climbing, even in a car.

Their only car was a 2007 Taurus, which they bought for Shannon and her commute to north Denver. If the trip were only three hours, one way, it would be considered a good day. It was a situation that neither Mark nor Shannon liked, but to keep their house, they did what they had to and hoped that someday something would change.

Mark reached the bottom of the hill and let Alan off his back. Alan smiled and held his father's gloved hand as they crossed the street, just as they did every morning. Thankful that the morning had not turned out as cold as it could have been, Mark unzipped his jacket a little, feeling the sweat building up inside. Alan was getting bigger, and Mark wondered how long he could carry him on days like this. When the day came, Mark knew he would miss it. The phrase "You never know the last time you will pick up your child" was something Mark was very aware of, and Mark cherished every moment while he could.

They walked along silently. Neither of them ever felt the need to fill up the space between them with pointless chatter; the silence and the feel of the tiny hand in his was all the connection that was needed.

"Bye, Dad," Alan said, letting go as soon as they arrived at his elementary school. Alan ran into the building as the bell rang. Mark walked away thinking of the school's silence after the bell rang, as all the tiny humans finally made their way inside. Within minutes, the absolute chaos of the playground was transformed into an empty shell, with only the sound of the highway in the distance.

Mark turned around and made his way to the restaurant, hoping that he would arrive early enough to get to the dishes the night crew typically left piled in the sinks.

The idea of being anything more than a dishwasher never occurred to Mark; he first got the job in his mid-twenties, and he met Shannon there when she was in college working as a waitress.

As was the case in most restaurants, the dishwasher was so low on the food chain that, at most times, he was invisible. Yet, for some reason, Shannon would talk to Mark more than any other woman ever had. They would stand outside during their breaks, and she would smoke while Mark leaned against the building and said very little but quietly listened to whatever was on her mind.

Shannon was not attractive in the traditional sense of the word. Although she did everything "right" with her makeup and clothes and didn't gain weight no matter what she ate, she simply was not attractive. The nights they talked in the alleyway behind the restaurant, Mark began to see that even though Shannon put on an air of confidence, she was insecure and hurting like everyone else. After a few weeks, they kissed, and then after a few months, they quietly got married with only Shannon's sister in attendance.

Mark never considered if he loved Shannon; she was simply the only woman who had ever paid attention to him, and he treasured that. He liked listening to her talk about everything under the sun and felt grateful to be with her. It was simply better than being alone; after all, he had always known he was no catch. To have someone…anyone… was enough.

Shannon left the restaurant quickly after graduating from college, and they found a small house on top of Fillmore that needed a substantial amount of work but at a price even a young married couple could afford. Mark's steady job enabled Shannon to bounce from job to job as she found new opportunities.

It was only two months after Alan was born that the opportunity came for Shannon to work in Denver. The pay was better, but the commute was longer, and with the added expense of having a better car that could make the drive every day, Mark sold his car and took over the job of caring for Alan, and began to walk to work each day.

The Upper Fourth Grill was one of many chain restaurants in Colorado Springs; not one of the worst, but not one of the best. Miles away from Paris or Napa, the people of Colorado Springs did not pretend to be 'foodies' in any way. They wanted a decent atmosphere, a price they could afford, and for the food to arrive quickly enough so that they could make their movie or get back to work on time. The quality of food was an afterthought, making The Upper Fourth Grill one of the most popular restaurants in town.

When Mark entered through the back door at eight-thirty every morning, he was met by the same damp smell that permeated his clothing. He usually finished mopping floors, wiping down the counter, and running the multiple tubs of unwashed dishes from the night before through the dishwasher around ten. He would then check the walk-in freezer and refrigerator to ensure any prep work that needed to be done was completed. By ten thirty, the rest of the staff would begin to arrive. Once the line cooks and the wait staff were in place, Mark would assume his position in 'The Cage' (as the rest of the staff called it) and wait for the lunch rush to begin. It was called The Cage because there was only a small entrance next to the deep sinks, and the other three sides were filled with the large industrial dishwasher, trash cans, and several wire racks where the busboys would drop their tubs full of dishes.

Once the lunch rush began, it would be three in the afternoon before Mark would stop taking the dishes from the tubs, place them on the thick plastic racks where he would hose them off above the disposal, and then run them into the industrial dishwasher. Over and over, this assembly line of one would repeat itself during the day. The staff never noticed Mark except for when the dishes and glasses did not magically appear when needed, and then, just like a hockey goalie, the rest of the staff would blame him. Not that the bus staff broke a glass at the bottom of the tub, forcing Mark to pull the pieces out one by one, or that someone on the wait staff let their tables pile up, waiting to pay their check so that the dishes flooded into the kitchen like a tsunami. Everything that went wrong was Mark's fault, for no other reason than no one on the totem pole any lower.

Mark ignored most snide comments and complaints, focusing on getting the next group of dishes out cleaner and quicker than the last. It did not matter if an entire glass of wine was spilled on him or if his back hurt so much that he could hardly twist and turn, as was needed to keep ahead of the rush. When he walked into The Cage, he simply turned off his higher brain functions and went to work. It was the only way he knew how to get through the day.

At the end of his shift, he would be relieved by one of the line-cook-drug-addicts-of-the-week and walk to meet Alan. Alan was far too young to walk up Fillmore Hill, so in the same place in the afternoon where he would let Alan down off his back in the morning, Alan would climb back onto his back, and Mark would begin the long, painful trek back up the hill carrying the boy.

Once they arrived home, Mark would start on another assembly line that he repeated each night by cleaning the house, washing the clothes when they piled up high enough, and picking up after Alan. Regardless of how often he went through the house, there always seemed to be something he needed to do. It never ceased to amaze Mark how much damage one small boy could do to a house in the time span between getting home and going to bed. Despite being such a calm child, Alan obliviously left a nightly path of destruction in his wake upon his joyful return to the house.

Mark thanked whatever luck he had that Alan was unlike many other boys he saw on the playground daily. The kind that never seemed to quit moving or yelling. The kind that when their mothers dropped them off at school, a visible sigh of relief would come over their entire being, only to watch at the end of the day as the child climbed back into the car, and the mother would mentally prepare herself to do battle with the child, even as they were driving out of the parking lot.

Alan, as much a creature of habit as his father, would come home and do his homework without being prompted and then park himself in front of the television until bedtime. He had a habit of doing several things at once and would often walk around the couch repeatedly as the loud myriad of noises from the cartoons he watched filled the room. He also had a habit of humming and sometimes talking to himself, even as he watched television. Since he was a baby, Mark called it his "chirping"; just sounds from a child who said very little, and it was one of the most comforting things in all of Mark's life.

Standing in front of the microwave, doing his best not to fall asleep on his feet, Mark would listen to Alan's chirping from the living room, and the day's problems would melt... at least for a little while.

When Shannon first got her job in Denver, she would always be home by seven, even if she had to leave work early to do so. After a while, she started to get home later; to the point where she would stay with a friend in the city and, on many nights, not commute home. Mark knew that Alan missed her, but there had always been a distance between the two of them that Mark did not understand. Shannon loved Alan because she was his mother, and Alan loved her for the same reason, but there was no true bond between their souls. Alan had always been Mark's and, in Shannon's mind, Mark's responsibility.

Mark walked upstairs with Alan and began the nightly routine of putting on pajamas, brushing teeth, and reading a story. Of all the hardship Mark faced during the day, all the disrespect he encountered, and the fact that no one saw or cared if he was there other than to put clean dishes in a rack, it was all worth it because, during the fifteen minutes, he got to put Alan to bed; he was the most important person in the entire world. Watching as the boy looked up with wide eyes as Mark read books and told stories was the single greatest accomplishment during his day.

They had been reading the Narnia Chronicles and were up to "The Silver Chair." Mark might get through an entire chapter on a good night, but most nights, it only took a few pages of reading before Alan was fast asleep. Mark would carefully bookmark the page and set it next to Alan's bed after he drifted off to sleep.

Sometimes Mark would stare at his son, wondering how he could have been so blessed. He thought of a movie that he saw when he was younger that said, "The only real wealth we ever achieve is our children." Watching Alan sleep peacefully for a few minutes, Mark did not feel as if he were an invisible dishwasher; he felt as if he were the richest man he knew.

After ensuring all the lights were off, and the doors were locked, walking up the stairs in the dark home was the hardest part of his day. Most nights, Mark did not crawl into bed but collapsed on top of it, asleep before his head touched the pillow. After years of the routine, Mark had learned never to shut the door to his room. Even though it was never done on purpose, the sound of Shannon coming into the room was something that would wake Mark up dramatically, regardless of how deep his sleep was. She could come in the front door, and all the way up the stairs, and Mark would not move, but when the door handle to the bedroom door was turned, it was as if Shannon had fired a gun.

Since the door was open tonight, the bedroom light being flipped on woke Mark up.

"Hey," Shannon said. If she noticed that she had woken Mark up, she did not say anything; she simply dropped her computer bag on the floor and walked into the bathroom, already removing one of her hoop earrings and kicking off her shoes.

"You know, Mark, I've asked you a million times not to wear those clothes to bed; they stink up the bed. Can you please just change out of those things when you get home? It's all I could smell when I walked in the door," Shannon sniffed disdainfully.

Mark sat up and tried to focus on anything in the room, doing his best to wake up. He knew trying to get any sleep until Shannon was ready to get into bed was going to be pointless. For lack of a better term, the energy she was putting off told him instantly that tonight would be a night where she would be talking until she finally closed her eyes.

Mark took off his shirt and pants and put on a loose-fitting t-shirt and a pair of shorts, sitting back down on the bed, waiting for Shannon to come out of the bathroom.

"I hate it when the Broncos play on Monday night. As soon as I got to the Colfax exit, the traffic sucked. I should have stayed with April, but I didn't know about the game, so I was stuck in traffic all the way down here. Forty miles with drunken fans being pulled over left and right; it fucking sucked," Shannon sighed as soon as she exited the bathroom. She began walking around the room, removing the clothes she had worn during the day. "Seriously, how stupid do you have to be to get drunk at some dumb football game and then try to drive all the way home in the middle of the winter...?" she continued. Mark knew he was drifting off, but that fact failed to lower the volume of Shannon's rhetorical conversation. He understood that she just simply needed to talk in order to wind down; if she didn't get the words out, she would just lay awake in bed and stare at the ceiling, so the best thing to do was to simply be in the room and listen as best he could. The commute was a favorite subject of Shannon's to complain about because it would always be there, and there was very little she could do about it, so to rage against it was how she dealt with it.

"There is no way I'm driving that tomorrow night. I'll probably stay up at April's for the next couple of days," Shannon said. Over the last year, she had begun to stay with April more often as her responsibilities at work increased. Mark had never met April and doubted if he ever would. Shannon had made it clear that she wanted to keep her home life and her professional life as separate as possible. She said it helped her relax, but Mark knew she was not a "relaxing" kind of person. Mark knew the truth.

Shannon was ashamed of him.

He didn't know why he did it when he was painfully aware of being so tired, but he said the words he knew would start a fight. "We could always move closer to your job."

Shannon's look stung him. "Oh, really? So, we are going to pull Alan out of his school; you are going to quit your job, lose our insurance, and then try to sell this piece of crap home in one of the worst housing markets in history?"

"I am just saying that if we factor in the time you spend on the road..."

"You know what, Mark?" she spat, "How about you don't factor anything to do with my day into your dumb idea? You don't know anything that I go through during the day. You have no idea how hard it is to have a real job with real responsibilities," Shannon said, sitting down at the foot of the bed and rubbing her elbows and arms with lotion.

"I was thinking about getting a new job anyway," Mark ventured.

Shannon's laugh was unabashedly mean. "Do you know how lucky you are to have the job that you have? You have no education or skills, yet somehow you managed to stay in one place long enough to get a benefits package better than I can get. That alone is worth more money than your pathetic paycheck. Why would you even think about leaving?"

"You know I hate it there," he sighed.

"So what?! Do you think I like my job? Do you think anyone *likes* what they do?" Shannon was now pacing the room as her rant accelerated. "I sit in a cube for eight to ten hours daily, reviewing spreadsheets. That's all! Do you think I like it? If I quit my job, we lose the house. I don't want to be there, but I do it because we were stupid enough to buy this place, and now we have to live with our mistake."

"Fine," Mark capitulated, totally regretting bringing up the subject.

"Look, Mark, I'm sorry you hate your job, but do you know how hard it is to find work right now? A guy in my department was fired six months ago, and he's still looking for something. This guy has a master's degree, Mark, master's! What chance do you have of getting a job when someone educated can't find anything? You are not quitting your job," she stated matter-of-factly.

Mark said nothing, turning to his side and closing his eyes.

Shannon would spend the next several minutes preparing for bed, and even though Mark knew she wanted to talk about her day, he did everything he could to stop the conversation from progressing any further. She was not in the mood to talk tonight; she was in the mood to fight.

He was angry with himself for bringing up getting a new job. He knew better than that. Shannon needed his medical coverage through the restaurant. One of the only benefits of staying at The Upper Fourth Grill was that employees who stayed over ten years received a benefits package unrivaled in the industry. It was easy to offer because almost no one stayed for nearly that long. Essentially, the corporation looked good because the package was on the books, and the number crunchers liked it because they never had to follow through. Mark was that rare exception, and Shannon had held onto it like a lifeline.

"Why do you always bring this kind of stuff up just before I try to go to sleep?" Shannon whined.

Mark had hoped that lying on his side and turning his back to her would be a major clue that he did not want to fight. It wasn't. The fight had begun, and Mark knew it all depended on how much pent-up energy Shannon needed to release. He did not move but did not close his eyes or try to sleep because now there was no point.

"I don't understand you, Mark," she continued. "We see each other so little these days, and yet, when I walk into the room, all you want to do is fight with me. It's amazing to me," Shannon said, now pacing at the foot of the bed. "Do you know what would be nice, Mark? It would be really nice if I could just come home and go to bed without having to deal with your jealousy. I am so sorry that I left being a waitress and decided to make something of my life. I'm sorry that you think it was so easy for me to finish college and then go get a real job rather than staying in the same place for the rest of my life!"

Mark sat up in bed but did not say anything. Tonight was when he knew he had to be strong and not fight; he had to consciously choose not to engage because Shannon lacked the strength to stop herself. He steadied himself against the rising tide, knowing that wave after wave of her barely-repressed anger would be slamming into him shortly.

Shannon stood in the doorway, fuming. "Mark, I don't understand what you expect of me. Do you even realize that I am staying up at April's as much as I am staying here? I would like to think that you'd do something to make me feel a little special when I come home. I think you would want to make sure that when I walk in the door, *my* paycheck pays for; by the way, you would at least try to make an effort. Do you know what I get instead? I get to drive down to this house and walk in with no lights on, not even the porch light, and it's as if you weren't expecting me at all. I get to walk in and smell that disgusting restaurant all over the house, like some kind of dead animal rotting in the attic. I come upstairs and find you passed out on the bed, stinking to high heaven like some kind of street bum. I get to come home to a man who can't speak or feel anything!" Shannon paced the floor and randomly jabbed the air to make her point as she spat her words.

"I used to think it was because you were quiet and contemplative. The truth is, I'm beginning to think that there is absolutely *nothing* going on in your silence and that you're simply too stupid to know any better. Do you know what I did last Friday? April and I went to a bar to meet with some clients. After they left, she and I talked all night about politics, books, and movies, and it was... great. The only problem is, as I sat there talking about all of this, I knew I could never share any of that with you. I knew if I came home and talked about any of it with you, I'd get nothing but the same stupid blank stare you're giving me now."

Shannon turned off the light in the bedroom and stalked into the bathroom once again. Mark could see her leaning against the sink counter. He did not move to comfort her. He simply remained motionless and waited for the next wave of vitriol.

She turned to him in the doorway. "Is this all that we are ever going to be, Mark? I hate myself like this, and I hate this life. I hate that when people ask me if I'm married, I have to lie about what you do. I mean, seriously, am I supposed to tell my boss, a man who went to Stanford, that my 41-year-old husband is nothing but a dishwasher? Oh! And not only is he nothing more than a filthy, sweat and bleach-covered dishwasher, but he was never anything else! My husband does the same job that a 16-year-old kid does after school and on weekends..." She paused to march up to him from the bathroom, leaned down in his face to make her final point, and continued, "...and will obviously never be anything else! Is that what I'm supposed to tell him? It's humiliating being married to you." She stood up and defiantly looked down at Mark, daring him to take the bait and finally participate in the argument.

Deep inside, he heard a voice he had known from childhood telling him that Shannon was right; he was not smart enough to be anything else, that this was all he was ever going to be, and that he had been fortunate even to get this far. He understood why she was ashamed of him. It was not surprising that she was embarrassed; what was really shocking was that at one time, she hadn't been embarrassed to be seen with him. Now there was nothing to defend.

"Your mother tried to warn me," Shannon sneered as she paced around the room and in and out of the adjoining bathroom as if the walk was responsible for coaxing the anger from her.

Only then did Mark react, but in the smallest of ways. His mouth tightened, and his eyes narrowed as if punched exactly where a bruise had already existed.

Shannon continued her verbal assault. "A week before we got married, did you know she called me? She called me and told me that she couldn't understand what I was doing with you, that I could do so much better," she said casually, knowing the words she was saying were flying across the room like knives. "I told her to go to hell. Can you believe that? The woman was reaching out to me, warning me, and I told her to go to hell." Shannon smacked her forehead in a mocking gesture of disbelief. "I thought I would show her. I thought, 'all he needs is a good woman behind him, and Mark could become someone.' I was so stupid. She was right, and as much as I hate her, she was right." Shannon slammed the door to the bathroom, flooding the bedroom with darkness.

Mark sat motionless with his fists clenched and his teeth pressed together. She knew exactly what to say, and even though he had prepared himself to be a rock against her wave upon wave of insults, he knew that inside, he was beginning to crumble. He could feel the pressure building to respond, to lash out at her as fiercely as she had attacked him. Still, if he even opened his mouth a little, the words would break over the levees of his restraint and flood the room, and another pointless battle would begin for supremacy over what neither one of them actually wanted.

He wanted to yell out at the top of his voice and say the foulest and ugliest words he could think of. He knew that it was only...

"Dad?"

Mark looked over in the darkness and saw his boy standing backlit in the doorway from the hall light that he was only now tall enough to reach unassisted barely.

"I had a bad dream..." Alan said, holding back tears of fear and tears of just being a young child in the middle of the night in need of his father.

Mark did not recall getting out of bed or walking over to Alan, but the minute the boy was in his arms, still shaking from fear, all the anger and frustration instantly left Mark, and time was frozen. He held Alan as they walked back to the bedroom, and Alan wrapped his tiny arms around Mark's neck as tightly as he could. Mark tried to put Alan back in his bed but the boy would not let go; so very carefully, Mark pulled the small mattress off of the bed and onto the floor, soundlessly lying down next to his son.

"Did you want to tell me about your dream?" Mark asked quietly.

Alan shook his head 'no' and let go of Mark a little, but left his arm over Mark's neck, and quickly went back to sleep. Mark lay on the floor next to his son, looking up at the plastic glow-in-the-dark stars on Alan's ceiling.

Shannon had been right about him through all of her bitterness and anger. He had never been anything more than a dishwasher and most likely never would be; Mark thought the most pathetic part of it all was that he never thought about how horrible his life was until Shannon came home and reminded him. Mark thought that he must really be as stupid as they said because, on the days when everything went smoothly and no one yelled at him for any reason, he was strangely content. There were times after work when he had a good shift, as he walked to get Alan from school, that he was actually happy. He would look up through the trees to the foothills and mountains of the Colorado Rockies and just breathe in and out as deeply as he could and be filled with joy.

His favorite part of the day was when Alan ran out of school with the other kids and hugged Mark like they had not seen each other for weeks. Alan never failed to hug Mark. It was all Mark needed, but it wasn't enough to heal him, and he knew it.

Alan turned over now, solidly asleep. Mindful of his son's warmth and innocence, the same old fear rose in his chest, and he had to consciously breathe. Even with the revelation that he was as simple as everyone had always said he was, Mark knew that it would not be long before Alan realized it too. It was only a matter of time before Alan would turn on him like everyone else, and it would only be a few short years before he realized what an insignificant person his father was. It seemed sadly inevitable that Alan, one day, would inevitably tell him what a disappointment he was.

Maybe that was why Mark was so happy right now; it was only a matter of time before the hugs after school would stop. It was only a matter of time before the stories would not be told at bedtime. It was only a matter of time before the shadowy look of disappointment would cross Alan's face just like it had with everyone else in Mark's life.

Mark closed his eyes and began to drift off to sleep. It may only be a matter of time before it all changed, but the time in Alan's life when Mark was his friend, father, and hero was happening right now, and he was not about to miss one minute of it.

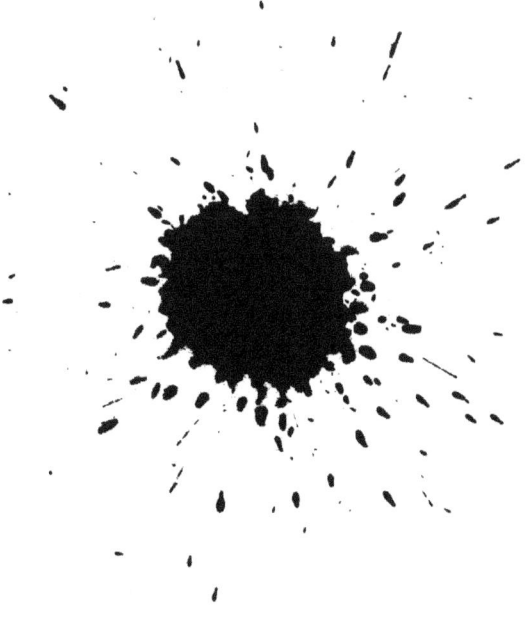

~ CHAPTER TWO ~

Riding the bus after a double shift was a form of sleep deprivation torture. Sitting in the back of the bus, Mark tried his best to find a balance between getting some rest but not so much that he would miss his stop. The worst part was that the moment Mark lost his grip on consciousness, the bus would stop; the bright white lights would turn on sharply and wake Mark up instantly. As soon as the bus began to move away from the bus stop, the lights would go off, and the engine hum would rock Mark back to sleep, only to wake him with another jolt a few blocks later.

The double shift was something Mark had not planned on. The kid who worked the night shift did not show up, so Mark picked up the extra hours, even though it meant that Shannon's sister would have to pick Alan up from school. On nights like these, Mark would walk the four blocks to the bus stop, ride it downtown, and then walk several more blocks to pick up Alan.

They would then turn around and make the trek in reverse, but thankfully, the bus would stop near the house, so on nights like these, they did not need to walk up the hill.

Tyler and Jenny Parker were, in many ways, the exact opposite of Shannon and Mark. Where Mark had no real goals, Tyler was one of the fastest-rising stars in his engineering firm and held a seat on the city council. Jenny was tall, blond, and pretty, the perfect politician's/businessman's wife. They lived downtown in a 130-year-old home, one of the first built in this prestigious area of town.

Jenny had never made it a secret how she felt about Mark (or Shannon, for that matter), but Mark was not blood, so there was no reason to even pretend with him. Jenny had been very clear about how disappointed she was that Shannon married Mark. Like a small drop of water breaking apart a giant stone, Shannon fought back at first but, over the years, had lost her resistance to the point that their equal disappointment in Mark was the only thing that the two sisters could ever agree on.

Even with the rift, the Parkers were always there when Alan needed looking after. All Mark had to do was ask, and Jenny would take care of everything.

Mark opened the rod iron gate in front of their house, and the motion sensor lights came on automatically on the porch. Even though it was unnecessary when he reached the porch, Mark rang the doorbell. The crisp, clean sound of the bells rang clearly, even muffled behind the etched glass insert of the front door. He thought that ringing the doorbell annoyed Jenny, but he secretly loved the sound of the bells, so he could never resist the urge.

As usual, Tyler met Mark at the door and invited him inside.

"Alan fell asleep upstairs; he'll be down in a minute. You want anything?" Tyler asked politely.

"No, thank you," Mark said. Whether in his worst work clothes or his best Sunday suit, Mark always felt dirty in their house. He stood in the always polished and clean entryway like a model home staged for beauty but not for use.

The stairwell's polished cherry handrails went upstairs under a small but bright chandelier. To his left, Mark could see a Norman Rockwell-esque dining room behind two glass doors. To his right was the living room, where the sounds of the nightly news could be heard. The air was filled with the warm smell of what remained of dinner from the kitchen in the back of the house. The home and the life it represented were the epitome of the American dream, yet Mark had never been more than three steps inside. He had never sat at the beautifully polished table or sat on the couches that looked as if they were as soft as a hug wrapped in colorful fabrics. He only knew the tile in the entry and, more often than not, the porch outside.

Alan came down the stairs with his jacket and backpack, ready to walk into the cold night air. He smiled at his father and then rubbed his eye with his small hand.

"Don't forget your..." Jenny said, coming down the hallway to meet Alan at the bottom of the stairs. She stopped short as soon as she saw Mark. Putting a small bag of food into Alan's backpack, she did her best to avoid catching Mark's eye. She and Mark performed a well-rehearsed dance around Alan as if he was a tiny DMZ between them that neither would ever cross.

Tyler walked back into the entryway with his coat in hand, breaking the tension. "I'll drive you guys home. It's getting cold out there."

With a look from Jenny, Tyler froze in mid-stride, not knowing what to do, as if he was a child being caught in a lie.

"Why don't you wait outside? Tyler will bring the car around in a minute," Jenny said politely while hugging Alan. Mark followed Alan outside and stood on the porch without saying a word as Jenny shut the door behind them. Without turning around, Mark could hear the intensifying voices inside, trying to keep quiet enough not to be heard outside. Their voices could be heard more clearly as the argument grew less restrained.

"I don't want him in the car, and I certainly do not want him in my house. I've told you that!" Jenny shouted.

"We agreed that we would do whatever we could to help Alan, and I am not going to let him walk home when it's so cold outside. Believe it or not, Jen, I have some say in what I do," Tyler barked back.

"I don't want him in my house again," Jenny snarled just before Mark could hear her angry footsteps retreat upstairs.

"Dad, look! It's snowing!" Alan cried out, standing on the path to the front gate, trying to catch the snowflakes on his tongue. Even with the tired old argument still ringing in his ears, it was hard for Mark not to smile at Alan with his mouth wide open, trying to catch the fat, wet flakes that were quickly beginning to cover everything in sight.

Mark loved it when it snowed. With the rain, there was always the noise of water bouncing off whatever it hit, but the snow was different. The world became perfectly silent. He did not know if somehow the new snow muffled the normal sounds of the city, but watching the snow gently drift down to the ground was one of the few joys of the cold. Tomorrow it would begin to melt, turning to slush and becoming troublesome, but on a night like tonight, it was the most peaceful event in the world.

Sitting on the front porch steps, Mark waited for Tyler to bring the car around from the garage behind the house. He appreciated the ride more than he could say; he was tired, and getting home in ten minutes instead of the forty-five it would take on the bus was an unexpected kindness.

He did not hate Jenny, even though she clearly despised him. He understood that her anger was not entirely his fault and that Shannon and Jenny had had many problems with each other long before he arrived. The ironic thing was that their mutual frustration with him had brought the sisters closer together, at least on the surface.

They still fought with each other in their own passive-aggressive ways. Shannon hated that Jenny was the 'pretty one,' so Shannon made a point of being the 'smart one.' This competition continued between them until a few short years ago when Shannon finally emerged victorious: no matter what Jenny would ever accomplish, Shannon would always hold the ultimate victory over her little sister for the simple reason that Shannon had a child. Only a month after Shannon announced that she was pregnant did Mark learn the truth. Tyler and Jenny had tried everything available in modern medicine, but Jenny simply could not bring a child to full term. To Shannon, Jenny's misery was nothing short of a delicious knockout blow.

Once Alan was born, the rift between the sisters grew even larger because as much as they did not like Mark, Jenny was appalled at how Shannon had left the child alone with him most of the time. In Jenny's mind, Shannon took the one thing that she would never have in life and carelessly tossed it into the world's most incompetent hands.

It was expected that Jenny would be angry every time Alan had to leave at night because not only did she have to let Alan return to the arms of a man she did not respect, but she also had to let go of the few moments that she ever felt like a mother. With all of the success and all the trappings of wealth, Mark knew that she would give it all up to have Alan as her own. Mark could not blame her for that, he would have done the same, and that was the one thing that kept Mark from ever being angry or hating Jenny in even the smallest way. As much as she loathed him and tried to make him feel small, Mark could always see the question in her eyes that asked, "Why you and not me?" He felt sorry for her.

Tyler's Audi moved silently through the wet streets. Alan sat in the back and, within only a few minutes, had dropped off to sleep in an impossible position that would have left any adult feeling sore for weeks afterward. His head rested at an almost 90-degree angle to the right side, propped up only by his tiny hand and held upright by the seatbelt.

No one spoke in the car. Tyler and Mark had a bond with each other much in the same way soldiers do. They also understood that their spouses would view any kind of relationship with each other as a betrayal. The problem was that, being men, they connected with each other simply by doing things together and not by words. Much in the same way that two friends will get up in the early morning to go fishing and speak only a few words throughout the day, Mark and Tyler had developed a mutual respect for each other without a word being said.

Mark felt the seat warming up and the purr of the soft engine as they made their way through the increasing snowfall and felt his eyes getting heavy again. He tried his best not to go to sleep, but the warmth of the car lulled him, and before he knew it, they were home.

Getting out of the car, still groggy, Mark waved his hand to thank Tyler and began to make his way inside.

"Mark, wait..." Tyler said abruptly, getting out of the car.

Mark let Alan in the house, watching as he immediately dropped his backpack in the entryway and his jacket a little further in. By the time he got to his bedroom, he would only have on his underwear, and his clothes would be strewn behind him like a trail of bread crumbs.

"Listen, Mark, I don't think you should come by the house for a little while," Tyler began apologetically. "Jenny is still trying to deal with... everything. She would hate it if I ever told you this, but she has hardly left the house in I don't know how long, and she's kind of a mess."

"Okay, I'll try to figure something out for Alan," Mark said quietly.

"No, no. Don't misunderstand me. We'll watch Alan anytime you need us to; in fact, we'd love it if he could spend the night now and then. I just think it would be better if I drove him home instead. Would that be all right?" Tyler said uncomfortably.

"Sure. That's fine," Mark sighed.

"Okay, I'll talk to you soon. Thanks, Mark," Tyler said a little too quickly, betraying his relief as he got in the car and drove off.

Mark had always understood that he would never be welcome and that he would never be family. Yet, as he closed the door and began cleaning up Alan's trail, Mark felt just a little more alone in a world that seemed to want nothing more than to push him into the shadows. Or off a cliff, he mused to himself.

The short discussion from the night before still bothered Mark in the morning. He did not want to be a part of their family or was surprised that they would ask him to stay away. It was that he knew so very few people in general. It was a hard realization that going to their house on the bus and standing on their porch to be glared at was one of the few social activities he ever engaged in. It was pathetic but true.

On the way to school that morning, they were about halfway down Fillmore Hill when pain shot up Mark's leg from his ankle so severely that he dropped to the ground. Adding to the pain was that he was forced to twist his back in order not to drop Alan, and he felt a blinding crack shoot up his spine that made his eyes instantly water.

Alan climbed off quickly and stood by, not knowing what to do.

"Dad? Are you all right?"

"I'm fine. Just give me a minute," Mark said softly, wanting to scream but holding everything inside not to scare Alan. He closed his eyes for a minute, trying to gain control. At work, he his back was always in pain, but he had never felt anything like this before; any movement at all caused a wave of sparks to shoot to every part of his body. With his eyes closed, he tried to feel anything but the pain was unbearable.

"Dad?" Alan said quietly, putting his small gloved hand on Mark's shoulder.

The voice seemed as if it were coming from another room. The blackness of the pain was overwhelming Mark while light danced around in front of him like fireworks, and he tried to do anything but move, hoping to find a way out.

"Dad? Look at me. Dad?" Alan said, now louder.

Mark opened his eyes, and the bright white snow around them seemed like a thousand camera flashes. Alan was standing in front of Mark, only a few inches away from his face, with a determined look.

"Dad, you're not breathing," Alan said, frightened.

The simple realization changed everything. Mark opened his mouth, and the crisp air flooded his lungs as he breathed in a few times deeply through his nose and then out through his mouth. The pain crashed against his spine one more time and then subsided.

Mark sat in the snow for a few more minutes, with Alan standing over him like a small sentinel, repeating the same words Mark had said a million times after Alan had skinned his knee or hurt himself in a million ways young boys knew how to do.

"You're okay. It's going to be all right. Shhhhhh," Alan said while rubbing his snow-covered gloved hand over Mark's hair. "You're okay. It's going to be all right."

After a few minutes, Mark tested his back and found that he could move again, and he stood up, taking care not to lean on the twisted ankle that had caused all the problems to begin with.

"You okay?" Alan asked, looking up.

"Yeah, but I think you're going to need to walk today," Mark winced while grabbing Alan's hand.

They walked down the remainder of the hill slowly as Mark tried to stay off his ankle as much as he could. Alan took the lead and pointed out ice patches and loose rocks along the way. In his small way, as they made their way down the hill, Alan did his best to take care of his father; constantly asking if Mark was all right and if he needed to rest.

When they finally got to the school, Alan hugged Mark goodbye and ran off as usual. However, before going inside, he turned and ran back. "I don't think we should let Aunt Jenny come inside our house until she starts being nice to you," he stated simply before giving Mark another quick hug and running inside.

Mark turned around and made his way to work, limping the entire way. He knew his back would be a problem all day and that it was beginning to feel warm from the injury, indicating he would be in pain for days, if not weeks, to come. His ankle hurt, and he was only now realizing his wrist must have hit the ground harder than he had thought because that was also beginning to throb.

Yet, even though he felt like he had just been hit by a car, Mark could not stop smiling.

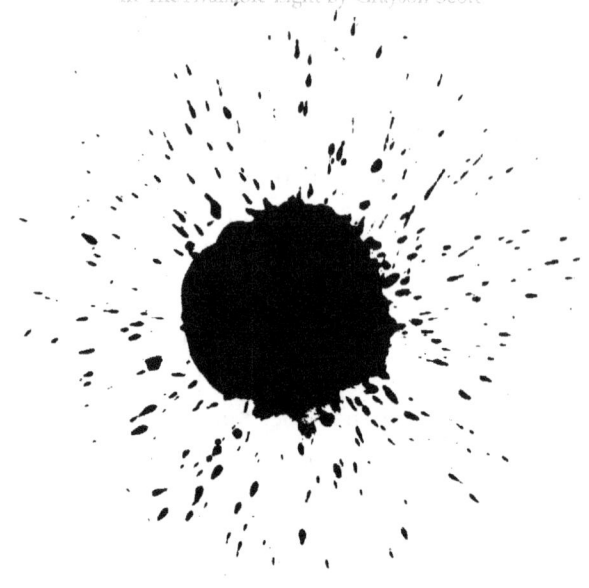

~ CHAPTER THREE ~

Erica Palmer stood on the playground of Holmes Elementary School, knowing that she was obligated to go inside and teach, but she found it hard to move. It was not that this was her first teaching assignment; far from it, in fact. It was not that she was not good at her job. It was the simple fact that she had never tried to teach so many children at once.

Two years ago, at her last school in Boston, there were only ten students per teacher. Erica was now keenly aware that she had not really comprehended the difference between teaching at a highly funded private school and the realities of an underfunded public school. She had applied for a second-grade teaching position a month ago, almost on a whim. Things had not worked out the way they should, so rather than going home to Boston with her tail between her legs, she'd applied for a teaching position, thinking it would be next semester before they would have a position open if they had anything at all. One month later, she found herself on the playground, not knowing what she was going to do.

Tom was a jerk, and she still couldn't believe she had given up everything to follow him to Colorado. He had been a friend of a friend for many years, and Erica had known him long before the two of them became a couple. He seemed to be one of the most solid individuals she had ever met, a lawyer at a respectable firm in Boston with political ambitions. The idea of being a politician's wife had a certain appeal to it. The problem was that she never considered what being a politician's mistress would be like. As it turned out, Tom understood the political process far better than he ever let on. He told Erica he would move to Colorado a year ago to work on a local senator's campaign. He resigned from his law firm and packed everything into his car, and was gone within a week. The funny thing about the entire situation was that Erica could not recall if he ever actually 'invited' her to come along. They were pretty serious and even talked of marriage, so she just assumed that where ever he went, she would go.

Erica's father had passed away years ago, and her mother still lived in the same house they grew up in Cambridge, surrounded by nothing but her charities and the empty rooms upstairs. Erica's brother was a lifetime student at Harvard, spending eternity 'finishing up' his doctorate. Her father was a professor of English Literature at Harvard and imparted his love for education to his children before he passed away when Erica was still in school. Doing anything other than being a teacher never occurred to her. It was what she had always wanted to be.

Going back to Boston was not an option, even though she knew her family would welcome her back with open arms. It was her friends she did not want to see, at least not right away. When she announced she would follow Tom to Colorado, her closest friends begged her not to go. Tears and shouted insults were all tried to get her to come to her senses, but she was determined. She hated that she had been so blind in the middle of a crowd of beloved people who saw the situation so clearly.

Tom was great for a couple of months. He was the campaign manager, and his horse in the race was ahead by fifteen points when all other opponents dropped out, handing him the nomination unopposed. The democrat running against them was caught in a DUI after a party in Denver, and by the time the polls closed in November last year, it looked to the political world as if Tom had run the perfect campaign for his candidate.

The problem was that by the time the polls were closed in November, Tom was practically married... and not to Erica. He told her on the phone the week before the election; the coward didn't even have the guts to face her in person. She found out later that the woman he would marry was the daughter of another politician and that the happy couple were moving to D.C.

It was so frustrating that she knew that her friends who had warned her against following Tom also knew she had been dumped, yet not one of them called her to see if she was okay. She knew it was foolish to wait on them, but she knew that if the situation were reversed, she would have reached out. She couldn't shake the feeling that they wanted her to come back and bow at their feet for having the audacity to go against them, and frankly, that wasn't going to happen.

Erica began to make her way into the school. She knew that the staring would begin once she emerged from her corner of the schoolyard. It was one thing if it only came from the men, which it did, but what really bothered her was how women looked at her.

It was frustrating because those that got to know her or even became friends with her kept in reserve a quiet jealousy. Those that did not befriend her simply looked on with loathing. The fact was that Erica was not just attractive; she was gorgeous, Hollywood gorgeous, and it defined much of who she was, whether she wanted it to or not.

Most of the time, she understood what horribly deformed people felt like in society because she could not go anywhere or do anything without her outside appearance playing a part in it. It was always out of the corner of her eye, the whispers and the staring everywhere she went. Her looks created a threshold that everyone else in the world felt that they had to work up the nerve to cross, and it kept everyone at a distance. In high school, she was not asked out by a single boy she liked and stayed home most of the time. In college, she was hit on constantly by those who considered themselves to be just as pretty as she was, with the ego to boot, or by those too drunk to care. Tom had been one of only three men she had ever had a relationship with, and sadly, it was the best of the three.

She always equated it to having money. Having money made many things in life easier, but it, by no means, solved all of your problems and, in many cases, created new ones. Yet, when you were overwhelmed, who would really understand? Her looks created problems that made her feel even more isolated because no one could understand. People always just assumed that because of her looks that life was easier for her. They assumed that all the problems they suffered due to their physical flaws, some real and some imaginary, were beyond Erica's understanding.

Her brother used to call her Clark Kent because of the amount of work she would go through to play down her looks. She rarely used make-up and made a point of finding less-than-flattering clothes. Still, it was there, hanging over her head like an ornate Sword of Damocles.

It was also one of the reasons she liked teaching elementary school. Unlike the staff, the children did not care one way or another. What the children cared about, for the most part, was her spirit, what was inside. They saw her for what she wanted to be, not for the thing that she could not control. She made her way inside and walked down the center of the hallway as the children hung up their jackets and made their way inside their classrooms while making as much noise as possible.

Standing by her classroom was the tall, thin African-American principal, Terri Evans, smiling politely at Erica as she approached.

"You ready for this?" Terri said over the din as children walked into the classroom, wondering who this new woman was but too scared of getting in trouble with the principal to ask. It was one of the things about this age group that Erica loved; the children craved boundaries because they were beginning to see that it was a much bigger world than they could have ever imagined, so, in many cases, authority still really meant something. If handled right, Erica felt that a healthy dose of gentle but firm authority could help any of these kids get off on the right foot.

"Absolutely," Erica said enthusiastically. As nervous as she was, she was excited to start this next phase in her life and to leave the mistakes of her past a distant memory.

"All right then, but please remember that these students have had nothing but substitutes all year. I don't know where they are, but we need to get them ready for testing, so you have your work cut out for you," Terri said. "Come on in, and I'll introduce you."

As soon as Terri started to move towards the door, the bell rang, and children in the hall and all within the classroom made a mad dash for their seats. Doors were shut as the last students entered, and the hallway quickly fell silent. Erica breathed in deeply and made her way into the classroom.

She did not know how she ended up here or for what purpose, but the moment she stepped over the classroom threshold, it was as if God Himself whispered in her ear that she was exactly where she needed to be, and suddenly she was at peace.

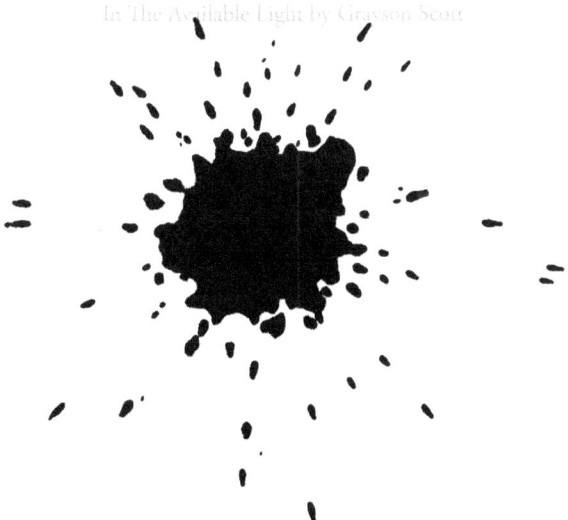

~ CHAPTER FOUR ~

There was very little doubt in Mark's mind that Rusty would not work out. Hired as the night dishwasher, Mark watched the horror in Rusty's eyes as Mark went over what the job entailed.

A senior in high school, this was Rusty's first attempt at a job, and the juvenile notion of not going to college and trying to make his way through life without an education was quickly beginning to wither. The first couple of mornings that he showed up, Mark was impressed. Rusty had completed everything he was supposed to the night before, but Mark knew it wouldn't last. It was as if Rusty was sprinting the first several yards of a marathon, and Mark knew he would get tired soon enough.

The next week, a few more dishes were left dirty each night, and by the end of the first month, entire tubs of dishes were left in the sink for Mark to deal with the next morning. Rusty did not last much longer after that, and Mark was told that he needed to work the night shift until a replacement could be found.

Jenny and Tyler were more than happy to pick up Alan from school and drop him off once Mark finally got home while he was working double shifts. Mark began to leave as early as possible to get home to Alan, but that meant that his mornings were more hectic than usual, trying to catch up from the night before and doing all the morning prep work in the kitchen.

The only light in the tunnel during these days was that the overtime pay he would receive would more than double his paycheck. He even began to look for a used car he and Alan could get around in.

When he opened his first paycheck after doing the double shifts, the amount was the same as if he had been working his standard shift. The next morning when the manager arrived, Mark was standing in the doorway of the small office just off of the kitchen waiting for him.

Jose Trussoni had been working for The Upper Fourth Grill almost as long as Mark. He had started out as a waiter in Dallas, then moved to Portland to be a part of the management training program offered by corporate. He then traveled around the country for several years as a trainer, making sure that every restaurant offered the same experience, no matter the location. The problem was that not only did Jose have a tendency to come on too strong with the staff (especially the female staff), but he also had a drinking problem that he was not ready to take any responsibility for. Three years ago in Tucson, the two vices were combined, resulting in a sexual harassment suit that led to Jose being dropped from the road and sent to Colorado Springs as a form of banishment. Jose held onto his job, but he was not happy about it. Maybe it was the addiction of authority or the proximity to the bar that kept Jose around, but he was never silent about his dislike of where he was. When things got really bad, Jose's favorite target to unload was Mark.

After all the times Jose had barked and yelled at Mark in front of the rest of the staff, Mark was anxious to confront him on the subject of his paycheck, but the hopes of getting enough money to get a used car left him no choice.

"What do you want, Mark?" Jose said without looking up from the paperwork on his desk.

"I didn't get my second paycheck this week," Mark began.

"What do you mean? It's the same every time. Why would you get a second check?" Jose sharply responded without looking up from the desk.

"I've been working double shifts for two weeks now. The overtime should have been sent out this week, but I didn't get the overtime check in the envelope," Mark explained, waiting for Jose's abuse to begin.

Jose scratched his unshaven chin and sighed deeply as if suddenly, a tremendous weight was just placed upon his shoulders. "Well, I don't do the payroll. That comes from corporate. I'll check on it once we open up."

"Do you want me to call? I just wanted to run it by you first," Mark said, already knowing that the odds of Jose staying on top of the situation were pretty slim.

"What do you want from me, Mark? I said I would handle it! Jesus! I'll talk to them today and have them put the extra time on the next pay period. Can't you see I'm busy?" Jose yelled and reached over to shut the door to the tiny office in Mark's face.

Mark stuffed his paycheck envelope into his pocket and walked back towards The Cage, knowing nothing would be done. There had been something in the way that Jose acted that made Mark suspect that he had known all along that Mark would not get paid his overtime. Even for Jose, he had been too defensive and too quick to anger. Jose was in charge of sending all the hours to corporate, so the fact that Mark was several hundred dollars short rested squarely on Jose's shoulders.

Instead of returning to the dishes, Mark walked outside to one of the last remaining pay phones in the city. It had always bugged

Shannon that Mark had no desire to get a cell phone, but not only did Mark not talk on the phone, he really had no one to call except on days like this.

"I'm going to have to work late again tonight. Can you watch Alan again?" Mark said into the hard plastic phone. It was so cold outside that every word caused white puffs of steam to cover the phone before drifting upward. Mark tried his best to keep moving and blew warm air into his free hand as he talked on the phone.

"We were hoping he could spend the night tonight. We wanted to take him to see a movie," Jenny said as politely as she could, but Mark could feel the coldness in her voice.

"Sure. I have the day off tomorrow, so you can drop him off anytime." Mark said. He was disappointed but excited for Alan. Alan loved going to the movies.

Jenny hung up the phone without saying goodbye, and Mark made his way back inside.

The rest of the day and night went as expected; the busboys and the wait staff brought more dishes to him than he could possibly keep up with, while the kitchen staff compounded the rush with both plastic and metal containers for everything they needed to cook, store, or prepare the dinner for the hundreds of customers on a typical Friday night.

In the restaurant, people laughed and ate while the staff remained stressed, jumping on each other for even the smallest hiccup in the assembly line. Mark did not care about either; the incident with Jose had been bothering him, and he was doing everything he could not to walk away from The Cage and never return.

He thought about when he was in the seventh grade and the two bullies that made his life a living hell.

Ralph and Chance. The two of them somehow always managed to be within a few feet of each other no matter what time of day and continually found Mark to be an easy target. They were like wild dogs who thought of Mark as the weakest within the pack and, unless restrained, would attack him repeatedly. In classrooms or out in the yard, day after day, the two of them would punch, shove, or make fun of Mark without reason or provocation.

Mark's few friends would encourage him to fight back, but he never did. He simply absorbed everything and never once responded. The problem was that over the years, as he absorbed the harassment, Mark found himself losing the few friends that he had once had. Mark never understood if they began avoiding him because they considered him weak or simply because they did not want to get caught in the crosshairs of his daily torture.

After making his life miserable for three years in junior high school, high school had a few unexpected bonuses. Apart from being three times the size of the junior high kids, the seniors found the cocky attitude of Ralph and Chance a challenge and taught the two boys a lesson about what it felt like to be bullied. Even though Mark never saw it with his own eyes, from what he heard, both boys had a pretty rough time of it. Ralph died only three weeks after high school in a car crash, and Chance continued along like a man who lost a limb, never the same without his friend.

Mark drifted through school like a broken ghost. The time in junior high painted an image of Mark that he never fully escaped from, not only from within but also from how everyone else saw him. In a nutshell, he was considered weak. It did not matter if the others in school actually knew Mark; his reputation followed him, and the best he could do was simply make his way through the halls as silently and invisibly as possible.

Since junior high, he had never had to deal with a bully in public until Jose came along. A part of him wanted to yell back at Jose and make him fix his check right away, but he simply did not know how. After years of being cast aside and ignored, Mark hated that he was being seen as weak and tortured all over again for it. He knew that Jose had no intention of fixing his mistake. Mark knew that Jose discounted him in every way possible, and the fact that Mark was upset about the situation simply did not matter in the least to Jose.

What bothered Mark the most was the very simple fact that he knew he would do nothing about it. He knew that he simply did not have it within himself to fight back. He would take the punishment and absorb it, just as he had done his entire life...and hated himself for it.

All night, Mark fought the anger and frustration within himself like a man choking to death. Sometimes, it took all of his self-control to stop his hand from throwing the glass he was washing against the wall. He knew that he could not let out the slightest slip of the anger that was building within because, if he did, he didn't know where it would stop. He could feel the cold white plates in his hand and imagined how they would be so much lighter after breaking them on the side of the sink. There could be no self-indulgent rage. There could be no response to the injustice. He could only continue and bury the pain until it went away.

Mark finally walked out of the back door at ten, an hour before the kitchen closed. The dining room was deserted, leaving only a single annoyed waitress by herself, texting furiously in the corner.

The cold night air bit into Mark's skin like pins and needles. The combination of the heat and steam made Mark's body acclimate to the tropical environment within The Cage, so the cold winter months made the transition from the kitchen into the night air painful at times.

His thick jacket did very little to help keep Mark warm. He could still feel his wet clothes underneath his jacket, pressing against him like a thousand ice cubes against his body. Pulling his hat down over his ears, Mark put his hands under his arms and pressed forward against the freezing wind. It reminded him of times when he would have to walk to the bus stop three blocks from his house in the morning to go to school. The children would often walk up the street backward, encased in so many layers of coats and scarves that they looked like ticks getting ready to pop. Unfortunately, tonight Mark only had one jacket, and the thin hat barely stretched over the top of his ears. The half-hour it would take to walk up Fillmore Hill on a night like this would be difficult and downright dangerous.

The cold night wind continued to penetrate his bones, and Mark knew he had to get inside as soon as possible. It felt as if the temperature had dropped well below zero, and he had no business trying to walk home tonight. He saw warm lights emanating from a small bar in a rundown shopping center and decided to go inside and call a cab.

The bar was having as slow of a night as the empty restaurant he had just left. One woman sat at the bar talking with the bartender, who looked at Mark with disappointment, clearly as anxious to go home for the night as Mark was.

Mark asked if they had a pay phone and was directed to the back near the restrooms. The bar was a much nicer place than he had imagined it would be from the outside. Having walked by it hundreds of times, the idea of coming inside had never crossed his mind, but it was warm and inviting. It was an American version of an Irish pub, with high wooden booths and a dark, worn bar in the center with three television screens silently playing ESPN highlights.

The cab company was as rude as he expected and told Mark that it might be two hours before anyone could make it out to pick him up, considering the snow and the frozen roads.

Mark hung up the phone, sat in the booth closest to him, and pretended to watch television. Sports were something Mark felt he'd always missed out on. Men watched sports and were as emotional about their favorite team as they were about their families, but Mark never got it. He wanted to, but it was all lost on him.

"Can I get you anything, honey?" a tall blonde woman said way too loud as she walked towards him. Attractive in the sense that maybe two decades ago, she was stunning, but time and life had changed all that. Yet within her was the confidence of a young woman who has grown used to men watching her, and she walked over to the table with a comfortingly bright smile.

"I'm sorry, I'm just waiting for a cab. I don't want to be any trouble. Maybe just a cup of coffee if you have any made." Mark said hopefully.

"Oh, it's no trouble. The kitchen's getting ready to close, but I can get you some chowder with your coffee. It looks like you could use some warming up."

"That would be great. Thank you." Mark said, smiling and taking off his jacket.

"Okay, honey, my name is Donna. Just yell if you need anything," Donna said, walking away and into the kitchen. She came out with a bowl of steaming white clam chowder and coffee in a few minutes.

Mark took a bite, and the warmth washed through his insides as if he had been wrapped in a warm towel. Under any other circumstance, the soup would have been plain and tasteless, but tonight, after escaping the cold, it was one of the best meals he had ever eaten. He was so engrossed in the food that he did not notice the woman sitting at the bar walk over to his table.

"I'm sorry to bother you, but you're not Russell, are you?" she asked.

Mark looked up and saw the thirty-something woman with short brown hair wearing a black dress, holding onto a giant gold flowered purse for dear life.

"No, I'm not," Mark said.

"Yeah, I didn't think so. I was supposed to meet him, and I've been sitting over there for an hour trying to figure out what I'm doing here in the first place, you know? Well, anyway... never mind. Sorry to bother you."

Mark smiled, not knowing what to say.

"Look, I'm sorry, but do you mind if I sit with you for a little bit? I don't want to seem pathetic. Well…any more so than I already do. But I got all dressed up and then got stood up. Maybe I could buy you a drink or something?" Something in her eyes looked as if she was reaching a breaking point. Mark motioned for her to sit down, not knowing what else to do.

"Thanks. My name is Amber," she said, sitting down and extending her hand across the table.

"Mark. My name is Mark. It's nice to meet you," Mark said, reaching for her hand.

The softness of her small, smooth hand felt good in Mark's, and suddenly the small wedding band on his left hand felt as if it shrank a full size and began squeezing his finger. Without consciously thinking about it, when he let go of Amber's hand, he reached down, slipped off his ring, and tucked it into his pocket.

Trying to keep up with Amber's many stories was like trying to catch a bullet train by holding out a hook and letting it jerk him inside. There were a few stories Mark was able to follow, but most of the time, he was completely lost with what she was talking about or how it related to the last story, but he had to admit to himself that she was entertaining to watch.

After an hour, every problem in Amber's life had been dropped on the table. No subject had been held in reserve. Mark sat back and listened while eating the rest of his soup and said very little. It reminded him of when he and Shannon were first getting to know each other behind the restaurant, as she would smoke and talk about herself, and Mark would listen. The only difference was that more ground was covered in substantially less time with Amber.

She had been married for a few years, only to come home and find that her husband had left her. No note or reason; he just packed up his clothes and disappeared. Since then, she has been meeting guys online and trying to make a connection. There had been a few prospects, but after three years, she was beginning to have doubts about the whole idea of online dating.

Amber perked up when Mark said he knew nothing about it. Excited, she explained the almost sacred process of proper online dating. First, someone meets and comments on a profile. If that goes well, the next level is to meet in a chat room, hopefully leading to a phone call. If the phone conversation went well, they would try to arrange a time and place to meet.

Tonight she was supposed to meet Russell, but even Amber had to admit that she didn't know if that was his real name or if his profile picture looked anything like the man in real life. After her third drink and second cigarette, she admitted that she had not expected much from Russell. He had moved them through the stages of online dating too quickly, and Amber was pretty sure he was looking for nothing more than a one-night stand. She laughed at herself, realizing that she just came out in the middle of one of the worst winter storms to meet a man she didn't even know and probably didn't want to.

Mark sat quietly, looking down at the empty bowl and cold coffee as the laughter turned to tears, and Amber hid her face as she sobbed quietly into her hands.

She stood up and quietly excused herself, and walked towards the restroom. Stopping, she suddenly walked back to the table, not caring that her makeup was ruined by her tears and feeble attempt to hide them.

"Please don't go anywhere," she said with quiet desperation. "I'll be right back."

"Okay."

Amber smiled apologetically and finally went into the women's restroom behind Mark.

Mark did not know what to do with himself for the few minutes she was away. He felt a thrill to be in the presence of a woman even though he knew she had no real interest in him. She was just lonely and hurting and wanted to be with anyone. He thought about Alan and wondered if they could make it to the movies, but remembering the plush Audi and how it cut through the snow like a warm knife, Mark could relax knowing that Alan was well taken care of. He had nowhere to be and no one to take care of for a change. Why not stay here with Amber a little while longer?

Amber came out of the bathroom a few minutes later, and even though Mark wanted to admit to himself that she was pretty, all he could see was how tired and embarrassed she was. For a moment, neither of them said anything, not knowing how to overcome the tears and the pain that had sprung up so suddenly.

"I think they're getting ready to kick us out of here," Amber said, leaning over the table towards Mark. "Do you want to come over to my place for a while? Nothing serious, but maybe we could..."

It must have been the look of surprise on Mark's face that caused her to stop suddenly. They both sat still, letting the words hang in the air, neither knowing what to do.

"I'm sorry. I shouldn't have..." Amber said, reaching for her things.

"Yes, I would." Mark blurted out. "That sounds like fun.

"Really? I mean, no pressure or anything. We can keep everything casual," Amber said.

"No, it sounds like fun. I need to cancel my cab, though. They should be here any minute," Mark said.

"Or, we could just take off and hope they don't get here before we get out the door," Amber said with a mischievous grin.

Without saying a word, Mark stood up and grabbed his coat without thinking about what he was doing, totally caught up in the moment. He walked towards the bar to pay his tab, knowing that Amber was behind him gathering her things.

Donna was behind the bar and looked at him with a knowing grin. "I thought you two would never leave."

Mark reached into his pocket for the cash he had earned in tips (something the wait staff absolutely loathed to share with him each night) and was pulling out the wadded bills when he heard his wedding ring dropping to the floor and bouncing away. In the silence of the bar, the tiny dings of metal against the wood floor sounded as though he had dropped a hammer as they echoed off the walls.

"You dropped..." Amber began to say as she picked up the ring. It took a few seconds for her to realize what she was holding before she offered it up to Mark with a confused look.

"You're married?" she said softly, still holding the ring to Mark. Her hand was beginning to shake.

Donna stared at the two of them and did not move. Mark looked at the two women, and the words of explanation remained stuck in his throat. He knew there was no easy way to explain what...

"YOU'RE MARRIED?!" Amber finally yelled, throwing his ring across the room and staring Mark down, not knowing if she would run out of the room or punch him as hard as she could. She opted for throwing a tepid leftover margarita that was sitting on the bar in his face, then stormed out into the frigid night.

Mark wiped his face with his bare hand and did not move from where he stood. It was only when Donna cleared her throat that Mark reached up and took his change from her. While Amber was furious, Donna looked at Mark with pity and disgust. She handed him a towel and then walked down to the end of the bar and began turning off the lights as if Mark no longer existed.

With everything he had been through at work and with Jenny and Tyler, and even Shannon, hating him so much, Mark had still always held a small candle of light within himself. Even though all of these people in his life hated him, that small amount of light he maintained reminded him that he was a good person. When the drink hit his face, and he realized what he had done, or rather what he had *almost* done, it was as if the flame had finally been fully extinguished. Mark held onto his coat with one hand and the small dingy towel in the other and walked back and forth in front of the bar where Amber had thrown his ring until he found it. Donna sat in the corner and acted as if he were invisible. The only sound was the humiliated shuffle of his feet dragging across the wooden floor as he looked for the ring.

> *Mark could feel her breath on his face as the spit from her screams made him feel even more worthless than the words she was spewing. The alcohol smell was pungent and made him want to throw up, but he did not give ground. He stood like a wall while she did everything she could to tear him down.*
>
> *She hit him in the face over and over. She yelled obscenities and scratched him, but he did not give way. He would never give in again.*
>
> *Suddenly, an explosion inside the back of his head caused everything in his vision to go black, and with all the strength in his body, he released the energy that had been repressed his entire life..., and he shoved back.*

When he finally found the ring under one of the benches, the front door opened on cue, and an annoyed man with a gray, alcoholic beard stepped inside and asked if someone had called for a cab.

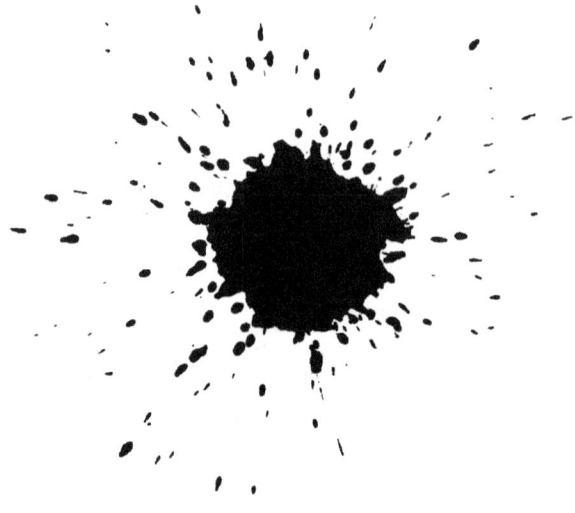

~ CHAPTER FIVE ~

Walking up to the retirement home, Mark was always reminded of a story he had heard when he was young. He did not remember when, but the fable always came to mind as he walked towards the sliding front double doors.

The story was about a young man named Puck who lived in a village at the bottom of a deep valley. High above the valley in the mountains, a tremendous dragon had lived for centuries in a deep cave but was now ancient and feeble, and everyone in the village was waiting for the old lizard to finally die. Every month, the village sent a volunteer to the cave to see if the dragon was still kicking. The volunteer would reach the cave, always careful not to get too close to the cave's opening because the dragon's breath could cook a man in a matter of seconds. So, standing behind a large boulder to the right of the cave every full moon, a volunteer would yell into the cave, asking the old dragon if it was still alive. The old dragon would say, "Still alive," and nothing more. One day, a young man in the village named Puck volunteered to check on the dragon. Boldly, Puck walked up to the cave, but instead of hiding behind the stone, he walked directly into the cave and stood only a few feet from the old dragon's snout.

"You still alive?" Puck asked confidently.

The old dragon that had been asleep for several weeks lifted his head, surprised to see someone so daring to enter his lair. "I am. You must have been very sure that I would be dead."

Puck shrugged his shoulders and said, "It doesn't matter to me either way. I just wanted to see you for myself."

"But weren't you afraid of being eaten?" The old dragon asked.

"No."

"Weren't you afraid I might cook you with a single breath?"

"No."

"And the thought that I could crush you under one of my paws didn't make you afraid?"

"No."

"And why is that?" the dragon asked, surprised by the young man's courage.

"Because everyone in my village is scared of you and avoids this entire mountain. They live boring lives of constant fear, and I wanted to see what we are all so afraid of with my own eyes," Puck said, standing with his chest out and arms crossed defiantly.

"Because you are so brave, I will tell you a secret no one knows about me," sighed the dragon. "I am so old that I can no longer breathe fire. My knees hurt so much I can no longer stand. Your people will be in no danger if they want to travel on my mountain," the dragon said.

"I knew there was no reason to be afraid of you! That is why I volunteered; to prove that everyone's fear of you is foolish," Puck said, extremely proud of himself.

"That is very brave of you, my young friend," the old dragon said, smiling. "However, there is one thing you forgot to consider: fear is not something we have been given to rule our lives. It is something we have been given to help prolong them. Even if you refuse to live in fear, you can still die because of stupidity."

With that, the dragon snatched up Puck and ate him with a single crunch.

The story's moral was that while facing our fears is admirable, it's still stupid to stand too close to what can eat you.

Mark had told Shannon that story many years ago when she had driven down to Canon City with Mark to check on his mother. She thought that the story was a cruel thing to say about a woman who suffered a stroke twenty years ago and had been stuck in a second-rate nursing home ever since. She remained appalled until she had been forced to spend more than just a few fleeting minutes with the woman. Since then, she had affectionately referred to Mark's mother as the 'Dragon Lady.' It had been early that Saturday morning when Mark received the call to come to the hospital to calm his mother down. Even though she had lost the ability to move her right arm and the right side of her face was paralyzed, Eliza Soderlind still had a wicked tongue, and if that was not enough to get what she wanted, she also possessed a violent temper. Mark did his best to come and see her once a month, but her outbursts rarely allowed him the luxury of waiting that long.

She lived in Canon City, one-hour southwest of Colorado Springs. With no public transportation to connect the two cities, Mark was forced to catch a Greyhound bus, making the one-hour trip into a minimum of four hours in each direction. Thankful that Alan was still away for the night, Mark had rushed out the door at just a little past five in the morning and walked through the hospital's sliding glass doors a little after nine.

The head nurse saw Mark as soon as he entered. She pinched her lips together and put her hand on her hip in disgust. Alicia Sanchez, a large Hispanic woman with a hairstyle out of the nineteen fifties, disliked Mark's mother intensely, but that was nothing new. In the twenty years she had lived in the hospital,

Mark had yet to meet any nurse who liked Eliza precisely because of days like today.

Ms. Sanchez motioned for Mark to follow her with a severe wave of her hand. Mark took off his jacket and began to follow her down the worn-carpeted hallways of the hospital. Mark caught glimpses of men and women in the rooms with oxygen tanks and walkers. Old men walked the hallways, taking only centimeter steps as Ms. Sanchez flew by them in her silent bulky white nurse shoes. When they arrived at the dining room, Mark saw his mother wearing the same clothes she always seemed to be wearing when he came. Unable to dress, the nurses and caregivers did their best to dress her, but more often than not, they simply let her wear her red worn-out robe over her hospital gown.

"She bit another volunteer," Ms. Sanchez said to Mark before angrily walking out of the room. This was not the first time; they both knew it would not be the last. Mark's job would be the same as it always was on days like these: try to calm Eliza down enough to get her back into her room.

"Mom?" Mark said, walking across the room to where she sat alone, stooped in her chair, looking outside.

"Oh, so they called you, did they? Useless," she snarled, looking at Mark as if she were sizing him up like a boxer before a fight.

"Yeah, they said you bit someone again. You can't do that," Mark said gently, sitting beside her and trying to act soothing.

"Why? What are they going to do? We both know they can't throw me out of here. I'm old and disabled; they're stuck with me until they either tear this place down or I die inside it," she said defiantly, her voice raising to a shout.

"C'mon, we need to get you back to your room. How long have you been in here?" Mark asked, standing up and taking hold of the handles on the back of her wheelchair.

"Who knows? Who cares?" she hissed like an old cobra. "They were trying to poison me, and I fought back, so they all ran off like cowards and called you. Like I give a..."

"No one is trying to poison you, Mom." Mark quickly interjected, relieved that she allowed him to move her away from the window. From what he could tell, she was having one of her better days.

"What the hell do you know? The applesauce they feed us here turned bad a week ago, but they keep shoving it down our throats as if our taste buds are as useless as our worn-out minds." Her eyes were wild as she continued her rant. "I may not remember everything, but I can taste when food is going bad, that's for damn sure!" she shouted, folding her arms for emphasis as Mark opened the dining room door and backed through it.

In the hallways, the other patients of the home avoided looking her in the eye to avoid provoking her. Thankfully, it only took minutes for Mark to return to her room and pull back the covers on her bed so he could lift her into it.

"Is your bitch of a wife dead yet?" she asked casually as Mark laid her gently down on the bed. "She might as well be. If she's not, she's most likely just trying to stay as far away from you as possible."

Mark ignored the comment and sat across the stale room in the rickety wooden chair. Even though she was mean, it still seemed like the polite thing to do. He knew he could only stay a few minutes because he needed to return to Colorado Springs in time for Alan to come home. He also knew that he would have to spend at least an hour apologizing to the staff and Ms. Sanchez before he left, but even so, a few minutes with his mother seemed like the right thing to do.

"You know what your father said to me the night before he left?" she asked, fidgeting to get comfortable. "Remember now; this was back when men did not just up and leave their families like they do now."

"Do we really have to do this now?" Mark sighed, knowing what was coming.

"Yes, we have to do this now! Do you know why? Because I have to live in this shithole! I have to have those fat women look down on me and dress me, even though their breath smells like chicken grease! This is why I'm here. It's not because of the stroke or the medical problems; it's because, in 1984, your father walked out the door and left me all alone with you!" she roared, spitting as she spoke and looking at Mark with naked hatred. "'If only we had waited before having a baby,' was what he said. We were married for only six months before you showed up, and he left because of you. And now I'm stuck here, waiting to die alone." Bitter tears ran slowly down her creased cheeks like hot rivulets of lava down an ancient but still deadly volcano.

Mark stood up slowly and began to walk to the door. "Bye, Mom."

She wasn't finished yet. "So when I ask you if your bitch of a wife is dead yet, don't think I don't know. Don't you think I don't know what happened!" she screamed as Mark turned the corner away from her room and left the building without apologizing to anyone. He had, once again, ventured too close to the teeth of the dragon.

~ CHAPTER SIX ~

Even though she was the new face at the school, her students considered Erica the coolest teacher in the history of all teachers. While most of the other educators at the school considered her a show-off, Erica had made close friends with the principal, so what the other teachers thought of her did not matter.

The source of the friction between her and her colleagues was that she did not use the equipment provided by the district but went out and purchased her own. While the other classrooms struggled with overhead projectors from the early nineties, Erica used her iPad, wirelessly attached to an Epson video projector, so she could walk around the classroom while she taught. She would use the web and its vast resources to show YouTube videos while other classrooms struggled with grease marker slides and ancient films. There was very little doubt that her modern approach to teaching had put her classroom ahead of the others; parents almost immediately began requesting their children's transfers into her classroom daily, even though hers was already completely full.

Today was the day that Erica had been waiting for all week. Because her students were performing so well, she had received permission to teach art classes on Friday afternoons. Every student looked forward to the lessons, especially today's lesson, because it would allow them to make a complete mess of themselves and the classroom.

The week before, Erica introduced the students to the artist Jackson Pollock. A modern artist that an untrained eye dismissed as nothing but paint splatters, his works were considered by the highest echelons of the art world as a master and sold for hundreds of millions of dollars. Erica promised the students that if everyone completed their homework all week, she would arrange for them to create their own paintings in the vein of Jason Pollock... and, most importantly, allow them to get as messy as they wanted.

To everyone's surprise, the bribe worked, and now it was Friday, and the students were holding their canisters of paint in their small hands like loaded weapons, ready to go off.

Erica had bought each student a plastic rain slicker from the local dollar store because even though she stressed not to get any paint on anything other than their canvases, no one had any illusions as to how messy this activity was going to get. After pushing the desks into the hall, placing plastic tarps on the floor, and spacing the children as far away from each other as possible, Erica gave the word, and the class-wide experiment in paint splattering began.

The noise went from silent to playground cacophony in an instant. Erica hid her iPad and computer at the last minute and then bounced around the classroom, getting the students who were overexcited to calm down and those that were too timid to be excited. Other teachers stood outside of the classroom wondering about the noise, even though Erica had provided plenty of notice as to what was going to happen, knowing many of them would want even the smallest excuse to find something else to complain about.

Principal Evans was also waiting for the event and was in the hallway to support Erica by herding the curious teachers back into their own classrooms. Terri stood outside and laughed as she watched Erica trying to control the chaos and mentally telling herself she would cancel her plans tonight to help Erica clean up her classroom. She would pick up some wine and make an event of it. Whatever Erica was, she was not scared of having a little fun with her students, even though the rest of the staff would be scoffing and snorting about this for weeks to come.

It was while trying to control the noise and chaos that Erica really noticed Alan for the first time. With so many children in her class at one time, it was often the quiet, well-behaved children that received the least amount of attention from a teacher.

However, in the middle of the chaos, it was Alan's lack of boyhood insanity that called so much attention to him. While the other children were flicking the paint onto the canvas, Alan had sat behind one of the tables against the window with his paintbrushes and was looking down with an intensity that was shocking to Erica. She had only witnessed that level of intensity from students at Cambridge, but never in a child so young.

Erica made her way across the room towards Alan, hoping not to disturb him. She felt as if she made one wrong step or moved too quickly, the intensity the small boy was experiencing would be as easily frightened away as a startled deer. Yet the closer she got to him, she could tell he was not paying attention to anything around him; he was lost in his own world. The brush moved on the canvas with purpose. While the other students slopped color after color of paint, Alan's brush moved with precision and determination. She noticed that he was only using black paint and dipping his brush into a small cup of water at times before returning to the canvas. She knew he was trying to get different shades of gray out of the black paint by watering it down, but this technique was hard to control. Even more impressive was that she had not taught him the technique, and her curiosity began to rise about what exactly he was doing.

The recess bell rang, jolting Erica back to reality and her duties. The children almost collectively sighed, knowing the painting time was over but quickly realizing too that school was over, so they threw off their painting slickers and ran for the door. When Erica thought again of what Alan had been doing, the classroom was empty and quiet.

Walking among the mess, Erica did not think about the hours it would take to clean everything up. She walked directly to the back of the room to see what Alan had been working on. When she got to the table, she was disappointed to see just another paint-splatter painting on half of Alan's canvas, just like the other children. She was about to walk away when she saw the original painting and then suddenly it hit her, and her jaw dropped in disbelief.

"What's the matter? You look like you just saw a ghost!" Terri Evans exclaimed, standing in the doorway of the classroom.

* * *

The next morning, Mark sat in the principal's office after dropping Alan off at his classroom. Alan had come home with a note from his teacher saying that it was very important that she meet with him right away. Thankfully, Mark was able to get one of the prep cooks to cover his morning duties, but even so, he fervently hoped this would not take too long.

As foolish as he knew it to be, he had tried to dress a little better than usual for the meeting. Even though he was a grown man, something remained intimidating about being called to the principal's office. He knew it was foolish because he had met Ms. Evans more than once but still reflexively felt he had done something wrong.

Mark did not expect to see the woman who walked into the room carrying a large book and a small dirty canvas in her hands. To Mark, it was like looking into the sun; she was so beautiful that he felt that he should not look at her directly. Never before had Mark understood the expression 'stunning' until that moment, as he was quite literally stunned. Even after she introduced herself, Mark could not find any words to say.

She looked away self-consciously, pulling the strand of hair that had come loose behind her ear, and sat down behind the desk. Mark sat down across from her and did his best impression of a dumbstruck lunatic.

"I wanted to show you something that Alan did in class yesterday," Erica began.

Mark snapped out of it at the mention of Alan's name and suddenly became coherent. Erica handed over the small canvas gently as if it was incredibly fragile. Mark took it from her hand and was confused. He had been expecting to see the typical anatomically inappropriate or violent drawing a student would make to get their parents called to the school. What he looked at was just a bunch of paint splattered randomly on half the canvas, nothing more.

Mark looked up at Erica, who was clearly very happy about something and was doing everything she could to contain herself. He looked at her with a dull expression. "I'm sorry, I don't understand."

As quick as a gunshot, Erica opened the large book she had brought and placed it next to the canvas. "It's a Pollock, Mr. Soderlind. Alan painted a Pollock! Specifically, "Lavender Mist" from 1950. Isn't that incredible?"

Mark looked down at the book and saw the same kind of paint splatter on Alan's canvas. His confusion must have been enough to tell Erica that Mark did not see what she was so excited about. She stood up and walked around the desk.

"Look at the two of them, especially the top left-hand corner of the original," Erica said, leaning over the desk and pushing the book and the painting next. Mark quickly put his hands in his lap as he had done hundreds of times as a student when he didn't understand what he was being told.

"See? Look here... and here," Erica pointed to the original and then to Alan's painting. "They're identical! In fact, the entire painting Alan created is identical to the picture he was working on to such a degree that I can't... wow," Erica trailed off, standing up and marveling at the two images side by side.

Mark looked at the painting in the book and the painting sitting before him, and suddenly the light bulb went off. She was right. The small portion that Alan had painted looked exactly the same as the original. Each splash of color was the exact shape. Each thin hairline of grey and black were in the same place. It really was remarkable.

"Alan did this?" Mark stammered when the truth finally sunk in.

"Yes, I watched him do it," Erica said absently, still looking at the miniature painting with pride. "Oh! There is one other thing. You are not going to believe this!"

Erica reached across the desk and pulled out a black and white photocopy inside the book. "You see on the original painting by Pollock, the small amount of flesh tone color throughout the painting? Since Alan only had black paint, he couldn't paint the color into this, so he substituted a shade of gray." Erica handed Mark the photocopy.

"This is a copy of the original in black and white, but look, the shade of gray Alan substituted for the color matches exactly. He only had grey tones to work with, but he somehow knew the exact shade of gray to substitute. Isn't that incredible?!?" Erica gasped.

Mark was beginning to feel stupid. He was proud of Alan for matching the painting exactly, and Alan had impressed his teacher, but all Mark could think was, "So what?"

Seeing the confusion on Mark's face, Erica walked behind the desk and put on her teaching face. Mark was not getting it and he needed to understand the magnitude of what they were talking about if she was going to be able to address why she had really asked him to come in today.

"Do you know anything about art by any chance, Mr. Soderlind?" Erica asked, already knowing the answer.

Mark replied, slightly foolish and deflated, "No, I really don't."

"That's ok. Imagine that someone, using only black and white, wanted to draw something." She reached down and flipped the book open to a picture of what looked like a barn. The pictures were labeled 'Wyeth'; even with Mark's lack of education, he knew it was remarkable.

"If you want to paint or draw with one color, you have to use all the different shades of that color. In doing so, you substitute a gray shade for the real color. Shadows become dark shades, while areas of light become very light shades. Does that make sense?"

She flipped the page, and there was a small image of a pair of boots, also by Wyeth, and the concept she was trying to teach him became clear. He nodded his head, indicating that he understood.

Erica flipped back to the Pollock painting and put Alan's canvas on top of the book.

She stared laser beams at Mark. "The fact that Alan, in the middle of a classroom of screaming second graders, could paint this painting so precisely and with the exact shades to replicate the original painting is nothing short of... a miracle."

Suddenly, it became clear to Mark what was really happening. "Are you saying that Alan cheated?" Mark asked, suddenly feeling very defensive.

"No! Not at all! I am saying that your son could be a genius," Erica said quickly, moving before him so he couldn't leave.

Mark looked at her to ensure her expression was serious and sat back down, aghast. "What?"

"Mr. Soderlind, many artists work their lives to develop this control. Your son did not randomly throw colors on the page. He took one of the most complicated pieces of art I know of and replicated it with such precision that it's... staggering. Something like this is unheard of! I talked to my brother last night, who is at Cambridge, and he didn't believe me. I wouldn't believe me, but I saw it happen with my own eyes. This little piece of work is simply beyond..." Erica's voice trailed off as her awe robbed her of the vocabulary to explain the magnitude of the product of Alan's afternoon.

Mark had never experienced true joy in his entire life until that moment. For the rest of his life, he would reflect on sitting in that small room as the first of three defining moments. Mark would never forget even the smallest detail as he realized who Alan really was and what a tremendous gift he held inside of him.

He reached over and picked up the small painting with the same kind of fragile care Erica had shown when she originally presented it to him. Mark stared at it as if she had just shown it to him for the first time all over again. Could it be true? Could the quiet boy who held his hand and sat on his back really be a genius? Just the thought lifted Mark's spirit as if it had been attached to a balloon. He smiled so wide it made his cheeks hurt because it had been so long since he had done such a simple thing as grin. It had been so long since he had a reason to. Today was one of the most perfect moments in Mark's life. As he sat in the uncomfortable chair in silence, looking at the painting, he felt as if the dark clouds that had always seemed to be hanging over him had drifted apart briefly, and he saw the beauty of sunlight for the first time.

"I wanted to get your permission to work with Alan, and to see if this was just a one-time fluke or if he really is... well, what I believe he might be," Erica said.

"Of course!" Mark responded, beaming with pride and holding Alan's canvas with two hands.

"Is it okay to meet after school for an hour or so? Does that work with your schedule?" Erica asked, finally standing up and walking towards the door. "If you need me to bring him home, I'd be happy to."

"No, I'll pick him up. Take all the time you need. I'll talk to him tonight about it, but I think he'll be fine," Mark said while walking out of the office, still clutching the painting.

"Mr. Soderlind, there is one other thing," Erica said as she walked with him down the silent halls of the school towards the big double doors that led outside.

She stopped in the hallway and gently touched Mark's arm to get his attention. Everything she told him had been leading to this moment, and she wanted to ensure she had his complete attention.

"A school in Boston is specifically created for extraordinary children like Alan. I think that if what I suspect is true, then you might be able to get Alan enrolled there. It would be an amazing opportunity for him because they could nurture his gift like...."

"I'm sorry; did you say it was in Boston?" Mark stammered.

"Well, yes. It's considered one of the finest schools in the country. In the world, actually. They have an academic program that's unlike anywhere else. If we... I mean, if you could get Alan into that school, it would open up so many doors for him," Erica said in a hopeful voice.

"Thank you, but I don't think so," Mark replied, still overjoyed. It was not that he hadn't heard what Erica had said, even though her beauty was still a distraction; it was that he knew how Shannon would react at just the thought of leaving Colorado and moving to Boston. It was simply unthinkable, so he didn't bother to consider it further. Mark smiled goodbye at Erica and walked towards the double doors to go outside.

"Mr. Soderlind, please wait!" Erica hurried to catch up with him quickly. "Mr. Sode... do you mind if I call you Mark? And by all means, please feel free to call me Erica." She held her hand to him as if meeting for the first time.

Mark took her hand in his and hoped that the grin he already had on his face for Alan was enough to cover the childish excitement of getting her hand for himself.

"Mark, I don't know if you truly understand what we're discussing. The Benton Academy is the most amazing school for his age. Alan would not only get the finest education possible, but he'd also be assigned a personal tutor, have access to the latest technology, and they would assign Alan mentors to help him grow in his skill. This school allows ten new students a year, and I think Alan has a real shot at getting in. I would be more than happy to help him in any way possible," Erica finished, suddenly realizing she had never let go of his hand.

Mark heard the words, and his heart soared briefly at just the possibility, but he knew the reality of the situation. A school like that would cost money, and they simply did not have any. Food, clothing, and shelter were what Mark could afford, and anything beyond that was simply a fantasy.

Mark pulled his hand out of hers gently and smiled sadly. "Thank you, but I'm sorry, it's impossible."

He walked the final yards to the double doors and pushed on the metal bar to open them. He turned to see Erica standing in the same spot.

"If it's all right, I'd still like you to work with Alan after school, as you mentioned. If that is okay." Mark said, his pleasant tone barely masking his creeping disappointment.

"Of course," she answered, still stunned at his refusal even to consider her offer.

Mark wanted to take the final steps outside, but before he knew why, he turned and looked at Erica, feeling a surge of emotion as he held the small canvas. Trying to control the overwhelming pride he felt in his son, and what she had told him, Mark felt a sting in his eyes as he quietly said to her, "I know you're disappointed about the school in Boston, but... you will never understand how much this means to Alan or to me."

With that, he smiled a tight-lipped smile without being able to look Erica in the eyes as he fought the emotions that were threatening to overtake him. He walked into the sunlight and felt the joy return as he walked off the school grounds, holding the small canvas with both hands, studying every brilliant centimeter.

Erica watched as Mark walked away and down the street. She was furious with him a minute before he had walked out the door. How any parent could not see the potential she was talking about was beyond her; in her mind, she was ready to make her case more forcefully than before, and then he had turned around and looked at her.

The look in his eyes broke her heart. What she saw in his eyes was a sense of pride and love for his son that she had never experienced before. This was not a man who was selfishly ignoring his son's potential; this was a man who deeply loved his child but simply could not do what she wanted him to do.

She watched him as he walked away, holding the painting and smiling. He suddenly reminded her of a small boy who had received a gift he had treasured as if he had never seen anything so beautiful.

Erica turned and walked down the hallway. She knew she needed to relieve Terri from taking care of her classroom. She smiled as she walked down the empty hallway with the heels of her shoes echoing off the tile floor and metal lockers, knowing she had done the right thing by asking Mark to come down and meet with her today. He looked like a guy who could use some good news.

"This isn't over by a long shot," she murmured as she opened the door to her classroom.

~ **CHAPTER SEVEN** ~

Mark loathed the taste of blood in his mouth.

As a child, on more occasions than he could remember after his mother had been drinking or just in a bad mood, she would hit him with an open palm across his face when she thought he got out of line. While her slaps stung more than anything, it was the nights when she clenched her fist and hit him in his mouth that he hated the most and remembered with perfect clarity. The metallic taste would linger, even if he fought the subsequent nausea it brought by eating something to give his mouth something else to do other than bleed. Nights when his mother's aim was off, and she hit him in his nose instead, were the worst because the smell of the blood, combined with what drained down his face and the back of his throat from his sinuses, would be all he could taste and smell for days.

Shannon never hit him with her fist, so when she did strike, it was always unexpected.

She had not been home for several days, which was not unusual at this point. Mark had spent the night talking with Alan about staying after school to work with Erica on learning how to paint and draw. Mark was careful not to press him too hard because he wanted Alan to want to do this on his own. If he was as gifted as his teacher thought, then the spark to work as hard as he would have to should come from within Alan and not out of some obligation to his father.

Alan, like any young boy, was excited and then immediately distracted. Mark understood that Alan had truly enjoyed making the painting that Mark had brought home. They hung it on the wall next to the front door so they could see it from just about anywhere in the house. Every time he looked at it, Mark could not help but glow with pride.

After putting Alan to bed, Mark sat back on the couch and stared at the painting for a couple of hours, thinking about the school, and when he could not stop himself...Erica. The entire experience was something that Mark had no way of relating to; it was completely new and unexpected. How does one accept that their child, who can't pick up their clothes from the floor, might be a genius? How does someone, who has only seen the ugliness of human nature, handle such news when it is told to him by the most beautiful woman in the world, who also happens to be looking at him with respect and even admiration? As if he had even the smallest part to play in the gift placed within the small boy.

She had been right, and Mark knew it. If Alan had an opportunity to go to a school that would nurture his talent, then he had an obligation to Alan to make it happen. But even as much as Mark wanted it to happen, there simply was no way. Mark knew that even if he managed to win the lottery and suddenly had all the money it would take to pay for the school, he would have to leave Shannon behind, and he knew he could not do that.

Mark turned off the lights and started to make his way to the bedroom when the image of Erica popped into his head again. He could not help but smile despite himself. How did a woman like that end up teaching at a tiny public school and not making millions in the movies or as a model? He had never seen a woman that remarkable with his own eyes before. When he was with her, he felt like he was suddenly in the center of the universe and then felt incredibly stupid for thinking so.

He lay awake in bed thinking about the woman from the bar a couple of weeks ago who had thrown the drink in his face. She had picked up on who he really was quickly enough. Whenever he thought back on the sound of his wedding ring on the bar floor, he wanted to jump out of his skin from embarrassment and humiliation.

Shannon strode purposefully into the room, turned on the light, and threw open the window to let in the cold night air. She had always habitually adjusted every room to her liking without asking if it was acceptable to anyone else, specifically Mark. When they had been friends, it was something Mark would joke about; but over the years, it became a source of frustration and then quiet resentment. Mark had surrendered to it years ago, but in the back of his mind, he felt that it told him how little he actually mattered to her.

"We need to talk about something," Mark said, sitting up and reaching for the extra blanket at the foot of the bed.

"I'm not in the mood tonight. Can't it wait?" Shannon sniffed, taking off her earrings in the bathroom.

"It's about Alan and a meeting I had with his teacher today. She wants to start working with him after school. She thinks he might have some real talent." Mark said cautiously.

"Okay, that's great. What do you need to talk to me about?" She asked, shutting the door to the bathroom before he could respond.

"I'll be right back; I want to show you something," Mark said, climbing out of bed. He ran down the stairs and took the small painting off the wall. By the time Shannon came out of the bathroom, he was standing at the door holding it out to her.

Shannon looked at it and then looked at Mark with the same expression he had when he first saw it.

"I know, right? That's what I thought when I saw it for the first time too, but Alan's teacher explained it to me," Mark continued, trying to mask his enthusiasm. "Apparently, he duplicated a really famous painting down to the smallest detail. She showed me the original, and it really is amazing what he did," Mark said, cringing a little as Shannon handled the painting roughly.

"So?" Shannon handed it back to Mark with only a glance at it.

"Well, his teacher told me that she would work with him after school and that he might be eligible to attend this amazing school in Boston. The school is only for gifted children and is supposed to be really prestigious." Mark could feel the mood in the room change and get darker.

"Yeah, okay." Shannon rubbed her forehead and let out a big sigh. Everything that had to do with Mark or Alan always seemed to be such a burden. "What does this have to do with me?" She sat and fixed her gaze on Mark, who could tell things were worsening by the minute.

Mark paused to think of another way to talk about the subject that he knew was ridiculous, to begin with. Looking down at the painting, he tried to find the right words, but his mouth remained frozen and silent.

"Oh, wait! Are you seriously thinking we should send Alan to this school?" Shannon retorted condescendingly as she walked away from Mark, unbuckling her black leather belt with the thick silver buckle. "What kind of absolute jackass are you? How could you send your own son away across the country so he could go finger paint somewhere?"

The comment struck home, instantly getting under Mark's skin. "I wasn't going to send him off alone. I was going to... or, I was thinking, we would go with him."

"Seriously, Mark, you want us to move across the country to a strange city with no jobs so that Alan can learn how to be a starving artist?" Shannon laughed cruelly.

"You don't understand!" Mark argued quietly. "He's really good. If you could just..."

The buckle of her belt hit him in his eye and temple, and suddenly there were bright lights and ringing around him.   Time slowed down, and even though the pain from the blow did not hurt yet, it caused his body to go into self-preservation mode instantly. Instinctively, his hands went up to cover his face, but the buckle struck one more time on the opposite cheek, and he felt and tasted the inevitable warm blood in his mouth. He instantly felt as if he was going to vomit.

Shannon shoved him, and he fell in a ball, knowing all too well that this was not over. He heard the leather belt hiss through the air as Shannon hit him repeatedly with the thick metal buckle like a cruel master whipping a dog. Her anger was explosive, all-consuming, and without reason or compassion when she got like this. He had tried to contain or to control her in the past, but that only made her feel caged, causing her to strike harder and more viciously.

She finally stopped hitting him and stood over him, utterly calm. "You try to take my son away from me, and I swear to God, I will kill you both."

When Mark finally uncovered his head, she was gone, leaving only the familiar taste of blood in his mouth.

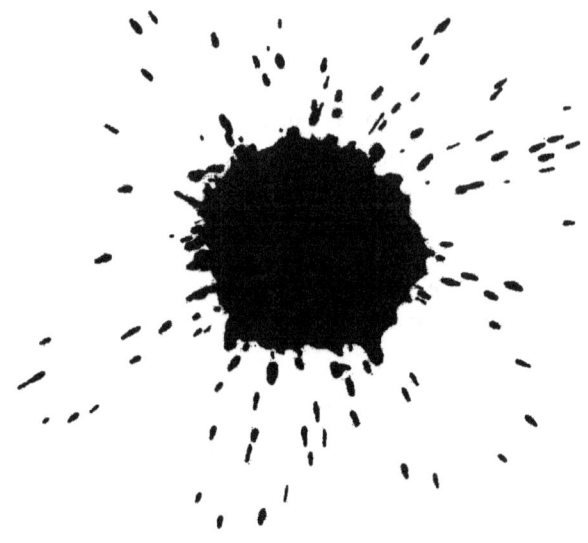

~ CHAPTER EIGHT ~

Erica had arrived early the next day at school and was waiting by the front gate, holding Alan's math book close to her chest, when she saw Mark and Alan walking towards the school.

Last night had been frustrating. She had been bouncing back and forth about what she should do; on the one hand, she truly believed that Mark would help Alan if he could, but she simply did not have the means. She doubted anyone had ever heard of the Benton Academy this far west, so naturally, the 'wow factor' of the school did not enter into the equation. If they were in Boston, just the mention of getting into the school would cause most parents to take a second or third mortgage on their homes just to get their child on a list for consideration.

Another part of her was telling her just to let it go. If they did not do this, the world would continue just as it always had. Governments would not collapse, and people would not suffer needlessly if Alan, for whatever reason, did not reach his full potential. Other things were more important than a small child learning to paint.

But she thought of something a friend told her a few years ago. After graduating from high school, it was inevitable that a small group of students would choose not to go to college but instead head off to New York or, if they were really brave, Los Angeles in hopes of being "discovered." A friend since childhood had similarly packed up her bags and left Boston for the "Great White Way," but within a few short years, she was back, enrolling in school.

Erica had lunch with her upon her return and was amazed at how much life had been sucked out of her. She said one thing Erica never forgot.

She said her agent told her that walking around New York and Los Angeles are potentially hundreds of Brandos, hundreds of DiVincis, hundreds of Tolkiens, all geniuses in their fields, but none of them working. The doorway is packed so tightly that it is almost impossible for any real genius to surface. All you could do was hope you get lucky or that your fame was destined by God, which it most likely was not.

Erica pulled down on her jacket in the cold wind as her determination to see Alan in the school solidified. She decided it had been fate for her to come out to Colorado on a whim. It had been fate that she, out of all the schools in the area, would be placed in a class with a student that only she could help. Her ties to the Benton Academy were strong, and she knew that her recommendation would carry weight with the board of trustees. She didn't care if it came down to dragging Mark and Alan across the country and throwing them through the front doors of the Benton Academy personally, she thought to herself. As God was her witness, that boy would be enrolled in that school this time next year.

As soon as Mark and Alan crossed the street, Erica left the schoolyard and walked directly to them with a heightened determination. She knew she was frowning as she marched towards them as if they had done something terribly wrong, but she could not stop herself.

Alan looked worried when he saw her, convinced he was in trouble. She couldn't help but notice how much they looked alike. Alan stared at her with wide eyes as she approached, while Mark kept his head down as he walked.

"Good morning, Alan," Erica said as nicely as possible, trying not to alarm the boy. "Could you go ahead and let me have a few words with your Dad?"

"Okay," Alan said softly while pulling Mark down by his hand. Mark leaned down, and Alan hugged him. Alan ran off to the school and through the fence to the playground but looked back just before going inside.

"I talked to Alan about staying late; I think he is really excited about it," Mark said, turning his head to look after Alan and making a point not to look at Erica directly.

"Good. I'm so happy to work with him," Erica said, smiling and waving at Alan. As soon as Alan was out of sight, she turned to Mark. "I wanted to show you something I found in Alan's desk."

She opened the math book to a blank page where a simple drawing of a hand holding a pen was in the center of the page. The detail was incredible, and it looked like a three-dimensional hand rising out of a two-dimensional surface.

"This is from the da Vinci notebooks I showed the class three weeks ago. I remember that I left it up on the screen for a little while as I showed the class a few images from a book. With this level of detail, Alan must have drawn it in only fifteen minutes at most."

Mark leaned in closer to the drawing, and Erica quickly turned the pages to the next marker and showed a grid-like pattern of birds that slowly morphed into a grid of fish.

"That one is Escher, we talked about that last week, but this one is my favorite." Erica turned the book quicker, slapping the pages down on one another. Mark could see that apart from the pieces Erica was looking for, hundreds of doodles in the book's margins would make any collegiate art major jealous.

"Look at this one! He must have spent hours on it," Erica marveled, handing the book to Mark. "I'm surprised he's not behind in his other schoolwork."

Mark looked down at the page, and the image took his breath away.

It was of a boy from several centuries ago standing with his hand on his hip, looking straight forward, almost as if he knew he was being watched. His clothes were ornate and detailed, and the boy held a hat in his left hand down by the high socks and bow-tied shoes.

"This is from a painting hanging in the room; the name of the painting is Blue Boy by Thomas Gainsborough. Unlike the others, he didn't copy the painting exactly. Can you see what he did?" Erica asked intently, standing close to Mark to look at the page together. "Look at the face..."

It immediately jumped off the page, and Mark saw his son looking back at him with his sad and serious eyes. Mark almost dropped the book and involuntarily took a step back. Erica took the book and pressed in close to make her next point.

"Can't you see what we're potentially dealing with here? Yesterday, when we talked, I suspected Alan's talent, his genius, but this leaves no doubt. Mark, please...you have to get Alan into the Benton Academy. It would be a tragedy if he grew up never knowing what his full potential was."

Yesterday, Mark had been distracted by Erica's' beauty, but he made sure he was ready for her today. As much as he wished the Benton Academy was possible, Mark sadly understood it was not.

No matter how much he wished things might be different, there was no escaping the truth.

"I'm sorry, but it... it's just not... I'm sorry." Mark tried to find the words without looking at her and then simply turned to walk away when he realized he couldn't.

Erica grabbed his arm, and Mark jumped involuntarily as if shocked. Erica stepped backward, puzzled by Mark's reaction. Before either of them could say anything, the school bell rang. She looked back at the building, knowing her time was running out.

"Mr. Soderlind... Mark..." Erica said, smiling while trying to calm the situation down. The look of sweetness in Mark's eyes was gone completely; she could sense she had crossed a line, but she wasn't ready to give up. "Do you know who Charles de Young was?"

Mark sighed and looked down at the ground, knowing that he was about to get a lecture. "No."

"He was a painter in England in the eighteen hundreds. You can find his paintings in museums around the world, and he's considered a Master. His work is considered raw and untrained, but the scope of it is amazing," Erica said as quickly as she could, knowing she had to go and that her audience was beginning to look as if he wanted to be anywhere but where he was.

"So what does that have to do with Alan?" Erica continued, "Charles de Young was a butcher and died broke. He was a butcher because his father was a butcher and his father before him. Charles did what any child would do and became the man his father wanted him to be. Decades after he died, a man found hundreds of canvasses and notebooks in Charles de Young's attic. The man that found the paintings became rich, while Charles de Young died penniless."

Erica took a moment to let what she was saying sink in. She could not tell if Mark was listening, but he had at least stopped fidgeting.

"Alan is a good kid, but he is going to become what he thinks you *want* him to become, and there is no way to avoid that because he wants to please you. You need to let Alan become everything he was destined to be, no matter what it will cost. If you need to move heaven or earth to ensure he gets the education he deserves, then that is what you do." She hated her scolding tone but couldn't stop herself because the point to be made was too crucial. "As his father, you need to do this. No excuses. No justifications as to why you can't. Alan is wired in such a way that literally thousands of people across the world would sell their souls to have a quarter of his potential. The idea that you would let him grow up without the opportunity to reach his true potential is...sickening."

Erica finally stopped, knowing she had gone too far. She could feel the heat from her frustration in her face and held onto Alan's school book so tight that she could feel her fingers beginning to ache. She instantly felt bad and embarrassed, but she still felt like she needed to get a reaction out of Mark. She felt he needed someone to shake him out of his complacency and wake him up to what was happening.

Instead, what she got was a man that, when he finally lifted his head, looked as if she had run him through with a sword. Her words had hurt him much deeper than she had meant to.

"I'm sorry," was all he said, and he turned around with his hands in his pockets.

Erica wanted to call out to him and apologize but found the words stuck in her throat.

She did not understand Mark. Every man she had ever known who'd taken a tongue-lashing like the one she just delivered would rise and fight back, even if they knew she was right. Men tended to yell and bang their chests like silverback apes, even if they knew somewhere in their brains that they had no clue what they were talking about, much less what they were fighting about. The problem was that even though she could not get Mark to react, she was an even bigger failure at getting him to change his mind. It was as if he could absorb her stress and simply walk away without any fight.

Erica turned and walked back to the school, only to find Alan standing at the gate looking at her. Instantly, she recognized the same intensity he had shown when he had been painting, yet this time it was quiet anger. As she walked up to him, he did not move even though all the other children had already entered the building. He simply looked at her as if he was furious with her.

"Alan, it's time to go inside," Erica said when she got close to him, bending down to his level.

Alan did not say anything but looked her directly in the eyes for a moment that seemed to last forever, and Erica got the message without Alan saying a word. She would never get whatever she wanted from Alan if she yelled at or hurt his father again. As sweet and innocent as Alan was, Erica understood that Alan was as much of a protector of his father as his father was for him.

The boy took his math book and went into the school. Erica stood up, feeling ashamed of herself.

In all of her pontifications about Alan being someone special, she forgot that she was dealing with not only a small helpless boy but with a family. She could not push and shove them into the school; it was something Mark and Alan had to do together. If she hurt Mark, she was hurting Alan, as if they were one and the same person.

She wanted to kick herself for being so self-centered and stupid. The wind picked up and began to blow the dust from the playground into her face as she walked into the school.

The same wind carried itself and pushed Mark as he walked away from the school as fast as possible.

Her words had hurt him more than any of the punches or abuse he had suffered at the hands of his mother or wife.

The idea that Alan would turn out just like him for no other reason than trying to remain loyal to him was like being sentenced to Hell itself. Visions of Alan living his life with a woman who did not love him and took advantage of him while doing everything she could to make him feel lower than the dirt she walked on shook Mark to his core.

The idea that Alan would live a life of washing dishes while going home at night and nursing his God-given talents like a drunk drinking from a flask was... sickening. Erica had been right; there was simply no way to avoid the truth.

Mark stopped and almost turned around and walked back to the school. He didn't know why, but it almost seemed as if he was being drawn back, as if unseen hands were stopping him from moving in the direction he was going.

Mark thought about what Shannon would do if he gave in and said that Alan would attend the school. She would be furious when she found out, and with just the slightest thought of his wife, it was as if the hands pulling him towards the school let go, and new hands were pulling him in the opposite direction.

He began walking towards the restaurant, knowing that today would be the same as tomorrow and the next day until he would wake up too old to do his job, and they would discard him as quickly as the rotting food from the night before.

The Cage and the stinking refuse of others was all he had been destined to see in life, but Alan was different. Alan was not meant for this kind of life. God had reached down and placed something within the small child that needed to be free, that needed to explore the world around him and capture it for others to see.

Mark stopped again, utterly torn. Feeling the hands pulling him back towards the school, he did not know why, but he knew that if he walked through the doors and spoke to Alan's teacher one more time, he would crumble, and he would give into everything that she wished for Alan. Nothing in his life would ever be the same.

Yet he did not move and did not change course. The legal battle for Alan would most likely end in not only Alan being taken out of the school (if they ever got there in the first place), but he knew that he risked losing Alan completely. He knew that the court would look at him and see that he was nothing more than a dishwasher that would never amount to anything. Shannon's entire family would join together and paint a picture for the judge that would leave the legal system with no choice but to move Alan as far away from his loser of a father as possible. So as much as Mark wanted to take Alan away and let him reach his full potential, he knew that, in the end, Alan would lose the one person who cared about him more than anyone in the world. Mark was finally released from the indecision and turned the corner and saw the restaurant and the rest of his life in front of him. Putting his head down and letting the wind howl in his ears, Mark walked away from the school and a life that would have been a joy to experience.

Erica walked into her classroom feeling terrible. The children, not sitting down, made their way to their seats and waited for her to start the class for the day as if sensing that something was wrong and that today was not the day to push boundaries.

Erica could not shake the feeling that she had done something terribly wrong. She had meant to help Alan but ended up ruining everything. She knew where Alan was sitting but refused to look at him for fear of losing control of herself in pure frustration. How could she have been so selfish? She had made the entire situation about...

The knock on the door broke her slide into self-pity but she was shaken to see Mark standing in the doorway of her classroom, looking as if he was doing something wrong.

Erica asked one of her parent helpers to get the class started, knowing as she was giving her instructions to the eager woman that she would get chewed out in the hallway and deserved every second of it.

She smiled at the class, walked out, and quietly shut the door behind her.

"Look, I am so sorry…" was all Erica could say before the wave of frustration, lack of sleep, and guilt washed over her and she felt the burning of tears flowing.

Mark was at a complete loss as to what to do, and just stood there with his mouth open.

Erica turned around, frustrated by her lack of professionalism, and did her best to stop the tears while fervently hoping that her makeup would not run down her face. It was one thing to be chewed out and something else entirely to be chewed out while looking like a watercolor painting caught in the rain. Of course, her frustration just made the wave of emotion that much more powerful.

"I'm sorry. You were going to say?" Erica blurted out, turning around and more upset for losing control than ever. She folded her arms across her chest and looked at Mark defiantly, almost daring him to say anything that would upset her further.

Mark remained dumbfounded but finally said, "Does the school you mentioned offer scholarships?"

"What?" was all Erica could say.

"Look, I want Alan to go to the school, but there is simply no way I can afford it. I thought that if they had some kind of scholarship, then maybe he could…. uh…. do… that." Mark mumbled, completely caught off guard as Erica covered her face with her hands.

Without thinking about it, Erica hugged Mark and cried in gratitude. Mark stood rigid and shocked for a minute and then finally placed his arms gently around her, and the two of them stood silently in the hallway.

When the wave of emotion released her, Erica let go and Mark stepped away, blushing.

"I'm sorry, but this is just... well... the best news," Erica said, looking at Mark and hoping he understood, still frustrated with herself. "They do have scholarships, but they only offer one per year."

"So, could you help him get one of the scholarships after school? It's the only way I can imagine being able to get him in." Mark said apologetically, not knowing how Erica would react.

"Yes, of course," Erica said, much more serious. "I'll call them today and get more information."

"There is one other thing," Mark said. "Until we know for sure, I was wondering if it would be possible not to tell anyone about... everything. I just...I don't want people to talk if this isn't a sure thing."

"Of course, of course." Erica sighed and was finally able to smile brightly. Erica looked up and saw for the first time that Mark was smiling a broad and wide smile, easily as excited as she was. She had never noticed that his eyes were so blue to the point that they looked like bright sapphires; they were truly beautiful.

Erica pulled herself together and reached out to shake Mark's hand but could not help but hug him one more time.

"I'm going to go clean my face and try and regain some of my dignity," Erica laughed shyly. "I'll call and find out about the scholarship. Will you be picking Alan up after school?"

"Yes."

"Okay, we'll talk then." Erica could not help but smile at Mark, who looked at her as confused as most men would be at her behavior, but she was so happy that it was infectious.

Erica turned and walked towards the girl's bathroom, trying her best not to dance as the tears of joy began to flow freely once again. This time, she did not feel foolish but energized, knowing she had just entered into something as close as she would ever understand to true destiny.

Mark watched her walk away, still smiling. He did not stop smiling all the way out of the school and down to the restaurant; for hours working in the pit, all he could think about was her body pressed against his and her arms around his neck. He had never felt so powerful in all of his life.

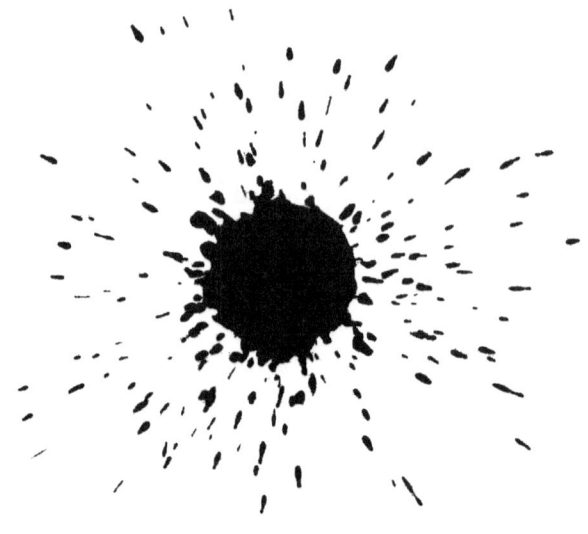

~ CHAPTER NINE ~

Mark knew he was going to have to talk with Alan about what was going to happen. The complexities of the path he had just chosen for them were hard for Mark to understand, and he did not know how he was going to break everything down into small enough bites so Alan would truly understand what was going to happen. It would not be fair to ask him to move forward without understanding what he would have to sacrifice.

Erica was true to her word, and that afternoon when Mark arrived at the school, she was waiting for him with a folder of forms and information about Benton Academy that she had printed from their website, along with several emails detailing the scholarship requirements.

She had good news and bad news, but to her credit, she had a plan, a good plan, and Mark said that as long as Alan was willing to do the work that was necessary, then Mark would be sure to do everything needed to see it to the finish line.

Back at the house, Mark stood over the stove and watched as the small grease bubbles popped around the edges of the hamburgers cooking in the skillet. He could hear the television in the living room around the corner, knowing that Alan would be lying on the couch in a vegetative state as the bright colors and hyperactive sound bombarded his senses.

As much as he hated himself for it, Mark could not stop thinking about Erica. He thought of the nights when he would watch his mother drink herself to sleep and the grimace she would make each time the brown liquid would be tipped into her throat; she looked as if she was just as likely to throw up the booze as she was to swallow it, and Mark never understood why she would do something over and over that was ultimately so destructive.

It was how he felt when he thought of Erica. He could still feel her body pressed against him, and as hard as he tried, he could not help himself from taking a small amount of pleasure from the memory; yet he knew he was only hurting himself with each moment that he thought about what it felt like to have her in his arms.

On the way home, as he walked with Alan on his shoulders up Fillmore, he vowed not to fantasize about her for no other reason than he did not want his judgment to be clouded as far as Alan was concerned. If everything went well, he and Alan would pack everything up and head to Boston at the end of the school year. With all the personal issues that it would create, much less the legal ones, the last thing Mark needed to do was to get all starry-eyed about a woman who was so far out of his league that he might as well be fantasizing about a movie star.

Yet, her touch was...

Mark coughed for no reason other than to stop himself from thinking about Erica. He thought of a movie he had watched several years ago where the phrase "a diet of the mind" was used.

He knew he would struggle with it, but he simply could no longer allow himself even the slightest thought in her direction.

Mark pulled the frying pan off the stove and called for Alan to turn off the television and get washed up.

Alan walked into the kitchen, still dazed from his television time, almost as if he was waking up. With the television off, the house was strangely quiet, and Mark knew that the time had come for the two of them to go over what Erica had given him at school and what it would mean for them.

Mark grabbed Alan, helped him sit on the tall barstool at the kitchen island, and then sat beside him. Even though Alan was big enough to get into the chair himself, Mark still lifted him now and then, just to remind himself how small Alan was, yet how much bigger he had become.

Alan took a huge bite from his hamburger, propped his head on his hand, and settled down for a nice long chew.

"I've been talking to your teacher about your drawings. She showed me your math book today," Mark said, sitting down and dumping a handful of french fries on both of their plates.

Alan immediately began to plead his case, convinced he was in trouble, even though his mouth was still full, making it impossible to understand a single word he was trying to say.

"It's all right, Alan. You're not in trouble. Don't choke," Mark said, trying not to laugh. "In fact, she told me she thought that your drawings were so good that maybe next year you should go to a school where they would let you draw and paint all day."

Alan just looked at Mark with a confused look and said, "Really?"

"Would you like that? Going to a new school is kind of a big deal. You would have to make new friends," Mark said, finally taking a bite of his own food.

They sat there for several minutes in silence. As strange as it seemed to outsiders, it was more common for Alan and Mark to sit and eat in silence with each other than it was for them to talk. The strong bond they had forged with one another was one of simply being with one another, and that was enough for each of them. The silence did not make either uncomfortable, and there was no desire to fill the space between them with empty words.

"That's okay. I don't really have many friends anyway. I used to play with Darrell at recess, but he's playing kickball now, and Tim only likes to swing, so that's okay. It would be fun to draw more. I'm always worried I'm going to get in trouble when I do it now," Alan said, staring at his plate with pressed eyebrows as if he was coming to a profound conclusion.

"Why do you think you were going to get in trouble?" Mark asked, concerned.

"Last year in Mrs. Peterson's class, she smacked my hand with a ruler when I was drawing during a test, and she made me go sit in the hallway."

"You never told me that," Mark was shocked at the revelation.

Alan just shrugged as if it was nothing to talk about and took another bite that smeared ketchup up his cheek.

Mark reached over and wiped his face. "How long have you been drawing like that?"

With his mouth full, Alan shrugged again and didn't look at Mark.

They sat in silence a while longer, but the question still lingered over the meal in Mark's mind. Even though it had been almost all he could think about since Erica had first unveiled Alan's painting, it had never dawned on him until that moment that even though he and Alan were close, he, too, had missed Alan's talent completely.

"Alan, hold on for a minute," Mark said, stopping the boy from taking another bite. "How long have you been drawing like you did in your math book?"

Alan looked at him to see if he was in trouble and then hopped down and ran out of the kitchen and upstairs. A minute later, Mark heard his small uneven pace as he returned down the stairs. Walking back into the kitchen, Mark saw Alan carrying a shoe box with some trepidation, but he quietly handed it to Mark.

Confused, Mark opened it up and first noticed several crayons worn down until many of them were only a few centimeters long. There were also a couple of small pencils that were covered in dark small fingerprints.

Underneath was a stack of construction paper that Mark lifted out of the box. He picked it up so gently that he looked like he was handling ancient papyrus rather than a second grader's artwork.

Mark looked at each page slowly, taking in the small drawings. Sometimes it would be nothing more than a leaf drawn with such detail that it looked as if it would fall from the page; other times, it would be a tree or a small toy Mark recognized from Alan's room. Each one was drawn and shaded to such perfection that it shocked Mark each time he saw a new page for the first time.

"How come you never showed these to me before?" Mark asked, in awe of the small boy.

"Because you got mad at me," Alan said.

"What? When?" Mark was instantly wracked with guilt that exploded inside him like a solar flare.

"You said I needed to stop when I got colors on my sheet. You had to throw away my sheets and buy me new ones," Alan explained.

Mark suddenly remembered. He had been tired and found Alan with his markers all over his bed. They had pooled out in large stains, and without thinking through his momentary frustration, he had told Alan to stop drawing. He never thought to look at what Alan had been drawing; all he could see was the mess that he was making and the extra work that it would create.

"I am so sorry, Alan. I didn't mean for you to be ashamed or to stop forever," Mark said, kneeling to Alan's level and hugging the boy. "I don't want you to EVER stop drawing. In fact, if you want to paint on the living room wall from now on, you can. You can paint or draw on anything! I don't care how messy it gets."

"On anything?" Alan asked, his eyes wide and laughing.

"Don't worry if it gets messy or drips on the floor, or on your bed, or anything. If you feel like painting or drawing and all you have is the kitchen floor, then go for it," Mark said in mock seriousness, pounding the wall gently to emphasize his point jokingly.

They wrestled for a few minutes when Mark suddenly remembered something. Picking up Alan and carrying him over his shoulder as the boy wiggled and laughed, Mark carried Alan out to the garage and opened up one of the cabinets. Setting Alan down facing the opposite direction from the cabinet, Mark opened up another door and told Alan to turn around and look.

The boy's eyes opened wide, and he gasped in delight as if he had just discovered a pot of gold at the end of a rainbow. Inside the cabinet was all the paint used to paint the inside and outside of the house. Twelve different paint colors in total in large gallon buckets. Mark and Alan opened each one of them, and Mark showed him how to stir the paint to get the full color to rise to the top. Alan was as excited as Mark had ever seen him. Each new color seemed to open up another world to the boy; it was Disneyland, Christmas, and a birthday wrapped up together.

They found themselves sitting back down to finish dinner long after their food had become cold and unappetizing. They talked and picked at the french fries for a few minutes until it was time for Alan to go to bed. After Alan ran upstairs to put on his pajamas, Mark then cleaned the kitchen.

It had been a good night. He felt terrible on one hand that he yelled at Alan about the mess he had made on his bed, but hoped that he had made up for it.

It had never dawned on him how the smallest word at the wrong time could have such a big effect on Alan. He thought of a river and how a single stone in a specific place could change its entire course. It had been over two years since the incident with the leaky markers on the bed sheet. It had been a bad day, and Mark had been exhausted and barked at Alan when he saw the mess, just like any other parent would. But to Alan, it had been a defining moment that taught him to keep his art a secret. Since Mark never raised his voice with Alan, the boy had simply interpreted it as best he could.

Turning off the light in the kitchen, Mark walked across the living room, locked the front door, and looked at the paint-splattered canvas Erica had given him. It was a miracle captured on canvas. If not for this little piece of art, Alan might have spent his entire life never knowing about his gift and never understanding why he had been put on this earth. Mark touched it and felt the small bumps of paint. It was a miracle, but he knew he still had another piece of news to tell Alan tonight. Suddenly, the joy of the last hour, playing with Alan and showing him the old paint cans, faded away. Mark sighed, turned around, and went upstairs, hoping that Alan was old enough to understand what was about to happen.

By the time Mark got upstairs, Alan had made a mess of his bathroom, not to mention a trail of wet footprints on the carpet from the bathroom to his bedroom. The clothes he had been wearing were now spread out all over the bathroom, not a single sock making its way into the hamper.

"He may be a genius, but he is still a child," was all Mark could think of as he picked everything up before turning off the bathroom light.

Mark walked into Alan's bedroom, and Alan jumped quickly into bed, pretending he was asleep and snoring comically. It was good to see Alan so relaxed and acting his age. When Mark heard parents telling their kids to "act their age," it usually meant to act older, but he wanted Alan to relax and be silly and not always so serious.

It was the news that Alan was not in trouble for wanting to draw that was the biggest relief, Mark thought. Doing something that you think is not allowed can be draining to keep that kind of secret, and Mark thought Alan seemed lighter for no other reason than everything was out in the open.

"Hey Alan, there is something else we need to talk about," Mark began, sitting beside the bed.

Alan opened up his eyes and smiled.

"That school I mentioned earlier... well, it isn't in Colorado. It's in a city called Boston way across the country next to the ocean," Mark said, talking seriously with Alan.

"Would we have to move there?" Alan asked.

"Well, yeah. It would just be the two of us out there. Your Aunt Jenny and Uncle Tyler would stay here. We would visit when we could, maybe even talk with them over the computer whenever possible," Mark chose his words carefully.

"You said just the two of us?" Alan asked, clearly confused.

Mark was at a loss for how to respond, so he sat in meditative silence. Alan caught on much quicker than he thought he would. All Mark could do was look at the floor and search for the right words to say while Alan processed the news.

"You mean, Mom would stay here?" Alan asked, sitting up.

"Yes," Mark exhaled, knowing there was no going back now.

"But she would be all alone," Alan pointed out.

"Well," Mark began slowly, "she would have Aunt Jenny and her friends, but you must understand something. You don't have to do this if this is too much for you. Besides, this isn't a sure thing just yet. I just wanted you to understand everything before we get started."

"What do you mean?" Alan asked.

"There is a special way we're trying to get you into the school: a 'scholarship.' And the school only gives out one a year to a very special kid, and I think you could get it. If you get it, it won't cost anything to go to the school," Mark said.

"What if they give it to someone else?" Alan was suddenly worried, and it made Mark both proud and sad that he, too, recognized one of the many concrete stumbling blocks in front of this nebulous dream.

"We'll worry about that if that happens, okay? I need you to think about painting or drawing the best picture you have ever thought of. Once you're done, we'll send it to them, and, of course, they will love it, and then we'll take you to that school in the summer," Mark was trying his best to sound as positive as possible.

"So, I get to paint anything I want?" Alan asked, suddenly cheering up again.

"Anything. You could paint my big, fat, hairy feet even." Mark said, smiling.

"Eeeewwwww." Alan squirmed, wrinkling his nose and laying back down again.

"So, you can think about all of this, and we will talk more tomorrow. Okay?"

"Okay."

Mark stood up, turned off the light, and began walking out of the room.

"Dad?"

"Yeah?"

"If we left, do you think Mom would miss us?" Alan said, sitting up again.

The words stung Mark. He felt bad for Alan that he would have a life that would ever make such a sweet boy think like that. He wanted to placate and tell him every wonderful thing about his mother, but the words escaped him.

"I don't know, Alan," was all Mark could say.

"Yeah... I don't know either." Alan said and laid back down again.

Mark walked into his bedroom and got ready for bed. He knew the answer and knew that Shannon would not miss them at all. Considering everything that had happened, she was incapable of it.

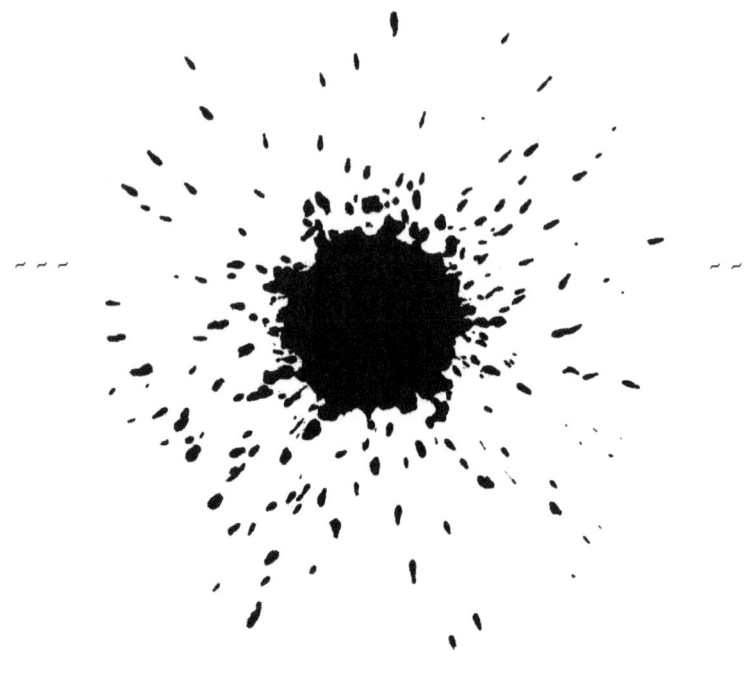

~ CHAPTER TEN ~

The idea of giving Alan free rein to paint and draw anywhere he felt like seemed like a good idea at the time but it quickly turned out to be a mistake. The fact that Alan could not remember to put his clothes in the hamper was magnified by ten with paint throughout the house.

Alan's small hand shook Mark awake the next morning. It really wasn't the touch on his cheek that brought Mark out of his stupor; it was the stickiness of the boy's hand on his face that alerted Mark that something was wrong.

When he finally opened his eyes, he saw Alan standing in his pajamas… covered in black paint. It was all over his face, and hair was dripping down his arms. Mark knew without looking in the mirror that wherever Alan touched was most likely covered in small black prints.

What Mark had not been expecting, although he really should have, was the small black footsteps from the garage, through the kitchen, up the stairs, and into the bedroom. With a small pool of paint collecting in the carpet where Alan stood, Mark sprang into action as quickly as his sleeping body would allow and dropped Alan in the bathtub.

Mark realized he was not upset about the mess as he looked for the industrial carpet cleaner. For some reason, it was relaxing to know that Alan was so excited about the road ahead that he took it upon himself to make the mess in the first place.

From what Mark could figure out from Alan's nine-year-old explanation (and the tracks around the house) was that Alan had been so excited he got up early and ran down to the garage to play with the paint. While trying to open the paint cans, Alan managed to tip one over and then, not knowing what else to do, ran upstairs to tell Mark.

As Alan splashed around in the bathtub after a good scrubbing, Mark crawled on his knees, doing his best to clean up every tiny footprint and paint drops. As he stood at the bottom of the stairs, looking at the footsteps and the handprints on the railing, Mark could not help but laugh. After doing his best to get as much of the paint out of the carpet, he pulled a wrinkled Alan out of the bathtub and helped the shivering boy get dressed.

After eating some breakfast, the two of them went out to the garage and took account of the mess. Thankfully, the gallon can had not been even a third full, so apart from getting it all over the other cans, there was very little mess to clean up. Alan looked around the garage and found old paint brushes that had not been touched since they first were used to paint Alan's room before he was brought home from the hospital as an infant. The smallest brush was three inches wide and was better for covering large walls than it was an artist's tool, but Alan loved it.

It took most of the morning to clean up the garage and clear a small corner of the garage out to give Alan enough room to have a place to work. Mark found an old blue tarp and laid it on the floor. Alan and Mark looked at the small corner with pride when they were done.

All they needed was something for Alan to paint on, which was surprisingly hard to find around the house. Mark finally decided that after lunch, they would head down to the local Hobby Lobby and pick up whatever they needed.

It was almost noon before Mark finally had the opportunity to make his way up to the shower, but before he did, he called the bank to check his balance. After ten minutes of navigating an automatic phone tree, Mark confirmed that he had no money to spend on art supplies and feeding the family for the week.

In the shower, the frustration over not getting his overtime pay began to rise again. They had a week to go before his next paycheck, and Mark hoped he would finally get the back pay they owed him to get Alan's needed supplies. He was sure they wouldn't come cheap, but that no longer mattered. Alan would get everything he needed very soon, and there was no need to worry about how it would happen. Mark promised himself he would just do everything he could and then have faith that the rest would come together. After all, if God had given Alan this overwhelming talent, then maybe God and the universe should get together and figured out how to pitch in.

The warm water rejuvenated Mark as he leaned his head up against the wall and let the water flow over his body. He had to admit that even though they had only recently started down this road, knowing they were moving down a path that could change everything was scary but far more exhilarating than anything that had ever happened to him.

"Dad!" Alan yelled from the other side of the closed bathroom door.

After the awakening he received this morning, Mark could only think that Alan had caused some new disaster and turned off the water and braced himself for anything.

"What is it, Alan?"

"There's someone at the door."

That was odd; no one ever came over. No one Shannon knew would ever drop by, and Mark certainly did not know anyone. Mark grabbed a t-shirt and a pair of sweatpants. They stuck to his wet body, and suddenly Mark felt very foolish, but the clear chime of the doorbell rang again, and he made his way downstairs.

All Mark could think of was that there would be news from the hospital; he hoped they did not send a police officer over, but surely they would call before they did that.

There is a certain scene that takes place in every sitcom that has ever existed when someone opens the door, and someone they did not expect to see is on the other side. In the sitcom, the door is always shut quickly while the person that opened the door takes a few minutes to collect themselves while the confused visitor waits patiently on the doorstep. Mark wished he could have found the presence of mind to slam the door shut, but instead, he could only stand there and stare with his mouth open.

"Hi, I hope you don't mind me coming by, but I wanted to give Alan a present," Erica said, looking confused at Mark's expression and damp appearance. Mark hoped he did not look as foolish as he felt, but he could not help looking at Erica like a man who had to let his eyes adjust to the sun after going outside from a dark room.

Her dark hair was pulled back, revealing her neck that reached up from her perfect shoulders to her elegant face. The white, purposefully wrinkled t-shirt under a brown jacket accented her flawless body on top of jeans, made Mark suddenly realize that no one had ever looked so good in a simple pair of pants since slacks had been invented. Of course, at the same time, he realized that he was standing there in a wet t-shirt and a pair of gray sweatpants with the paint from this morning all over them.

With superhuman effort, Mark managed to shut his mouth, stop staring at her, and somehow even managed to invite her in. Once Erica crossed the house's threshold, Mark became aware of every imperfection in the living room, and suddenly his house was an epic disaster. The sterile white walls, with no artwork except for the small canvas by the door, suddenly made the house look as if it had just been moved into. The furniture was suddenly worn and embarrassing.

With Erica standing among his things in his home, it felt as if he had woken up from a long sleep and saw all the compromises and complacent decisions he had made his entire life. She was real, she was alive, and his home was nothing more than basic shelter. It did not seem right that she was there because in the few seconds, it took her to walk over the threshold of the doorway, Mark could not help but come to the conclusion that she was just "better" than anything he had ever known.

Mark looked up and saw Alan standing at the top of the stairs looking down at Erica but not knowing what to do.

"Hi, Alan," Erica said warmly when she saw him.

"Hi," Alan said quietly. Mark stood by, watching his son.

"I brought you something. Do you mind if I bring it into the car?" Erica asked, already moving out the door.

She walked back outside, and Alan began to make his way slowly down the stairs with the thought of the unexpected gift. Without shutting the door, Mark ran up the stairs and into the bathroom with the slim hope that he could put himself together in some small way to look less like a vagrant. Throwing off the wet t-shirt, he put on one of the few clean button-down shirts he owned, ran a comb through his hair...then quickly admitted defeat. He tried to walk from his bedroom calmly and then downstairs without falling on his face.

Standing at the top of the stairs, Mark watched for a few minutes as Erica showed Alan the present she had brought him. It was a beautiful easel with at least ten canvases in different shapes and sizes. The easel had a small drawer at the bottom, and when she opened it up for Alan to see, it was stuffed with small tubes of paint in every color imaginable. Alan took each tube as if made out of glass and then gently moved his hand along the surface of the easel. Alan's face was stuck in an expression of joy as if his young brain could not process the overwhelming wonderfulness of the gift before him.

Erica bent down and watched as Alan silently looked at the present, smiling as wide as she could. Turning her head, she looked up the stairs at Mark, smiling wide and radiating happiness like a streetlight in their small home.

All Mark could think was that he was falling in...

Her body rolled over, pinching her neck unnaturally, as she fell down the stairs and slammed into the front door. Her clothes were twisted and bent around her, and she did not move. Mark stood at the top of the stairs and did nothing, frozen. All he could think was that she must have blacked out before her head hit the tile at the bottom of the stairs because she never tried to stop or brace herself; she just rolled down the stairs like a rag doll.

She lay there, and the sound of the cracking and snapping bones as she fell seemed to echo off the house's walls.

"Dad, did you see?" Alan blurted out, his tiny hand pulling Mark down the stairs towards the easel and the radiant woman who stood smiling, waiting for him to join the celebration.

Alan carefully showed Mark everything Erica had brought, becoming increasingly excited with each new item.

When Alan got to the part about how to take the easel down, he carefully loosed the butterfly screws and let the easel down to the floor, carefully following Erica's instructions.

"So, I was hoping we could go somewhere today and help Alan get started on his project. Did you have a chance to go over the scholarship with him?" Erica asked, looking up at Mark as she helped Alan finish breaking down the easel so it was no bigger than a small suitcase when they were done.

Alan did not give Mark a chance to answer but simply cheered and ran into the living room and began to put on his shoes and jacket.

"You'll have to let me pay you for all of this. We were going to go tomorrow and pick up... well, exactly what you brought, to be honest." Mark lied knowing he would have had no idea what to get or, for that matter, how he would have been able to afford it.

"No, please; I wanted to do this. I was at the store as soon as they opened and made sure Alan had everything. It was the least I could do, considering how I acted yesterday," Erica said, picking up the canvases still wrapped in plastic.

Mark wanted to protest, but decided against it. The look in her eyes told him she had needed to do it as much as Alan had needed it, almost as if she was paying a penance.

"Well, thank you. It is... incredible." Mark said, reaching out and taking a few of the larger canvases from her.

Mark forced himself to not look in her eyes and took the extra canvases into the garage, gently putting them against the wall that they had cleared out for Alan this morning.

Reaching for the garage door, he stopped himself from opening it and stood in the on the cement staring at the door. He could feel his blood pumping and knew that in his own way, he was just as excited about seeing Erica as Alan had been to get his new easel. It was stupid and childish, but something happened to him when he got too close to her; it was as if he was toy who had run out of energy, and just her presence charged him up and brought him back to life.

"This is stupid, this is stupid, this is stupid," he kept saying to himself.

What did he expect to happen when he walked out of the garage? Did he honestly expect her to react like he was with her? It was insane, but he needed to do it for Alan. If she was willing to show up here on a Saturday and work with Alan, he needed to stop acting like a lovesick child and move past these stupid fantasies.

Mark breathed in deeply and then found the strength to go back into the house.

By the time he returned, they had already put all of Alan's equipment in Erica's four-door hardtop Jeep Sahara and were waiting for Mark. They drove together down the other side of Fillmore Hill and made their way to the Garden of the Gods on the western slope of the city.

The park was one of the main tourist attractions in southern Colorado and breathtakingly beautiful. Considered a holy place by the Ute Indians that had populated Colorado before the Gold Rush deposited thousands of eastern settlers all around the Pikes Peak area, the Garden of the Gods was 400 acres set aside by an industrious family during the founding of the city, mainly because of its magnificent rock formations that reach hundreds of feet into the air in long panels of stone. They were so large that they could be seen from all over the city. The Garden of the Gods seemed the perfect place for Alan to begin.

It was one of those rare February days where hints of spring were in the air, and the first warm days were a pleasant change from the past and future snow storms. They parked in one of the first lots, and Mark took the collapsed easel while Erica took the canvas. They walked down the cement trails that made their way around the magnificent stone walls that reached three or four stories into the air. Behind them, ancient oak trees stood in the same place they had for hundreds, even thousands of years, untouched by the civilization that now surrounded them.

"If you see something interesting, just tell us, and we'll stop," Erica said quietly to Alan, who was walking between them. Mark held the easel on the same side, almost like a small shield that would protect him from her.

Alan looked up at her, confused. "I don't know what I'm looking for," he said quietly as if he was doing something wrong. Mark looked at him and wished he had an answer for him, but, in all honesty, he did not know either.

Erica stopped them and had them set up the easel just a few feet off the path and faced it in the opposite direction of the hundreds of people who were walking around the park without their heavy coats for the first time in months.

"See this pine tree, Alan?" Erica pointed to a tree that seemed to be growing right out of the stone structure. Its roots could be seen at the base like long tentacles reaching for moisture. A small fern contrasted the brown and black of the bark, while the red stone and green needles on the tree stood out in contrast to each other.

"Why don't you just try to draw this tree? This doesn't have to be your final project. Just practice. Okay? You don't have to make it perfect, but play around with the paint and see how it all feels," Erica said reassuringly while bending down and talking to Alan quietly.

Mark stood back and watched silently as Erica unwrapped the brand-new paintbrushes and reached into the little drawer where all the paint tubes were. She handed Alan the brush, squirted a small amount of the paint onto a palette, and handed it to the boy. Alan looked at the bright colors in small lumps, then at the tree, then at the canvas. Erica stood back, and both she and Mark held their breath.

All Mark could think as Alan held the brush in his hand was the video footage of the space shuttle when it took off. There was a tremendous amount of fire and noise when the engines kicked in, and then slowly, the giant space shuttle began to lift off until it finally was shooting toward space. They stood behind Alan, collectively waiting with bated breath, hoping to see the genius inside the small boy leap forth and onto the canvas while he continued to look at the tree, then the canvas, and then the paint over and over again.

Alan finally turned around and looked at the two of them and said simply, "I have no idea what I'm supposed to do."

The tension was broken, and both Mark and Erica relaxed. Erica stepped forward and began to instruct Alan while Mark turned around to look at Pikes Peak through the pine trees and red and white sandstone sentinels that covered the foothills. He said aloud to himself, "Today is a good day."

* * *

Erica worked with Alan for a half hour, showing him the basics of painting and spending a surprisingly short amount of time mixing the colors together to get a brand new color. It was as if Alan could sense the color he needed and knew exactly how to get it. She was happy that she decided to buy acrylic paints rather than starting Alan off with oil paints. They were easier to control and would be a good first step for him.

The first breakthrough came when she finally was able to show him that each stroke did not need to be perfect; how sometimes it was better just to get the most basic shapes down and then, like a sculptor, slowly work towards more detail. As long as he knew where he was going with his painting, making as many mistakes as needed was acceptable until he finally got it right. She ensured he knew it was all right to start over by painting over the last try and that all would be forgotten forever.

At the end of the half-hour, it was as if a switch flipped in his brain, and Alan stopped asking questions. The intensity that Erica had witnessed for the first time in the classroom came over the boy like dark clouds that finally began to unload the rain as he used the brush confidently. Erica stood up and looked up to see Mark was a few feet away, sitting quietly on one of the many stone benches found throughout the garden, looking at her the same way that Alan was now looking at his painting. It was a look she had noticed come over Mark for only split seconds, but it was at least ten full seconds this time before he realized she was looking at him in return. Then he blushed and looked away.

Men had looked at her before, but it was different with Mark. Usually, a man who looked at her that way would step forward, say something stupid, or just keep blatantly gawking. Mark just looked at her, and when he did, she felt a strength in him that made her want more. She had to admit to herself that she liked it when Mark looked at her, but it happened so infrequently that it made the short glances all that much more valuable. He had an attractive raw masculinity, not intrusive or aggressive, but mutely powerful nonetheless.

For the first time, she wondered about Alan's mother and what the story was with her. Erica had checked on all the forms the school had on Alan and never saw any mention of a mother, only Mark. There was no other contact information other than an aunt that lived downtown.

Erica looked down at Alan to see how he was doing and saw that he was still concentrating, but making an absolute mess of the canvas, like any other eight-year-old boy. Erica's first instinct was to continue to instruct him, but something stopped her, and she instead chose to walk away and sit next to Mark, letting Alan's inspiration direct him instead of her words.

Mark tensed up and looked down at the ground, but Erica did her best to keep her distance and not sit down next to him. She looked up at the blue sky with the bright white clouds that seemed to move so slowly that they did not look like they were moving at all. The warm sun washed over her face, and she closed her eyes, letting the sunlight cover her in a shower of warmth and light. She had not realized how cold it had been that winter until she felt the warmth of the sun once again.

She finally opened her eyes and looked over at Mark, who was smelling a pine cone. He looked over at her and smiled, then gently handed it to her. She smelled it, and the aroma of pine and earth filled her senses, almost as if she had taken a bite of rich chocolate.

"Thank you for this. We never get the opportunity to come out here," Mark said after a few minutes of silence. "I remember when I was a kid before they put in all of this cement down, my dad brought me out here to look for arrowheads. We didn't find any, but it's one of the last memories I have of him."

"I'm sorry. Did he pass away?" Erica asked.

"I don't know. He left not long after that," Mark said, and Erica wished she hadn't asked.

"I'm sorry," she ventured.

"It's okay. It was a long time ago," he shrugged, but Erica could sense his sadness.

They sat silently for a few minutes, and Erica looked over at Alan to see how he was doing. The sun was bright, and she could not see the canvas from where she was, but he was still working hard.

"My dad was the one who taught me to paint," Erica said. "I remember when I was young, he was sitting in his office painting an apple just for the fun of it. He was a professor, and he used painting as a way to relax, nothing more. He would have been the first to tell you he was never that good, but I still have that picture of the apple. It was the moment when I first understood that we could capture moments in time that were beyond simply taking a picture. It may not be as accurate, but it was more emotional?"

Mark nodded in agreement and looked away without responding. Erica watched him for a moment and then turned her body to straddle the bench so she could watch Alan.

"You're doing a great job with him," Erica said without looking at Mark.

He chuckled. "Thanks, but I have no idea what I'm doing. I just try to get him to school and sleep each day."

"You should give yourself more credit," she said, pointing at him in mock disapproval. "I have students doing everything their little minds can think of just to get their parents to notice them. You and Alan are doing just fine."

Mark was silent for a few moments and then finally said, "Thank you. That is nice of you to say."

Erica was beginning to see something about the two of them that she had overlooked before. It reminded her of a conference she attended several years ago where several of the people attending were from schools all around the globe. The conversation was fast-paced when she spoke to the educators from America, but the teachers from Europe conducted themselves differently. Maybe it was the language barrier, but when she spoke, she could tell they were trying to understand her, not just trying to think of what they would say next. It created a slower-paced conversation but a better understanding of what was being said.

It was the same way with Mark and Alan, for that matter. Their speech pattern was slower but much more refined than most people in many ways. They thought about what they were saying and did not just speak because they needed to hide behind their words.

They sat under the warmth of the sun and the garden's beauty in peaceful silence with one another. It was only when Mark stood up that the silence was broken. "I'm sorry, but the stone is getting to be a bit much. Do you want to go for a walk?"

"I'll go see how Alan is doing," Erica said.

"It's okay. We will keep him in sight. I'm not used to sitting down like this. Shall we?" Mark said, motioning down the cement path.

"Sure," Erica replied and stood up, smiling.

They strolled lazily at a snail's pace, each checking on Alan over their shoulders every few minutes. When they reached the end of the path, they walked back towards Alan and then as far as they could in the opposite direction without losing sight of the small boy in front of the easel.

Erica could not hold it in any longer as they strolled. "Do you mind if I ask about Alan's mom?"

Erica saw the muscles on the corner of Mark's mouth tense for a minute. He walked with both hands pressed firmly in his pockets, looking down. With the question still hanging in the air, Mark breathed in but did not exhale. Erica could tell he was searching for the right words but suddenly felt like she had crossed a line.

"Look... I'm sorry," she began.

"No, it's fine," Mark said, looking at her briefly. "She... Alan's mom is not around."

Mark looked as if he was fighting to find the right words. "She just... well... she just did not like me that much. We thought that Alan would make a difference, but..."

The look in his eyes told Erica everything that he could not say. Whatever the specifics were, they did not matter to Erica any longer. What she saw was a man who was doing his best to take care of a wonderful child and keep his head above water when he had been let down by the people who should have been helping him. He was taking care of Alan with dignity and grace, and if she knew nothing else about him, in that quick moment that passed between them, she knew that she respected him.

"People sometimes suck, huh?" Erica said, trying to lighten up the situation.

Mark chuckled once to himself and then put his head down again and began to walk back towards Alan.

When they got closer, Erica could see that Alan was no longer painting.

"It isn't any good," Alan said, frustrated.

Mark walked back to the bench, and Erica stood back from the canvas and looked at what Alan had been working on.

He had followed her instructions and had painted the color of the stone without any detail and put the color of the tree where it should be, but when it came to the parts where he had tried to sculpt down, it had turned into a mess.

Erica saw what Alan had been trying to do and asked him, "Alan, where are the lines on that tree?"

Alan pointed to the edges of where he had been trying to separate the tree from the background. He had separated it with two strokes on either side and had been trying to fill in the center.

"No, Alan. What I want you to do is to find those big solid lines on the actual tree. Go walk over there and show me these two solid lines." Erica said.

Alan looked up at her with squinted eyes and then looked back at the tree but did not move.

"Well, there are no lines on the tree..." Alan said, almost as if he was asking a question.

"Very good! So, if there are no lines on the tree, why did you paint them?" Erica asked.

Alan just shrugged his shoulders and continued to look at the tree, then the canvas. "I guess I was just trying to draw a tree."

"Good answer, Alan!" Erica exclaimed. Alan smiled brightly.

"You want to learn a huge secret?" Erica asked, getting on her knees and looking around as if she was worried that someone might hear her.

Alan's eyes got big, and he smiled, wondering what game she was playing with him. "Yeah..."

"Okay. This is what all great painters know that no one else does." Erica said barely above a whisper. "When you are painting, you can never paint what you *think* you are painting; you have to paint what you are *actually* painting."

Alan was incredibly disappointed and looked at Erica as if she had lost her mind. "That doesn't make any sense."

Erica kept the intensity and continued looking around, ensuring no one was listening. "What you painted here is what you thought a tree should look like, but you did not paint the actual tree in front of you. The most important part of being a painter is to see life as it IS, not as you think it should be."

Erica took the paintbrush out of Alan's hand and made two little adjustments to the small tree.

"The best way to see the world as it is, Alan, is to start by looking at the shapes and colors of everything around you. When you look at the tree, don't look at it as a whole tree, but pay attention to each small shape within the tree and try to capture each shape, one at a time. You see, Alan, life is about how many small things combine to make something bigger."

Erica painted two small shapes on the tree, and suddenly the tree began to look like the tree in front of them.

"That same principal goes applies to everything you try to paint. If you tell yourself you will draw a rock, your mind will tell you what a rock *should* be, and you will not see what is right in front of you. If you simply look to see everything that makes up the rock, you will see the truth of what you are looking at. Do you see?" Erica asked, still painting the small shapes here and there that brought the mass of colors and shapes into perspective on Alan's canvas.

Alan looked at her, and then back to the canvas, and then gently took the brush from her hand. Like he was in a trance, he began not to trace what he thought he was looking at but to finally paint the world around him.

Erica stepped back and saw Mark standing only a few feet away. The powerful explosion that they had been waiting for finally lifted Alan off the launch pad, and Erica and Mark stood back, holding their breath again, as the fingers of God reached down and brought that small, insignificant tree to life on the white canvas.

After a half hour, Alan stopped and turned around and only said, "I'm hungry."

~ CHAPTER ELEVEN ~

"No, Alan."

"Pleeeeease! I won't do it this time."

"Alan, not now."

"Dad, I promise."

"I'm sorry, but what are we talking about?" Erica finally asked. She did not want to intrude, but the debate between Alan and Mark had been raging quietly for a while now, and she could not ignore what was happening around her any longer.

They both stopped and looked at her as if she had just appeared out of thin air.

Alan smiled at her as if he had just found the leverage he had been looking for. Mark smiled to himself and just shook his head.

"Dad hates it when I order buffalo wings in public," Alan said, smiling.

Mark rolled his eyes, not letting Erica in on the joke, and said, "Just order something else, Alan."

"So why not, Alan? Are you allergic to them?" Erica asked, intrigued because Alan seemed so happy to tell her, but she could also tell Mark was not upset. For the first time, it actually seemed as if he was on the verge of laughing.

They had packed up all the equipment after Alan had finished his painting, and Erica offered to take them to Applebee's to celebrate the project's kickoff. It was just after four, and Alan was starving. However, the debate about the buffalo wings had started almost immediately upon the suggestion of eating somewhere.

"I'm not allergic to them; I love them. But my dad said that watching me eat them was the most disgusting thing ever happening on the planet. Anywhere. Ever." Alan said, laughing.

"I did not," Mark said.

"You did too! You said that lions eat zebras with more dignity!"

Mark lowered his menu and said nothing but gave Alan a quick look that was half joking, but it also told Alan he was treading on very thin ice.

"Well, I think I need to see this for myself," Erica said, taking the bait.

Alan cheered and reached up and gave Erica a high five.

"You don't want to do this. It's... just horrible." Mark said, leaning back in the booth, almost begging Erica not to do this. But both Erica and Alan stared at him with raised eyebrows, pleading with him to give his permission.

"Fine... okay. But no ranch dressing."

"Daaaad! It's no good without the ranch dressing." Alan whined.

Mark could not help but chuckle, knowing what would happen in the next few minutes. "Okay, because you did so well today. But

I am not sitting with you while it happens." Mark said, standing up and moving to the other side of the table, sitting next to Erica.

Erica was taken aback for a minute because Mark had worked hard to keep his distance from her, and it felt strange to be so close to him in the small booth. On the other hand, Alan looked like he was in heaven, having an entire side of the booth to himself, and he spread out his arms and reached to each side of the table.

"It's such a shame that we have to ruin a perfect day like this, Alan. I think it would be best to apologize now for what you are about to do." Mark said, smiling at Alan.

Alan just laughed and fell over in his seat.

After ordering, the waitress brought over a kid's menu with games and a couple of crayons for Alan. Alan began playing the games and was silent, which created an awkward silence between Mark and Erica, who found themselves sitting next to each other unexpectedly. It was not the kind of silence Erica had noticed before that was peaceful and relaxing; she could sense Mark's nervousness and trepidation around her. She could almost feel it emanating from him like a heat lamp in this proximity.

"Thanks again for doing this. I felt just awful about the things that I said." Erica finally said.

"It's okay. You were right." Mark said. "I don't think I would have been able to live with myself if we didn't even try. I owe him that, you know?"

Erica turned her head and looked at Mark for a moment. He looked down at the table and played with a napkin as if he was a 16-year-old boy on his first date, scared to death and completely out of his element. The fact that he was so unpretentious, almost vulnerable, made her almost as fascinated with him as she was with Alan. When he was with Alan, he seemed to have a level of confidence... no, that wasn't it... it was purpose. It was that he seemed to have a clear purpose that turned him into a different man. Mark was always well within his shell in the few conversations they had without Alan. He was withdrawn and distant, ensuring he did not reveal even the smallest part of himself.

Yet, all day with Alan, Mark had been relaxed…even funny. He almost seemed as if he already knew that Alan would be something extraordinary and that his job would be to exist in orbit around the boy. Never taking over, but always there if Alan ever needed anything.

It made Erica sad. On the one hand, she was happy for Alan, knowing that she had been wrong and that Alan did have someone to look out for him for as long as his father could do so. Erica just could not help thinking about Mark and how alone he would be when the world learned about Alan. They would scramble to know everything about Alan, and Mark would do everything to protect his son; but who would be looking out for Mark? Who would be there to help Mark if it all got overwhelming? It made her appreciate his sacrifice and hesitancy that much more.

The food arrived, and Alan and Mark began laughing at the private joke Erica was about to be privy to. They set the basket of buffalo wings, dripping in sauce, in front of Alan, and his eyes grew three sizes. Next to the basket, the waitress placed a small metal cup of ranch dressing, which immediately had the opposite effect on Alan. His eyes looked up at the waitress and then looked at Mark, pleading for him to fix whatever had just gone terribly wrong.

"Is there any way you could bring a small bowl of ranch dressing?" Mark asked, smiling, causing Alan to smile again and look up at the waitress, who walked away without expression.

Alan watched her intently as Mark began to shake his head. Erica watched in silence with a curious anticipation of what was in store. She wasn't sure if she had heard Mark right when he asked for a *bowl* of ranch dressing. With Mark's warning, she knew this was the beginning of Mark and Alan's secret shame.

The waitress brought a shallow bowl filled halfway with ranch dressing and walked away quickly so they would not trouble her again. Erica could not help but think that even though the waitress was rude and inattentive if what was about to happen was half as bad as it had been made out to be, she would earn her tip with just the cleaning up.

Mark had been right; it was disgusting. Fun to watch, but it did not take long for Erica to give up trying to eat while Alan made a complete mess of everything around him.

Each small wing was dipped at least one knuckle deep in the bowl and swirled around. Then Alan would eat the wing as if it was bone dry. By the time he was done, Alan had white ranch dressing and red buffalo sauce all over his hands, arms, hair, shirt, and face. After only two wings, Mark had to wipe Alan's face clean, so the mess would not get into his eyes. The more he ate, the more boy looked like a wax figure of a clown, melting right in front of them.

Mark sat back and laughed quietly, partly out of pride but mostly out of pure shame. Erica could not help laughing because even though Alan was a total mess within minutes, she could see that, in his mind, he was trying to be as neat as possible, but it was just the price that needed to be paid to get the taste just right. It became even worse when Alan would laugh and open his mouth, showing even more of the mess slopping around over his tongue.

Mark and Erica watched as Alan ate the entire basket of wings, following the same process each time and somehow making a bigger mess with each new bite than before. Erica could not recall a moment when she had laughed so hard for so long. Sometimes, she thought her sides would burst, and all she could do was laugh until she cried.

By the time they left the booth, they had made a pile of napkins in the center of the table. Erica focused on cleaning up the table while Mark focused on trying to get the red and white sauces off of Alan's face, out of his hair, and, to the best of his ability, out of the boy's clothes. Alan was happy and laughed himself silly every time Mark found a new place where Alan had managed to make a mess.

It was dark before they arrived back at the house. Alan fell asleep in the back of the Jeep during the ten minutes it took to get from the restaurant to the house. He was 'fat and happy,' as her father used to say, and the only way to follow that up was with a nice long nap.

Erica pulled into the driveway and turned off the engine. Mark began to get out of the car, but Erica reached over and touched him on the arm.

"Today was fun," was all she could think to say.

"Yeah, it was," Mark said, looking out the front window, smiling crookedly.

"He is a great kid," Erica said, looking back at Alan sleeping peacefully.

Mark turned and positioned himself to look at Erica, leaning against the car door. "How much of a chance do you think he really has to get the scholarship?"

"I don't know. The board of trustees will review whatever he comes up with, but they have only given out a full-ride scholarship a couple of times. It's a long shot." Erica answered honestly.

The car's silence was comforting as they sat there thinking in the dark. Mark seemed far away, but Erica did not press him.

"Regardless of what happens, you should know that you were right to say what you said. Even if he doesn't get to go to the school, I will make sure that he gets whatever kind of education he needs so that he can become... whatever it is he is capable of." Mark said. "If it weren't for you, I never would have known."

"Thank you for saying that." Erica smiled.

Mark returned her smile for a second and then got out of the car, folded his seat forward and retrieved Alan, who collapsed around his shoulders. Mark shut the door as quietly as he could and Erica watched as they walked up to the front door and disappeared inside.

Pulling away from the house, she found it odd that she felt disappointed that she had to leave them behind. For a few brief moments, she had felt as if she had been welcomed inside of their world, and now that she was on the outside headed far away, she wanted to be back inside again. As selfish as she knew she was being, she felt for the first time since her father had passed away what it was like to be part of a family.

She could not help but think about what a wonderful father she had been fortunate to have, even if it had been for far too short of a time. She remembered that as they crossed the Charleston High Bridge when she was a little girl, her father would tell her that all the lights in the water were actually an undersea kingdom full of mermaids. The small wooden sticks and poles sticking out of the water, he told her, were the very tops of tremendous castles so tall that just the poles where the flags should be stuck out of the water. He told her that, on very special occasions, she could see flags waving just above the waves.

Even as an adult, and long after the bridge had been torn down and replaced with the ultra-modern suspension bridge, she still looked down at the water, hoping to see even a glimpse of the undersea kingdom.

Being with Mark and Alan reminded her how much she missed her father and how special he was. As she drove, she wiped away the tears, knowing that even though he was gone, he was still somewhere watching her. She suddenly understood Mark and his relationship with Alan. Yes, he would be in orbit around Alan his entire life, but it was nothing as crude as a planetary orbit. Just like her father was to her, Erica finally understood that Mark was Alan's guardian angel.

For a moment, she felt she could feel her father in the car and turned around at a stop light to look, and then began to laugh as she saw multiple stains of ranch dressing and buffalo sauce that Mark had missed, that were now a permanent part of her back seat.

~ CHAPTER TWELVE ~

The following week passed by with remarkable ease for Mark. Three distinct highlights of the day energized Mark through the rest of the day. The first was watching Alan paint or draw at night. He was searching for his inspiration and producing many sketches on anything he could get his hands on. Mark finally bought him an artist's sketch pad and some number 2 pencils, which Alan carried with him no matter where he went.

Flipping through the book and seeing the world from Alan's perspective was a treasure and the main topic of conversation during the second highlight of his day.

Erica was now beginning to wait for them out by the fence with coffee each morning. Mark logically knew that her interest in him was only professional, so it was nice to see her waiting for them and speaking with him. As he walked to work drinking the coffee she gave him, winter was beginning to settle back into the front range of Colorado, and the temperatures began to drop again, but Mark was as warm as if it had been the middle of summer.

His time in The Cage flew by, and Mark was out the door each day, ensuring he was waiting for Alan as soon as he was done working with Erica after school. At this point, it was Erica's turn to show Mark what Alan had created during their time together. While her time with Alan was much more technical, they both agreed that new moments of inspiration took their breath away each day.

Mark asked Erica if they should be concerned that Alan would not be able to find the proper inspiration for the piece that they were to submit to the school. Erica was not worried and told Mark that the piece they would submit was something that would be very personal to Alan. They could not force him but only give him the tools he needed.

She explained that it was like growing food. If a farmer went out into the field every day and worried and fussed over each seed, then the entire process would be painfully frustrating. However, the farmer's job is not to grow the food; it is his job to create an environment where food can grow naturally, knowing that if he did his job properly, the food would appear when the time was right.

Each day, Alan was learning something new, and each day, Mark and Erica felt that they would see the piece Alan would lock onto and finish to the best of his ability.

By the end of the week, Mark stopped struggling with the idea that Erica would ever be interested in him and just settled into a boyhood crush on the pretty school teacher. Mark figured it was harmless as long as he did not act upon those feelings or let his guard down and do something stupid.

Everything that used to be so difficult seemed easier; it was almost as if Mark had received fresh batteries. Nothing seemed to slow him down, and he was three steps ahead of everyone at work.

He was in a groove for a change, and the lack of friction in everything around him was energizing.

Friday was different. After Mark dropped off Alan, he and Erica stood outside in the cold and talked about nothing for several minutes. When he finally could tear himself away, Erica asked him if it would be all right if she gave him a call. She said she wanted to talk to him about something she could not discuss at school. Mark agreed, of course, and as he walked away from her, his mind began spinning out of control.

One moment, his fear took over, and he convinced himself that she was going to call him and tell him that he needed to stop acting like there was something between them; and the next moment, he hoped she would call and tell him she wanted to see more of him. Both sides of the equation were as unrealistic as the other, but with everything going so well, Mark chose to fall on the opposite side of cynicism from a change.

The phone call came an hour before he was to get off that evening. One of the wait staff returned to the kitchen and said he had a phone call waiting for him in the office.

Mark placed the rack he was working on into the dishwasher and walked out of the kitchen, making sure not to be seen by the general public in the dining area. He thought it was odd that Erica would call the restaurant during the day, especially when they would see each other in just a few minutes, but it did not matter. Getting another opportunity to feed his schoolboy crush was all that mattered.

"Mr. Soderlind, I am sorry to bother you at work, but your mother refuses all food and medication. We need you to come here right away to try to help us resolve this situation," the nurse on the other end of the phone said.

The disappointment was significant, and even though Mark agreed to come right away, the frustration was profound.

For the next half hour, Mark did everything he could to get a hold of Jenny or Tyler, but was greeted only by voicemail repeatedly. By the time his shift was over, he knew he would have to pick up Alan and take him to the hospital in Canon City. Not only would the bus fare cost twice as much, but Mark hated taking Alan anywhere near that hospital.

During the rare times, his mother recognized her only grandson, she would be friendly for a few minutes, but the complaining and language would set in, and Mark would be forced to have some of the nurses watch Alan until he could get her to calm down.

More so than the inconvenience of the entire situation was that it felt like storm clouds had just arrived and ruined a perfectly good picnic. Everything had been going so well that a trip to see his mother would be the perfect antidote to everything going in the right direction.

He knew he would eventually have to tell the hospital that he was moving and that they would no longer have a contact number for someone local to help with their most difficult patient. This was just one of the many people he would have to tell he was abandoning and suffering their disappointment and condemnation for not living up to his responsibilities.

Mark put on his coat and gloves and made his way to the school as the sun was beginning to set, and the deep cold was setting in and chilled him to the bone. His leather gloves were shoved deep into his pockets, and he pulled the wool cap over his ears, doing his best to keep his head down as he walked along the ice-covered sidewalks to the school. Bright headlights zoomed past him as he walked while the cold set into his cheeks, mouth, and eyes. The cold air was getting through his thickest jacket, making his face numb every time the wind picked up and blew more ice into his eyes.

When he finally made it to the school, the warmth of the hallway was like stepping into a furnace, making the skin on his face hurt as it did its best to warm up slowly. Mark went to Alan's classroom and was getting ready to knock on the door when he saw Erica working with Alan inside.

She was so beautiful that it made his heart ache as much as his cold face. It was as if all the coldness he had ever suffered in his life was slowly melting off of him under the heat of who she was. She was as warm as the sun to his soul, and regardless of her feelings for him, he would always be grateful to her for waking him up. Even if it were for a short time, he would always try to remain unthawed for the rest of his life. He shook his head at his own foolishness... he had it bad, much worse than he wanted to admit to himself.

The hinges squeaked as he walked into the room, and Erica looked over and smiled wide as soon as she saw him.

"Dad!" Alan shouted and ran over and hugged him.

Erica had been showing Alan several different watercolor techniques, which Alan quickly declared that he hated. He said the colors were too thin, and he wanted to return to working in acrylic and, hopefully, oil soon. It was hard to believe that such a small child could have such strong opinions, but he did, so Erica shrugged it off as a lesson learned regardless.

"I'm sorry. I have to cut the lesson short today. We have to go see Mark's grandmother tonight." Mark said.

"Awww. Can I go to Aunt Jenny's instead? The hospital smells like salt. It's gross." Alan said as he walked over to get his coat with his arms hanging as limp as his bottom lip.

"Sorry, but you have to come with me this time. We have a long night ahead of us, so let's grab your stuff and go." Mark said, trying to keep his frustration with the situation at bay. "I just need to call a cab, and we will be out of your hair."

"Call a cab? Why don't you let me give you a ride?" Erica asked, gathering up her things.

"That's nice of you, but we have to get to Canon City. It's too far away. Whenever we do this, we just grab the bus." Mark said.

"It's not a problem; I have nothing to do tonight. Besides, since I moved here, I have not had a chance to see much of Colorado. It will be fun to go for a ride." Erica said, pulling on her coat and turning off the lights. "I won't take no for an answer. I'll even let you buy Alan and me dinner on the way there."

Mark was mortified at the idea of being in a car with Erica so close after getting off work. He knew how he smelled, and there would be no way to keep his coat on the entire time.

"Dad, can we go by the house first? I forgot my sketch pad." Alan asked as he fumbled with his gloves. Mark was so happy to oblige that he could have kissed him.

After quickly changing clothes and searching for some of Alan's pencils for the road trip, they finally headed down highway 115 to Canyon City within the hour. After they left the city, the sun had set so that the only sites were the road ahead in the headlights and lights on the horizon. It was then that Erica asked the question that Mark had been dreading since she offered them a ride.

"Is your Mom sick?" Erica asked.

Mark did not know how to answer the question. Having Erica near his mother was a terror growing in his stomach with each passing mile. If it was only having to deal with his mother being mean or saying something inappropriate (which was much more of a certainty), that was something he could handle, but ultimately, Mark knew that his mother would not miss an opportunity to talk about Shannon. The idea of having someone like his mother tell Erica about Shannon before he had a chance to was far too horrible to contemplate.

"She is… uh… she is not well." Mark began. "There are really two things wrong with her. First, she has a really bad case of lupus and is unable to walk or take care of herself. Essentially, her body's immune system is at war with itself and is causing all sorts of physical problems for her. The other problem is that she was an alcoholic for many years and, to be perfectly honest, has the temperament of a wolverine."

"I'm sorry," Erica said. "My mom and I aren't close, but at least she is healthy, I guess."

They continued to ride in the car in silence. Mark waiting for the other question that was bound to come.

It was hard sitting next to her. A part of him just wanted to exhale and relax, but he knew that if he did so, he would regret it by saying something stupid. Yet, he could feel the walls he had so effectively built beginning to crumble every time he looked at her or smelled her perfume as it filled the car.

"If Alan gets the scholarship..." Erica began to say as Mark's heart sank. "What are you going to do about your mom?"

"Honestly, I don't know," Mark said, turning and looking out the passenger's window.

The hum of the engine and the sway of the car on the pavement was relaxing, but all Mark could think about was how little Erica would think of him if she knew the entire truth of his situation. How could he hope to earn and keep her respect when she discovered the magnitude of secrets he was keeping from her? He wanted to tell her the level of sacrifice he was willing to make for Alan to get into the Benton Academy but knew that the minute he did so, she would pull away from him.

How could a woman like Erica, who seemed to have more compassion for him than anyone he had ever met, possibly want anything to do with him if she knew he was actively planning on leaving his wife and mother without so much as a goodbye the minute Alan received his scholarship?

"Look, I'll take Alan to get something to eat while you deal with your Mom. I feel bad that I forced myself into this." Erica said after a while.

Something happened to Mark that had never happened before; he began to talk about his mother to Erica without holding back any of the sordid details. He told her about the drinking, about the beatings he had suffered at her hands, and how she blamed him for everything that ever went wrong with her life.

The frustration with being raised by a monster came to the surface, and, at times, he knew he was speaking too fast for Erica to understand, but once he started, he could not stop himself. He tried to keep his voice down as Alan sat in the back with his headphones in his ears, but the more he spoke, the more he forgot about anything other than the words coming out of his mouth. He was not emotional or angry; it could have been a story about a bad day at work or a minor disappointment in his life. Mark knew that the atrocities he had suffered were out of the norm, but for him, it *was* the norm, and all he had was a gut feeling that things should have been different. He was not feeling sorry for himself, but seeing how sweet life could be when he was with Erica was addictive, and he did not want to let the feeling go of how great the past week had been.

In a small way, it was nothing more than a man rising above the waves and letting the fresh air fill his lungs again; but the closer they got to the hospital, he knew there was a possibility of being dragged down underneath the waves again. Opening up to Erica was not a sad or pathetic act; it was simply a man looking for someone to throw him a lifeline. Someone to tell him that his gut feelings about the way he had been raised were correct.

Erica listened intently, stopping Mark now and then to ask short questions that usually set Mark off in another direction. Every few minutes, Mark would apologize for dumping all of this on her until Erica insisted that he stop apologizing to her. The only time she took her eyes off the road was when Mark finally told her that she was the only person he had ever told any of this to.

"So when Alan gets the scholarship, I don't know what to do... I am the only family she has," Mark finally said before falling silent, exhausted from the conversation.

They pulled into the hospital a few minutes later and parked.

"Come here," Erica said to Mark. Then looking back at Alan in the rearview mirror. "We will be right back, Alan. And then we will go to that 'Mr. Ed's' place back on the highway."

Erica walked with Mark to the back of the car and wrapped her arms around him. He responded, regretful that they were both wearing their heavy coats, wanting to feel her body pressed against his again.

"You listen to me, Mark," Erica said intently, grabbing his shoulders. Mark noticed the intensity in her eyes only in the snow-flurried light under the parking lot lights. "If Alan gets this scholarship, you take him, and yourself, as far away from that woman inside and never come back. I want you to promise me that!"

"I appreciate that, but...." Mark said, looking down and taking a step back.

Erica did not give up. "You listen to me, Mark. That woman is not your family. She raised you, but she is not your family. Alan is your family. A family is the people in your life that you would throw yourself in front of a bus to protect. A family is the very select people that would give anything to see you become everything you are supposed to be. It is not the people who try each day to beat you down so they can feel better about themselves. It is not the people who have no love for you. That woman may have your DNA, but she sacrificed her right to be in your family the first time she hit you. The things she did were nothing more than her severing ties with you. You keep the door open for her because she is not doing anything to be a part of your life. She is only interested in you being in hers, and then she kicks you in the teeth when you oblige her."

Erica finally backed away from Mark as if she had only just realized she had, with all the best intentions, practically assaulted him. "Now go inside and do whatever you must to get her to calm down. I will go get a chili dog or whatever comfort food this town offers and think about how I can apologize to you when I pick you up."

Mark did not move as Erica walked around and returned to the Jeep. The crunching of the snow under her tires woke Mark up, and he finally began to walk towards the hospital. With each step he took, he could not help but let the smile on his face, and in his mind, grow bigger and bigger.

Walking into his Mom's room, Mark was ready for anything besides what he found.

The woman he had feared for his entire life looked as if she was so frail that a gust of wind could simply blow her to dust. Her hair was no longer gray as he remembered it but stringy and as white as the bed sheets she was lying in; curled up on her side like a child. The woman he once feared was now completely helpless.

Mark stood in the doorway for a few minutes, shocked by the vision, and then slipped off his coat and sat down in the chair next to her bed. On the table next to the chair was a tray with untouched food. Mark picked up the glass of juice and positioned the straw so he could help her drink.

"Mom. You need to eat something." Mark said softly. "Take a drink."

She looked at him with unfocused eyes and took a small sip. Some of the juice flowed out of her mouth, but she swallowed what she could. Mark quickly cleaned her mouth and helped her take a few more sips.

For the next hour, Mark helped her to drink, eat a little, and finally sit up in bed. The entire time, she was weak and limp, but the more she ate, the more responsive she became, even if the difference was barely noticeable. A nurse came in, and Mark worked with her until all the medication was taken.

She finally closed her foggy eyes, and Mark began to move to get his coat, knowing that Erica and Alan were ready to head back. He moved to grab his jacket when he felt her weak hand gently touch his. She did not open her eyes or move, but with her little strength, she did her best to hold his hand, and Mark knew she did not want him to leave.

In all his life, it was the only sign of affection from his mother that he had ever known or would ever know. Mark stopped moving and just stared down at the weathered hand that barely had the strength to wrap her finger around his. He finally moved the chair in closer, wrapped her hand with both of his, and sat bent over, holding on to her.

He finally felt her release several minutes later as she fell into a deep sleep with her chest moving up and down slowly. Mark looked at her and could not see the monster that tortured him, but simply an ancient woman under the wrinkles and dark eyes that looked remarkably like Alan's.

Mark sat there for a few more minutes and then leaned down and kissed the hand still pressed between the two of his.

Mark walked out of the hospital to see Erica's black Jeep sitting in the parking lot with the lights on inside and steam rising from the exhaust pipe in the back. The snow was now falling again silently. Walking to the car, he saw Alan in the front seat, smiling almost as wide as Erica.

As soon as they saw Mark, they both looked like they had been caught doing something bad but could not stop laughing. Alan crawled into the back seat, and Erica cleaned napkins and empty food wrappers off the dashboard as Mark climbed inside.

Mark smiled and felt the warmth of being with the two of them return but could not get the image of the old woman under the textured white blankets in the hospital room out of his mind.

The trip back was loud initially as Erica and Alan told Mark every silly thing they had been doing since he left. Mark smiled and listened but could still feel detached from the joy they were trying to share with him.

After a half hour, Alan finally settled back down, put his headphones in again, and then closed his eyes, content once again, in the back of Erica's car.

The silence between Erica and Mark was potent but not aggressive. Erica asked if he was all right. Mark said yes, but did not offer anything about what took place with his mother.

It was not until they were back in Colorado Springs and only a few minutes away from the house that Mark finally spoke.

"You said that she was not my family because of the terrible things she did to me," Mark began.

"I am so sorry, I... it is just so frustrating to hear..." Erica stumbled.

"You were right. Without question, you were right. But there is just one thing..." Mark said, interrupting her.

"She had no love for me my entire life, much less anything that could be considered compassion. The easy thing to do would be to walk away, but I can't do that for no other reason than that is the choice she would have made if she could have. I hate the things she did to me and the life she forced me into, but I now have the choice I did not have as a child as an adult. I have the choice to rise above her garbage and not let a single ounce of who she was into my son's life. So I go whenever they call because each time I walk into that horrible hospital, I know I am stronger than she ever was and may not be much, but at least I am not her. Does that make sense?" Mark asked.

"Yes." Erica quietly replied.

The rest of the ride home took place in silence. When they arrived at the house, Mark did not say anything but got Alan out of the back seat, took him inside, and laid him on the couch. When he returned to the car to get the rest of Alan's things, Erica was silent until Mark began to shut the door.

"Mark, I am sorry for what I said... again. I just... I am just not as strong as you are. I don't know how you do it," she said, her voice raw. "But if Alan does get the scholarship, you will have a choice."

"I never have a real choice in anything," was all Mark could say.

Mark shut the door and smiled a tight lip smile, and waved goodbye.

After taking a groggy but content, Alan upstairs to bed. Mark sat by his bedside and read a story to him long after Alan was asleep. Mark looked down at the boy's smooth face and once again saw the reflection of his mother in the boy. He could not help but wonder what had happened to her to cause her to be so full of hate. She must have been young and as happy as Alan at some point in her life, but to end up like a withered vine seemed unfair, even to someone like her.

Mark walked out of the room and downstairs. He saw Alan's notebook and casually leafed through it to see if anything was new. On the last page was a picture of Erica and him sitting in the front seat of Erica's Jeep, talking to one another. Alan must have sketched the two on the way to the hospital.

This picture was not as detailed as some of the other drawings, and the lines were jagged and rough due to the car's bouncing, but it was striking nonetheless. What stood out most was the look in Erica's eyes reflected in the mirror between the rearview mirror. There was happiness and a joy in them that captured who she was.

Mark touched the picture gently, once again amazed at seeing a snapshot of the world through his son's eyes, just as the eight-year-old saw it. His gift was amazing, not in his technique but in how he could capture moments so perfectly with nothing but a pencil.

Mark could not help but smile as he put the pencils and sketch pad away and finally made his way to the bedroom.

Shannon was fast asleep in the bed with her back to the door, and the covers pulled to her side. Mark removed his clothes as quietly as possible and laid down gently, ensuring he did not wake her up. The bed creaked, and she rolled over so that their backs were to one another, being sure to leave a pillow in between so that they did not accidentally touch.

Mark fell asleep, wishing he was with Erica. What she said was true, but she had no idea of the depth of the decisions before him.

~ CHAPTER THIRTEEN ~

Mark and Alan did not hear from Erica the next weekend, and when they returned to school the following week, the smooth and easy banter they had the week before was gone. Alan was unaffected and announced on Monday at the end of the day that he knew exactly what he wanted to paint for his final project. He seemed really excited about it but told Erica and Mark that no one was allowed to see what he was working on until he was done. Both adults tried to protest, but Alan held fast and quickly got his way.

Alan spent all night in the garage after Mark helped him secure the largest canvas that Erica brought over on the easel. The temptation to look at what Alan was creating was overwhelming after Alan went to bed, but Mark stopped himself. It felt like he would break some kind of protective spell around the painting if he intruded, so even though it was killing him, he let Alan keep his secret.

By the end of the week, Alan asked if it would be okay if he did not stay late with Erica so he could come home earlier to work on the painting. So even though it was only a couple hours earlier, that small change almost completely cut Erica out of their lives. On a couple of occasions, Mark tried to speak to her after school; but with all the madness of what the school became at the end of the day, it was impossible to talk. After a few days, they stopped trying.

The following Thursday was one of the worst days Mark had ever experienced at the Upper Fourth Grill. The temperature had settled down to a freezing ten degrees above zero, and the frost seemed to collect and grow day to day around the city like dust in the summer.

When Mark arrived that morning, he found the entire kitchen covered in water after the pipes in the building had burst. Thankfully, it happened just before he arrived, and he could turn off the water before it flooded the front of the restaurant. Adding to the problem was that it took the entire staff to get the mess cleaned up so they could open the doors again, and they did not jump in and help without a substantial amount of grumbling and complaining.

Mark did his best to keep his head down and do his part as best he could, but once the front doors were open, the dishwasher was no longer functioning, and everything had to be washed by hand. This upset everyone more and put an even bigger target on Mark's back. He worked as hard and fast as possible, but a dirty fork or plate inevitably slipped through, and when it did, the customers and wait staff seemed to take it as a personal attack and made sure they let Mark know.

After the first day of working without the dishwasher, Mark's back and shoulders felt like they were on fire all night long. He found that he could not sleep in the bed and ended up sitting in a chair with his feet propped up all night. He strategically placed pillows all around him before he could get even the smallest semblance of rest. It was far too little sleep, and the next day he started out exhausted, and it only went downhill from there.

The dishwasher was still broken, and he continued to have to wash each dish by hand, but the plumber kept turning off the water all day long. Even if Mark could keep up, with no water, there was only so much he could do. The temperature of the staff began to rise until it seemed as if everyone was fighting with everyone, which ironically was a break for Mark. If they were fighting with each other, then the target became a little smaller on his back.

Mark remained relatively unscathed for the most part as the fighting escalated; that is, until Jose strutted into the kitchen and told Mark he was going to have to work double shifts until they got caught up. Jose did not ask or discuss it with Mark; he simply told him what would happen with not so much as a sideways glance in Mark's direction.

"No," popped out of Mark's mouth before he could stop it.

"What did you say?" Jose said, stopping with his hand on the swinging door that led out of the kitchen. "What did you say?" He repeated twice as loud this time.

The entire kitchen went silent as his voice echoed off the walls.

"I said no. I am not working a double shift tonight." Mark said without looking up from the deep sink filled with white bubbles and dirty dishes.

"Then get out. You're fired." Jose shouted, standing at the edge of The Cage.

"I don't think you want to do that, Jose." Mark calmly replied, turning around to face Jose while wiping off his hands with a towel. It was a weird moment because as he turned around, he suddenly realized that he was at least three, maybe four inches taller than Jose. When he turned around and faced Jose directly, Jose took an involuntary step backward, intimidated. After worrying about this man for so long, it was odd to finally see that he was as small physically as he was intellectually, and suddenly Mark felt empowered.

"I'll do what I want. It's my restaurant." Jose said, noticing that the rest of the kitchen staff was watching.

"That's true, but the problem is that you still owe me all the overtime on my time card. Since I know that you process the overtime and that I am not the only one missing their overtime checks, maybe we should call corporate to find out where the checks have been going.". Mark said with increased confidence.

With this, the tension in the room suddenly changed, and all eyes were on Jose. It was a lucky guess on Mark's part, but after being invisible to the rest of the staff for so long, it was amazing what they would say next when they didn't think you were listening.

"What are you talking about? I don't deal with the paychecks." Jose said, looking as if someone had just reached down his throat and stopped his heart.

"I know you don't, but what you *do* control is the distribution of checks when they arrive. What you also control is letting the employees cash the checks at the bar when we need to. Since the overtime checks come in separately, it would be pretty easy for you to cash our checks and pocket the cash without anyone knowing." Mark continued, walking out of The Cage. "I think it would be pretty easy to trace, don't you? All I need to do is call corporate and ask if the overtime checks I never received were cashed." Mark said.

"You're out of your mind... Okay, fine! You're not fired but get back to work. And you are working late tonight, if you like it or not!" Jose said, exacerbated, turning pale and moving quickly towards the door.

Jose did not make it. Even though Mark was taller than Jose, the rest of the kitchen staff were far more intimidating than Mark would ever be. The shouting began, and in only a few minutes, Jose was lucky enough to escape the front door without being harmed. By the end of the day, Jose was fired, and a corporate rep was pulled down from Denver to keep the restaurant open, along with getting to the bottom of the missing overtime checks.

While all the commotion was taking place, Mark smiled to himself and quietly went back to work. It had been an educated shot in the dark, and he was thrilled to learn he had been right on the mark with it. In many ways, Mark no longer cared about the money that was owed to him; just seeing the look on Jose's face when Mark finally called him out was worth the few hundred dollars that were owed to him.

Mark called Jenny and asked her to watch Alan that night when the corporate rep called an All Staff meeting at the night's end. Not only was he able to get caught up, but suddenly Mark was a hero to the entire staff. As the news spread, everyone came by The Cage and shook Mark's hand, and even a few of the wait staff hugged him. Overnight, the invisible punching bag became everyone's best friend.

It turned out that Jose had been running his scam for years. Anyone who had ever called him on it had been fired, so the ones that suspected, but needed their job, kept their mouths shut. The bartender at night had a part to play and was immediately fired, but also provided enough information as to what had been going on to avoid being charged. By the time it was all accounted for, Jose had stolen over sixty thousand dollars from his employees over the years and was arrested within forty-eight hours of ordering Mark he had to work overtime.

At the staff meeting, everyone was assured that a complete audit of the time cards would take place and that everyone would be paid for the hours owed to them. The corporate rep, Manuel Ybarra, turned out to be a great guy who stuck around for several weeks afterward, ensuring that everything was taken care of, and personally handed out the checks when they came in with an apology letter from the president of the company.

By Saturday, everything had settled down, apart from the industrial garbage disposal in The Cage going on the fritz and the plumbers who just fixed the broken pipes being in the way again. It did not matter, though; the minute Jose had left, the entire atmosphere in the restaurant had changed, and the staff had a sense of camaraderie as if they had survived combat together.

Mark was in such a good mood that when he dropped off Alan at Jenny's house, her anger towards him did not affect him whatsoever.

That day, while they were doing their morning prep, Manuel Ybarra asked to speak with Mark. Manuel asked Mark what a typical day was like for him, and Mark went through everything from opening up in the morning and doing the prep work to the drudgery of keeping in front of the rest of the staff with the dishes. Manuel was amazed at how long Mark had been working at The Upper Fourth Grill and asked if he had ever considered applying for a management position. Mark said no, but Manuel encouraged him to look into it since a new management staff would be brought in after the mess that Jose had left in his wake. Manuel said he would be interested in interviewing Mark if interested in the position.

When he returned to The Cage, the disposal exploded in a shower of old food and a red mush of a liquid that smelled like wine mixed with sardine juice. Mark got the brunt of the blast, but the plumber was right next to him in the alley a few minutes later, trying not the throw up as they cleaned themselves up while trying to stay warm all at the same time.

As fate would have it, a waitress poked her head out of the back door and told Mark that he had a visitor in the restaurant waiting for him.

Walking inside into the humid warmth of the kitchen, Mark looked through the round window within the kitchen door and saw Erica standing by the bar, looking as if she was unsure what to do with herself.

If he could see his own expression, he would have looked just as frightened as Jose did when the kitchen staff cornered him. Even on a normal day, Mark would have been mortified to have Erica see him at work, but with the red, smelly stains all over his clothes, it was a disaster.

Mark grabbed the waitress, who told him Erica was there when she returned to the kitchen. "Can you please tell her I will be out in a minute? Can you get her a drink or something?"

"Is she your girlfriend? She's hot!" The waitress responded, way too loud.

Suddenly the prep and line cooks were looking at Erica from the kitchen window. Erica's presence instantly tripled whatever credit Mark had gained from getting Jose fired. Mark was not amused but distracted by looking for a way to cover up his clothes.

Suddenly, everything went dark as his head was covered with something white. Pulling it off, he saw that it was one of the chef jackets that the cooks wore and were cleaned each night. The waitress stared at him, trying not to laugh, while the rest of the kitchen staff told him to change and get out there. Mark took off his shirt (to the whistles and catcalls of everyone else) and put on the uniform. He looked around silently, asking if he looked all right when the waitress reached up and did her best to comb his unmanageable hair.

Mark walked through the swinging door amid pats on the back and instantly forgettable suggestions for what to do with Erica. Once outside of the kitchen, smiling to himself, he kicked the door without turning around, hearing it thump against those that were still trying to watch.

Mark made his way slowly to Erica, who was still looking around the restaurant's front end. The room was strangely silent as it always was before opening. In Mark's mind, it was one of the few times the Upper Fourth Grill looked remotely promising as a place to eat. The brass was polished, and the floors were clean. The lights were dimmed so that the only light entering the room was from the pulled shades on either side. In a few hours, it would be filled with screaming children, bright lights, and generic food created as fast as possible, made from recipes developed in a lab on the west coast. But right now, it was almost romantic. Even more so with Erica standing in the center of it all, waiting for him.

When she turned and saw him, she smiled brightly. It was an odd moment because even though Mark knew how pretty she was, it was as if he was seeing her for the first time. Her thick black hair was down and falling over her shoulders just below the color of her grey t-shirt. Her body, for lack of a better word, was perfect, and she stood at the end of the bar without saying anything with her crooked little smile as if she was in on a secret that no one else in the world knew about. She truly was the most beautiful woman Mark had ever seen in his entire life.

"Hey," Mark said, rather unceremoniously, when he got close enough. "Is everything okay?"

"Oh, yeah. Everything is just fine," She said, looking at the white-pressed chef's jacket Mark was wearing. "I have never seen you at work; you look great."

There were a few seconds, nothing more than an impulse, where Mark contemplated letting Erica think this was what he wore daily and that he was some important person in the kitchen. His consciousness got the better of him, and he quickly told her the story of the broken disposal and how he was scrambling to find something that did not smell like rotting fish to come out to talk to her in.

She thought it was funny but simply closed off the subject by saying, "Still, it looks really good on you."

The thought that he looked good to Erica was more than his brain could handle at that moment. It was like too many concepts trying to get through the small door of his brain simultaneously; he would eventually be able to process everything that was happening but he was still shocked at the fact that she was standing in front of him and was having trouble seeing or hearing anything else.

After hearing a thump behind him in the kitchen, Mark walked Erica across the room to a booth that he knew was hidden from any prying eyes looking out the kitchen window. He wondered if Erica heard the "Awwwww's" coming from the kitchen when they sat down, but it didn't matter.

"So, you're probably wondering how Alan is doing with his project," Mark said once they sat down.

"No... I mean... yes. Yes, I am. Have you seen it?" Erica asked.

"No, I haven't. But the curiosity is killing me. He has stopped watching television almost completely. I had to get a space heater because he just wants to be in the garage working, whether night or day. He came in the other night shivering! I have never seen him so happy, though." Mark said, feeling as if he was rambling.

"What do you think it is?" Erica asked.

"I don't know. He won't talk about it at all. I had no idea an eight-year-old could be so stubborn." Mark said.

"Yeah, they are. I have twenty of them each day. Sometimes all I can hope for is to keep them alive until I can return them to their parents." Erica said with a smile and then immediately remembered something, saying, "Oh! I got a letter from the Benton Academy, and they said that the board of directors would review all scholarship entries the first week of June. Do you think he will be ready by then?"

"I think so. I can't imagine it being much longer at the rate he is working." Mark replied.

To his surprise, the waitress that alerted Mark to Erica's presence in the first place appeared at their table with a suppressed smile and put down silverware and plates.

"I hope you like omelets; they are making some for you right now." She said, looking at Mark with wide eyes, approving of Erica. Mark had worked with the waitress for who knows how long but did not know her name. It was an odd feeling, knowing that the people he worked with could see him in any other manner than the weird guy who worked in The Cage.

"I really wasn't planning on staying for breakfast. I know you have to get everything ready to open." Erica said, worried that she might be in the way.

"Don't worry. We owe Mark for dropping the house on the wicked witch. It's the least we can do." The waitress retorted. "Besides, it's hard to hear what you are talking about from the kitchen, which gives me an excuse to eavesdrop."

Erica looked puzzled as the waitress left.

"It's nothing," Mark said, wanting to avoid the subject.

"Okay, I'll tell her," the waitress said, returning to the table. "This guy is a hero. As long as I have been here, he hardly speaks to any of us, so we thought he was all stuck up…or weird… Sorry about that. And then, suddenly, out of the blue, he turns out to be freakin' Superman."

For what seemed like an eternity to Mark, the waitress told Erica about everything that had happened with Jose. In her version of the story, Mark came across as practically grabbing Jose by the ear and throwing him in jail personally rather than letting the kitchen staff scare the crap out of the guy until he left. By the time she was done, Mark wanted to thank her from the bottom of his heart, wishing she would also drop into a hole right where she stood.

When they were alone again, Erica sat in the booth, looking at Mark with laughter.

"You really hated that, didn't you?" Erica asked with a crooked smile.

"So much," Mark said. "It really wasn't that big of a deal. I mean, it is so much better here with Jose gone, but I was just trying to save my job. The rest was a bonus."

"Well, you are just a bag full of surprises, aren't you, Mr. Soderlind?" Erica said, leaning forward.

All Mark could do was raise his eyebrows and look away from her. It was one thing for the people he worked with to act differently around him, but having Erica think he was something he wasn't bothered him. In a few months, if not a few weeks, he would most likely be the invisible man in the restaurant again, and all of this Superman garbage would be forgotten. Everything about the restaurant, apart from himself, was in a constant state of flux, and this time next year, anyone who ever cared about what happened would be long gone and the entire incident forgotten.

Erica was something different. She was more permanent in Mark's mind, and he was already keeping too many secrets from her.

The waitress appeared with the omelets and, this time had the good sense to leave immediately. Erica and Mark began to eat to fill up the space that seemed to be widening between them.

"You haven't asked me why I'm here." Erica finally said.

"I'm sorry. I thought it was to check up on Alan." Mark said, a bit confused.

"I'm here because I was raised by a woman who taught me that it was wrong for a girl to call a boy and ask him out on a date," Erica said, turning her head and sighing as if the sentence had been building up in her for a while.

Mark could not help but wonder how he managed to have his mouth full at such a pivotal moment in the conversation. As the words bounced around in his head, he found he could not chew and was more afraid of the meal coming up from his stomach than going down. After he was finally able to get his mouth empty, he still found what his ears heard hard to believe.

"A date?" Mark asked. "As in…. a date? No Alan?" Mark continued, wishing suddenly that he had not swallowed until he could have thought up something more intelligent to say.

"Yes, but *you* have to ask *me*. My mother would never forgive me if she knew I threw myself at you like this." Erica coyly replied.

This was the second moment in his life that a single detail would never fade away. Sitting in the booth as the sun streamed over the table, Erica was doing everything she could to be as strong and secure in herself as possible, but seeing just a glimpse of insecurity on her beautiful face as she waited for Mark to say the words she came to hear.

It was also one of the few miraculous moments in life when exactly the right words are presented by your brain at the right time, making Mark seem substantially cleverer than he ever had been before. He did not know why he said it; maybe it was the fact that the woman across from him was being so ridiculous, acting as if Mark would not jump at the chance to be seen in public with her. They both knew it was a done deal, but for some unknown reason, Mark said, "No. I'm sorry, but I only date attractive women."

The look on Erica's face was priceless. Complete shock, horror, and confusion passed in front of her eyes as she tried to fix the apparent malfunction between her ears and brain. Mark played it cool and took a bite of his omelet, hoping to keep a straight face and stop his own laughter.

Within a couple of seconds, she was in on the joke and looking playfully hurt as she threw her napkin at him as they both began to laugh.

"Erica, would you give me the honor of taking you out tonight?" Mark finally asked, looking her in the eyes, hoping she could see he wanted nothing more.

"No. Piss off." She responded while looking around as she began gathering her things, then stopped moving, paused, and smiled brightly. "I would love to."

Six hours later, Mark stood in front of a mirror, wondering how he had become so old without knowing it. He also could not help wondering if he would ever grow any brains before he became too old to care.

He left work early and caught a bus down to Old Colorado City. Before they made plans, Erica told him she wanted to try a small Italian restaurant called Paravicini's that a friend had told her about. So, not wanting to be picked up, he told Erica he would meet her there at seven.

After asking if Jenny could watch Alan again, Mark made the long walk up Fillmore Hill to change out of his work clothes and then walked down the other side of the hill, which was only a few minutes outside of Old Colorado City.

Old Colorado City was really nothing more than a single strip of road in the oldest part of town. It was initially the capital of the entire state of Colorado, but the money brokers from Denver refused to travel there, so the capitol was moved to Denver, and that city flourished; while Colorado City became something of a ghost town. That was until the merchants from Colorado Springs moved in and made it a tourist destination full of 'Ma and Pa' stores and some of the best bed and breakfast hotels in the entire state.

Mark immediately walked into a hair salon with a name he could not pronounce to get his hair cut. He could not remember the last time he'd gotten his hair professionally cut but remembered that the local barber made him feel more like a sheep getting sheared than a human being hoping to improve his appearance. Upon finding out that Mark was getting ready for an important date, the small Brazilian cutting his hair asked him if he would wear what he had on and then quickly told Mark that it was completely unacceptable. She gave him the name of a store a few doors down and then decided it would be best to walk him there personally.

Within minutes, a tailor with a bald head and thick glasses was measuring him for a suit; but as grateful as he was, all he could think about was how much it would cost.

Standing in the dressing room with the blue suit and black shoe, Mark knew this was as good as it would get. He was not a model, and his proverbial warts and age lines would prevent him from looking much better than he did then. He was satisfied that he had done everything he could to impress...

> *Mark knew that he should do something, yet he stayed on top of the stairs, looked down as she laid on the floor against the front door, and realized she still hadn't moved. All he could do was watch at a distance and wait for her to get up at any moment, but she just lay there. The blood started to pool out behind her head across the white tiles with the consistency of syrup but darker than any blood he had ever seen.*
>
> *Turning around, Mark picked up Alan and walked him into his bedroom. The small boy sometimes cried until he threw up, so Mark held him close for several minutes and walked around the small room in a circle until Alan was calm enough to lay down.*
>
> *When he finally got Alan to sleep, Mark walked out of the room, half expecting her body to be gone, but it was still in the same place and the blood continued to flow.*

"You still in there?" the tailor's voice burst into the dressing room. Mark looked at himself one final time and sighed, knowing that even though it was the best he could do, she deserved much better.

"This woman you are seeing, she is beautiful, no?" The old tailor asked in his thick Italian accent.

Mark stood by the counter as the tailor put his old clothes in the bag and smiled. "She is the most beautiful woman in the world."

The tailor opened his arms wide and announced in a loud voice. "Well! The most beautiful woman in the world!" and then laughed. "You bring her by here when you are done so I can see this beauty for myself!"

Mark held on to his debit card with his breath tight as he waited for the total. As much as he loved the dark suit, he knew he was eating caviar on a Carl's Jr budget; but he was too far in at this point to turn back.

"With the shoes, that will be $2,789." The tailor said, taking the card and running it before Mark could exhale.

Quickly, Mark did the math, and with the overtime and overdraft protection, he should still be able to buy dinner with no problem. Since the horror of having his card declined at the restaurant after the date was too much to bare, he decided to quickly stop by the ATM on the way and get out cash before the suit transaction hit his bank, just in case.

Mark took his old clothes in the new shopping bag and headed towards the door after thanking the tailor. Mark stopped momentarily, then turned and asked, "Is there any way I could leave these here with you and pick them up tomorrow? I don't have...."

"I will do you one better! I will take them out back and burn them," the tailor said, laughing. "No, go. Men like us should not keep the most beautiful woman in the world waiting." The tailor took the bag from Mark, practically shoving him out the door.

Paravicini's was everything anyone could want on a first date. First of all, and most importantly, the food was amazing. The kind of Italian food makes you wonder why the French attempted to be culinary masters when Italy is next door. A single bite makes you forget every chain restaurant in the world, as you are temporarily blinded by how food should really taste.

The atmosphere was bright and crowded, with a main room by the front door, a second room much smaller to the side, and a porch during the warm summer days. Even though the line was out the door and the cramped quarters would lead you to think that the small room was impersonal, the family that owned and ran the place made each customer feel like they were the only one in the room. Attentive, professional, and as warm as the food they served, the family-owed atmosphere of Paravicini's separated it from every other Italian place on this side of the Atlantic.

Yet, sitting at his table by the window twenty minutes after he was supposed to meet with Erica without ordering, he knew he was beginning to get on the family's nerves.

Mark could feel the tension as those standing crowded by the door trying to stay warm while waiting for an open table burned their stare into the back of his head as he slowly ate the once warm bread one small bite at a time. The waiter came over for the third time and asked if he wanted to order yet, and Mark looked up and asked if he could wait a little longer.

He never took off his coat as he wanted to put his best foot forward when she arrived, although the idea that she might not be able to make it was becoming more of a reality with each passing moment. He looked up at the clock and began to think about the walk home.

The temperature was dropping outside, and his coat was in the bag at the tailor's. Suddenly, the joke about his clothes being burned took on a new importance, and as Mark was wondering how he was ever going to get out of the restaurant gracefully, he saw her walking down the street.

He would have noticed that she was in a hurry if he had been able to. If he could have, he would have noticed that she had a look of frustration on her face at being so late. Instead, all he could think about was how poets and musicians had all come up short throughout history. There were simply no words. When she got to the curb, if he could have, he would have thrown his new suit on the ground in front of her so she would not get a single toe wet.

As she finally entered the front and took off her wrap, she revealed a slim black dress over her stunning figure, and all the oxygen was sucked out of the room. The small room full of about a hundred people collectively looked at her as she revealed herself and in one accord, thought, "Daaamn!"

Mark found the strength to stand, and she saw him immediately. She smiled and skirted between the tables as men did their best to watch her every move without being caught, while their dates noticed everything from her shoes to her earrings, wondering where she bought them and hating her for showing up at all.

When she got to Mark, she smiled apologetically, knowing he had been waiting for her a long time. Instead of hugging him, she simply reached out her hand and touched his jaw. It was as if she had rubbed rose petals on his cheek, her soft palm resting on his face.

Seeing it cut professionally for the first time, she looked up at his hair and ran her fingers through it in approval. Her touch made his knees weak but energized him at the same time. All he could think to himself was, "holy crap" but what he said was:

"You look amazing."

"Aww, thank you," she said. "I'm SO sorry I'm late. It's been a long time since I got to dress up like an adult, and I almost forgot how."

They sat down, and Erica reached over and touched the sleeve of his jacket. "I love your suit. Where did you get it?"

Mark told her, and the awkward moments of not knowing what to say, and the strained silences that they had dealt with since Canyon City all fell away. They took their time and talked peacefully, and relaxed about everything and nothing.

"How is it that you have managed to raise a perfect child?" Erica asked once the final plate was taken away, and they were waiting on their dessert and coffee. "Of all my students, I never have to worry about Alan doing what he is supposed to do. He gets good grades on every assignment, like clockwork, and he could be the sweetest eight-year-old on the face of the planet. How are you doing it?"

"I wish I could say it has anything to do with me, but Alan has had to grow up faster than most kids… considering everything that has happened," Mark said, leaning back in his chair, feeling relaxed and content from the wine and food.

"Does he ever do anything bad?" Erica asked.

"Sure, but it takes so little to get him back in line that it is hardly noticeable."

"Like what?"

"Well, he hates taking showers, for one. I guess that's normal, but he doesn't fight back in the normal way. A while ago, he decided he was too old to have me in the bathroom with him when he was in the shower, so I would get the shower running and shut the door behind me. After a couple of weeks, I noticed that he was filthy even though he had been taking showers every other night. Oh, he smelled just awful. It was amazing that he could walk around like that. So one night, I stood outside the door and listened, and then halfway through his shower, I walked in, and he was lying naked on the bathmat, just as calm as can be. This had been going on since I left him alone to shower alone. Just hanging out in the bathroom long enough for me to think he was taking a shower and then walking out." Mark said, laughing right along with Erica.

"If that's the biggest thing to worry about, then you are doing just fine." Erica said, still laughing.

"It isn't, but that's the fun stuff." Mark said, taking the last sip of wine.

"So what is?" Erica asked, intrigued, leaning her perfect elbows on the table. "What *is* the hardest part? I want to know."

Mark could not help but see the seriousness in her eyes. He suspected that, at this point, she might know all about Shannon, and she wanted him to tell her personally. He knew it had to come up eventually, but tonight seemed so perfect, and he didn't want to ruin it.

"Why are you here with me, Mark?" Erica asked.

"You're kidding, right? Why I am here with you is obvious to everyone in the room. The real question is, why are you here with *me*?" Mark responded flippantly.

"So, you are here with me because I look good in a dress and am pretty? Is that the only depth of this, Mark?" Erica asked intently.

Mark knew he had crossed a line and breathed in deeply, looking at her. "Yes, I am here because you're pretty. I'm sorry if that is offensive, but it is true. Do I think that you are only pretty with nothing else to offer? No, of course not." Mark answered truthfully. "But I have been around ugly people my whole life. Not just ugly on the outside, although that is probably true, real, deep ugliness. The kind that permeates the soul. So, could I be here because you are the most beautiful woman I have ever known? Yes, but your beauty only starts with what I am looking at. I feel your beauty when I walk away from you each morning at school. I feel it all day long like some angel is walking beside me. I never knew the kind of beauty that you carry around with you every day even existed in the world."

"There is one other thing," Mark unabashedly continued. "I may not know the kind of beauty you know, but you also don't know the level of darkness that exists out there. You have no idea what it is like to be spit on, to be berated for no other reason than you looking the way I do. You will never know that kind of life. So if you want me to apologize for wanting to be with you, day in and day out, so I can just stare at you, then I'm sorry, I won't. Because when you are in the gutter, doing whatever it is you can to get by, you tend to want to stare at an angel when she appears, even if it's for a minute, and you want to take it in like fresh water."

Erica stared at Mark as he spoke, impressed and slightly embarrassed at his flattery and his honest tone. "Wow," she said when he was done. "You never spoke to me like that. I am the one usually giving the lectures."

"Yeah..." Mark said, smiling. "I have been doing that lately, but only because of you."

"It was kinda hot; you know that?" Erica said, squinting her eyes.

Mark couldn't help laughing. "Well, that's a first for me. I can rest assured that I have never been called 'hot' before."

The waiter brought the dessert, and they laughed and spoke about the other students as they sampled one another's desserts while sipping on their coffee.

"So, I'm going to turn the tables on you. Why are you here with me?" Mark asked between bites of cheesecake.

"Oh, no! You never answered *my* question. Apart from my beauty..." Erica returned, fluttering her eyelashes. "What are your intentions with me?"

"You have to see that this makes no sense at all," Mark said, knowing the wine was loosening his tongue. "I have worked in a nothing job for my entire career. I have nothing to offer you. Even asking questions about my intentions makes no sense because I have no options. I could walk around this room and ask every woman out; they would all say no without a second thought. Yet, you have all the options in the world. I would bet half the men in here would leave the table they are sitting at right now if you so much as batted an eye at them. Can't you see that? The real question is, why are you slumming with someone like me?"

He said it with laughter in his voice, and Mark really was not trying to be as cruel as he came across, but he had enough sense to finally stop talking.

"So, what are you saying? You think I'm out of your league?" Erica asked, clearly not amused.

"Erica, you are so far out of my league, we aren't even playing the same game," Mark said.

"So right off the bat, let me say that you are, by far, the oldest guy I have ever been out with. You also weigh more than any guy I have dated. You have more mental baggage than anyone I ever *contemplated* being with. You have no money, and that is coming from someone on a teacher's salary. Does that just about cover it? Does that give you some sense of validation, hearing me say the things you know to be true?" Erica asked in a serious tone.

Mark sat with his eyes wide. "Yeah, I think that just about covers it. And I have to tell you, I am feeling SO much better now that we agree I am old, chubby, broke, and potentially psychotic."

"Good, but here comes the hard part. Today when the waitress at your work told me about how you stood up and got the money owed to the staff, you looked like you would have preferred to run out the door rather than listen to some girl give you a compliment. The problem here is not that you don't have anything to offer me. The problem is that you refuse to see it. You refuse to see yourself. You may have been down in the gutter for a long time, but it's about time to roll over and look at the stars for a change. I am sitting across from a man who treats me like I am something precious and fragile, a man who loves his son and takes care of him better than any parent in my class. A man willing to give up everything to help others, and what's more is he does it when the opportunity presents itself."

Mark shrugged, not knowing how to respond.

"Mark, can you ever imagine cheating on me?" Erica asked, leaning in and taking his hand.

"Never."

"How about hitting me? Can you ever conceive hitting or hurting me in any way?"

"No."

"I know you want the best for me, and even if every woman in here is missing it, I find you sexy as hell. So to answer your question, *that* is why I am sitting across from you."

Mark did not want to move. He sat there holding her hand, staring at her perfectly manicured fingernails.

"Wow," he said with a smile. "That could be the nicest thing anyone has ever told me."

"I don't know… I think I come in second to the 'angel descending' analogy," Erica quickly replied, laughing.

"Too corny?" Mark asked, wincing at his own analogy.

"It's one of those things that if you saw it in a movie, the guys in the audience would think it was lame, but every woman in the audience would secretly wish the guy they were there with would say it to her. I know I enjoyed…"

"I owe you an apology!" a man said loudly in Mark's ear, interrupting Erica.

Mark turned and saw the tailor standing next to the table, who quickly began patting Mark on the back hard enough to save Mark's life if he was choking.

"She is as beautiful as Sophia Lauren herself, lei è bella come il cielo!" the tailor said.

"Grazie, sei troppo gentile!" Erica cheerfully replied, thanking him and letting him kiss her hand.

"Perché sei in una data con un tale uomo?" the tailor asked, surprised by Erica.

Erica smiled and looked back with a fiery intensity, "Lui è un eroe, e lui è l'uomo che amo!"

The tailor clapped his hands against his chest and grabbed Mark by the shoulders.

"I have done you wrong, my friend; the suit is on me! You come by tomorrow, and we will tear up the receipt." He said, clapping his hands together again and waving his hands in the air, refusing any protest Mark might have.

A small and rather stern-looking woman next to the tailor smacked him on the shoulder with her handbag, more upset by the loss of the sale than the affection bestowed upon Erica. The tailor was pulled away to the table across the room as the two of them had a not-so-subtle argument.

Mark looked up at Erica, who was smiling at him. "Yeah...um... so you speak Italian? Yeah sure, I'm in your league." Mark said, rolling his eyes and smiling back at her.

"Is this going to be an ongoing thing with you?" Erica asked.

"You have no idea."

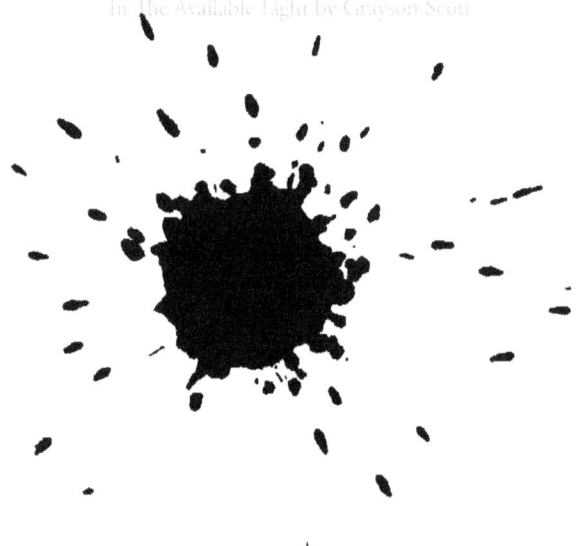

～ CHAPTER FOURTEEN ～

Jenny looked at Alan eating and wondered if Mark made the poor boy eat from a dog bowl, considering his table manners. How Shannon let this happen was appalling to her. They were raised in the same house by the same parents, but Shannon... well... it wasn't Shannon's fault, apart from being responsible for marrying Mark.

"Alan, please remove your elbows and sit up straight," Jenny said quietly, but her tone was not mistaken. Tyler would look at her to say anything, but there needed to be some decorum when eating. He thought that she should take it easy on the boy when he was with them. They hardly got to see him anymore, and Tyler was worried that if she continued the feud with Mark that a day would come when they would never see Alan again. Jenny would remind Tyler about how Mark ruined Shannon's life, or at least what was left of it. Tyler would respond by saying that until things changed, Mark was essentially a single father, and they needed to help whenever they could, for Alan's sake.

Jenny knew that Tyler was right and did not need to be guilted into helping raise her only nephew, but the anger that would rise up every time she saw Mark was beyond her control. If she could ever hate anyone, it was him; but for Alan's sake, she did her best to hold her tongue.

"Can I have some more chicken?" Alan asked, licking his lips, almost out of breath from eating so fast.

"May I have more chicken, please?" Jenny said slowly, enunciating each word as if Alan was still learning to read.

"May I have more chicken, please?" Alan repeated as Jenny slowly handed him the bowl of chicken and rice. They sat in the formal dining room under a small chandelier. The dining room could comfortably seat ten people if needed, but on nights when Alan would stay over, the three of them would sit at one end of the table and eat. When Alan was not there, it was as if Jenny and Tyler were spirits haunting the same home. Tyler had his office on the third floor and even a small kitchen, so some nights, he would not come down at all while Jenny would wander the house, cleaning and dusting as if she was constantly waiting for friends or friends relatives to drop by. They knew of each other's presence in the house and heard the bumping around but never interacted unless it was absolutely necessary.

Thankfully, Alan piled on the chicken and rice and did not make a mess. Jenny thought she should have helped him with it, but once again, Tyler would have told her that she had to let the boy do things for himself if he was going to learn anything. It was all well and good for Tyler to talk about letting the boy learn, but *she* would be the one on her hands and knees cleaning the carpet when they were finished eating, she thought with more than just a little twinge of bitterness. She would be the one with the cleaners, scrubbing the table to clean off all the dirty little fingerprints. She did things for the boy not because she was trying to stunt his growth but so that he could learn what it looked like to do certain tasks right and make less of a mess in the process. It wasn't fair that she had to be so worried about teaching the boy and then also have to worry about what Tyler would say to her when Alan was gone. As much as she loved Alan, it was work to have the eight-year-old tornado blow in, blow up, and then blow out of the house randomly. All the lessons she tried to teach him were diminished, if not forgotten completely, each time Alan walked out the door with his father. Jenny knew all the time and effort she had spent on him while he was there was for nothing.

"Slow down, Alan. There's no need to eat so fast," Jenny scolded, putting her fork on the table. "If you don't slow down, you're going to choke.... don't use your sleeve! You have a napkin in your lap, don't you?!"

"Thowwry" Alan apologized through a mouthful of food.

"That was really gross, buddy," Tyler said with a smile, causing Alan to laugh, still with his mouth full.

Jenny was mortified. It was one thing to have bad table manners, but it was something else entirely to encourage them. Tyler did nothing more than shrug his shoulders, knowing she was upset with him, but if she was honest with herself, she could not think of a time when she was not upset lately, so she could see why it no longer mattered. Alan asked if he could be excused from the table so that he could work on homework. Within a few minutes of uncomfortable silence, Tyler politely thanked Jenny for fixing dinner, picked up his plate, and carried it into the kitchen.

Jenny knew that even though the dishwasher was empty, she would find Alan and Tyler's plates in the sink and maybe rinsed off if it was a good night. If it were a bad night, she would find their plates on the countertop with the cold remains of their dinner rapidly hardening. Cleaning the kitchen was never thought of, nor was bringing the rest of the plates and dishes in from the dining room. Those, too, would be left for her without a second thought.

She sat in the silence of the dining room and finished the rest of her meal alone. After finishing a second glass of wine, she poured herself a third while she put away the food she had spent most of the early evening preparing for them, only for them to eat like animals and then run away again.

On the one hand, she knew it was unfair for them to leave everything for her without even asking if they could help, but if they did help, they would most likely make a bigger mess. So while it would be polite to ask if they could help out, in truth, she did not want them to get in the way. Tonight, her glass appeared to leak because it seemed that every time she lifted the glass, it was empty again. The bottle she had opened for dinner was empty before she knew it. She went down into the cellar and took a bottle off the shelf, feeling a little guilty, knowing that the second bottle would be empty by the time she went to bed.

It wasn't as if there was anything for her to do tonight anyway; Alan would be up on the third level watching television or doing his homework, and Tyler would be in his office watching the Avalanche, the Rockies, or the Broncos. She lost track of whatever sports season it was, but it did not matter because now that she'd served her purpose of putting food on the table, there was nothing left to talk about. She would sit in the dining room, or maybe the formal living room on the main level, and think about what could have been...and drink.

She reached up and took down another wine glass and rinsed it out. Even though she would be drinking tonight, there was no reason to act like a barbarian. Jenny secretly wondered if she was on track to become one of those stereotypical, disheveled, crazy old women who sat in their huge, empty houses' dark rooms, ranting and crying while drinking straight from the bottle until they passed out. Even though she was drinking more than she ever had in her life, she felt she was not out of control because she did it with a sense of dignity and class. She would never agree that she may have a problem as long as she could control how she maintained herself.

She walked to the front of the house with her glass in hand and looked out the front window, past the lawn and the wrought-iron gate surrounding their house on Wood Avenue. It was going to be a cold night tonight, and she could not help herself from secretly hoping that Mark would trip and fall on the ice as he walked home. Maybe he would hit his head on the sidewalk, and no one would see him lying by the side of the road until morning because of the snow flurries, but then it would be too late. She knew that with everything that had happened with Shannon, she would be happy that Jenny and Tyler would look after Alan.

Jenny was under no illusion that having Alan around all the time would save her marriage or restore anything that had already been lost. However, it would mentally release her to raise Alan the way he should be raised. There would be no more cartoons and coloring after dinner. Alan would be in the kitchen scrubbing the dishes, just as she had done when she was young.

Even though she watched Alan, she knew it was not her job to "raise" him. She knew she wasn't the boy's mother. She knew that with Shannon gone, Mark was raising Alan alone and that she and Tyler were nothing more than free daycare. She sat down in the wingback chair and kept looking out the window until both the bottle and her glass were empty. She stood up and felt the wine but pulled on her blouse and did her best to steady herself as she recycled the bottle and made her way upstairs and into her bedroom.

Neither Tyler nor Alan were anywhere to be seen, so she maintained her control over the room that was trying its best to spin until she got next to her bed. She told herself that she was only going to lie down for a minute, but she was fast asleep before she could pull herself fully on top of the covers.

From down the hall, Tyler heard Jenny come up the wood staircase, listening as her uneven footsteps slowly made their way toward the bedroom. It was becoming a habit for Jenny to drink herself to sleep lately, but Tyler also knew that if he tried to intercede, his action would be met with either anger or weeping about how everything had gone wrong in her life. He stood up from behind his desk and turned off the television that hung on the wall opposite where he found himself sitting almost every night lately. He found it ironic that as he walked through the home that Jenny had dreamed of since she was a girl, surrounded by all the trinkets she could buy, Jenny would have the nerve to tell him how unfulfilled she was. He knew that it was because she had been denied the one thing in life that was the last excuse left to her. Tyler thought that even Jenny would not be able to complain about her life if she had been able to have a child, yet she refused to adopt and had given up on anything other than making her baby the old-fashioned way. In truth, she had given up on that a long time ago also.

Tyler found her lying on top of the bed the same way he had several other nights lately. He lifted her legs up on the bed and entered her closet to get her clothes. As he was looking through the rows of hangers and drawers, he mentally told himself to set the alarm a half hour early tomorrow and to get out of the house as quickly as possible. Jenny was going to wake up with a headache, and she would be in a foul mood the instant her eyes opened. If he could leave the house before that happened, he could avoid it until he got home at night.

He slowly and methodically dressed her for bed, hoping that she was not genuinely awake even as she sat up. When he finally got her under the covers, he sat by the bed and brushed her hair out of her face. She was as beautiful as the day he first saw her; maybe her eyes were older, and the drinking was beginning to affect her skin and how she smelled, but it was nothing compared to the memory of who she used to be. When everything happened with Shannon and Mark, it was as if Jenny no longer had a lifetime adversary to fight with and, therefore, lost a big piece of her identity. Tyler could see how she treated Mark and how it was the same way that Jenny had treated Shannon when she was around. The difference was that Mark never fought back. He looked at her blankly, like a deer in her headlights, as she ran over him repeatedly, which was more maddening than if he yelled or made snide comments in return.

Jenny stirred and rolled away from Tyler, as if she could still sense his touch and reject him even in her drunken stupor. He sat by the side of the bed, silently praying for the right words or actions that would bring Jenny back to him. She was mean, controlling, and cold inside as the weather outside, but he could not imagine his life without her. He still saw her for the young woman she used to be, and there were rare moments when the person she still was inside would appear out of nowhere, and his heart would be refreshed, even if it was only for a short time.

He loved her, warts and all.

Tyler walked away and shut the door to the bedroom as quietly as possible. He walked to the stairs and made his way upstairs, expecting to see Alan either sitting upside down in a beanbag or fast asleep on the couch, with the television providing a flickering blue light throughout the room. However, to his surprise, the upstairs was pitch black, and Alan was nowhere to be found.

Making his way back downstairs, Tyler checked Alan's bedroom and found that the bed was still neatly made.

Walking down the stairs, he finally called for Alan, hoping he would not wake Jenny.

Breathing a sigh of relief, Tyler finally saw the small footsteps in the snow from the back door to the separate garage. More curious than concerned, he followed, seeing that the lights were on in the garage.

Opening the door to the garage, Tyler found Alan in the corner of a room holding a notebook, looking as if he had just been caught red-handed after committing a heinous crime. Alan quickly shut the notebook and did his best to hide it.

"Alan, what was that?" Tyler asked, not really upset but curious about what a great kid like Alan thought was so wrong that he had to hide it.

"Nothing," Alan visibly gulped. "It's for school, but I'm not allowed to show it to anyone." Alan stood up quickly, still looking like he would run out into the freezing night air if Tyler spooked him.

"If it's for school, then there's no reason for you to hide it from me," Tyler said calmly, being sure to block the door and not approach Alan simultaneously.

"I can't. I'd get into trouble." Alan said, pleading.

"You won't get into trouble. Now let me see it," Tyler said sternly.

Alan looked like a caged animal, knowing he had no way out of the situation but frightened by what it all meant. Tyler put on his most serious face, even though he was not upset. He simply held out his hand and expected Alan to place the notebook in it. Even though it took several minutes, Alan eventually handed the book over and burst into tears. Tyler felt horrible and put the notebook down and silently hugged the boy tightly. Whatever it was that Alan was trying to hide was something that Tyler had never witnessed before. Alan was genuinely scared that he would get into trouble or that he had done something wrong. Still, he also did not have the emotional capacity to lie or keep something hidden, so the tears flowed as the tiny man crossed over into unknown mental territory.

Tyler refused to believe that Alan had been the one to draw the sketches in the book until Alan let him watch as he quickly drew a paint can full of nails and screws Tyler kept within one of the many cabinets in the garage. As he watched over Alan's shoulder, his small hands flew over the page while magically bringing the paint can to life on the page. Tyler suddenly felt like he were the child and the small boy the adult. It gave him the feeling of being in the presence of true greatness, as if the boy's spirit illuminated the garage, and he was lucky to be in his presence. Afterward, Tyler sat on the floor with Alan in his lap as the boy went through his entire sketchbook, explaining each small drawing and his challenges when working on it.

One sketch specifically seemed to bother Alan. It was of Mark and a woman (Shannon?) driving, drawn in Alan's perspective from the back seat. It made Alan jittery, and he quickly flipped the page as soon as Tyler said it was okay. When they were done, Alan stood up and said, "You can't tell anyone about this. This has to be a secret, or I'll get in so much trouble." His eyes clouded again, and he looked like he would cry again at the thought.

"Alan, why would you possibly get into trouble for this?" Tyler asked while brushing off his pants. "What you can do is...amazing. You should never think that this is wrong."

"I know, but my Dad told me not to show you," Alan said. "So you can't tell him, you know, okay?"

Alan held out his hand with his little fist clenched but his pinky was sticking out. Tyler just looked at him, not knowing what to do.

"It's a pinky promise. No matter what, you can't break a pinky promise. If you do, your arms will fall off." Alan explained in his most serious tone.

"Sounds serious," Tyler said, furrowing his brows at the magnitude of the pinky promise.

"It. Is." Alan said emphatically.

Tyler hooked Alan's pinky with his own, and with that, Alan breathed a sigh of relief.

"You promised, and you can't tell Aunt Jenny about the school either," Alan said.

"What school?" Tyler asked, now totally confused.

"The school in Boston where I'm going to go next year. My teacher at school is helping me get in so that I can draw and paint all the time," Alan explained.

"What? Are you moving, Alan?" Tyler was trying to follow Alan's explanation and wondered if he was just making up a very detailed story.

"Yeah," Alan said proudly. "I'm going to go to a school in Boston. Boston is by the ocean."

"Do you know when?" Tyler was becoming slightly alarmed.

"As soon as I get into the school, my teacher found. My Dad knows more about it; I think he said it would be this summer, but you can't say anything. You promised." Alan said, waving his pinky around again like a small maestro conducting a tiny orchestra.

Tyler smiled reassuringly at him. "I won't. Why don't you get ready for bed? We can talk about all of this later."

Alan cheerfully ran out of the garage and into the house like a bird set free from his cage. Tyler watched the boy go inside and then shut the door to the garage again. Raking his hands through his hair, all he could think about was Jenny's reaction when she found out, and he grimaced in the dim light. He knew he promised Alan that he would not say anything, but he also knew that if this news was not brought up to Jenny in exactly the right way, then his marriage would be over, and Jenny would be irretrievably lost. Tyler kicked at the tires of the Audi and then propped himself up on the trunk of the car. Even as Alan let the words fall from his mouth, Tyler could already hear the clock ticking. He thought of the woman who was up in his bed, passed out again from frustration with her life, and he could not begin to guess how she would react to the news that Alan would be leaving. Jenny would definitely take it personally, as if the incredible talent Alan had displayed tonight was a personal attack against her. "How dare he have the talent and potential to be something greater than her own plan for his future?"

Tyler thought sarcastically. As soon as she found out what was happening, she would make it about her; she would instantly become the victim, but he would be the one to pay for the crime.

Tyler rubbed his face hard and then jumped from the car, knowing he should go inside, but...

"Well, damn," were the only words he could think of as he sighed heavily. He knew that his marriage was hanging on by a thread and that this could be the last weight on his shoulders that would snap the last hope of keeping it all together. The idea came into his head slowly, but he knew that to make it a reality, he would need to do something he would find personally repugnant. To even conceive of the idea was wrong, yet as he stood there, he realized that while it might hurt Alan in the short term, it would help him in the long run. He had to be careful because, while the news that Mark was going to try to take Alan away would cause Jenny to explode emotionally, if he told her what he was thinking now, it would only add fuel to the fire, but at least it would channel her fury.

It would be simple enough; he had more resources and connections than Mark. His reputation was impeccable, and he knew most of the judges by first name. A simple golf trip would set the wheels in motion, and Tyler knew that the process would be easy and heavily swayed in his favor. His simple idea would solve some of his anger issues with Jenny. If Alan was around more, it might even solve the drinking… or at least be a huge step in the right direction. Tyler shut the door, and the cold air cut through him like a welding torch. Once he touched this flame to Jenny, her excitement would not allow it to stop until all of their lives were changed forever. As he walked across the lawn, crunching the new-fallen snow under his shoes, he knew that to do this, he had to do one very important thing, and he did not know if it was possible.

The warmth of the house was welcoming, and after turning off the back porch light, he knew he had no choice. On Monday, he would make a few phone calls to confirm what he was already thinking; if he were right, he would come home from the office early and tell Jenny everything, including his plan. That would leave him tomorrow to come to grips with the only part of the plan he was unsure of... Could he do this? Could he do something so wrong that he felt he would have to sacrifice a piece of his soul to accomplish it?

He stood over, snoring and muttering Jenny, knowing that he would do anything he could to bring the woman he used to know and love back to life. He just wished that there was some way he could apologize to Mark for taking Alan away from him.

~ CHAPTER FIFTEEN ~

About the time Alan walked out of Tyler's garage, Mark and Erica were sitting in The Golden Bee Tavern at the Broadmoor Hotel, hoping that the feeling would come back to their extremities as they sipped on hot chocolate.

"That was just a terrible idea," Erica said with laughter after they had each taken a few drinks and began to feel as if they were no longer walking snowmen.

After dinner, neither wanted to call it a night, so Erica suggested they walk around the Broadmoor Hotel for a while. The hotel was one of the premier five-star hotels in the United States and had been so for the last fifty years. It was an antique taste of elegance not seen in today's culture, and Erica had only heard about it but had never seen it with her own eyes until tonight.

The terrible idea had been hers while they stood in the hotel's warmth, looking over the lake outside. The lights were reflecting off the water, and it looked like the most romantic place on the planet, so they decided to take a stroll.

Unfortunately, the temperature dropped quickly, and even though they were bundled up, the romantic walk turned painful when they reached the other side of the lake. Exactly at the point where it did not matter if they finished the walk or backtracked, they agreed to hurry up and finish the path they had started. Shivering, they held onto each other and did not speak, hoping to get back inside as soon as possible. Yet, as horrible as it could have been, they at least were able to laugh at their bad choice even as their teeth audibly chattered like children. On the plus side, they held hands the entire time, even though they both had gloves on. It was a silly and almost juvenile thing to do, but the fact that, in some small way, they were connected made everything better.

"At one point, I thought I was going to die of exposure," Mark said, laughing. "And all I could think about was you finally getting warm while you broke a sweat by having to drag me back around the rest of the way."

Erica reached over and took Mark's hands and placed them over hers as she held the warm cup.

"Oh my God, your hands are freezing!" Mark said but did not let go of her.

They talked and giggled as if they were the same age as Erica's students for the next two hours until they both knew without saying a word that it was getting late and they would soon have to go home.

"I had a great time tonight," Erica said, sitting back against the rich brown leather of the booth. "I mean, apart from almost freezing to death. I could have done without that."

"Well, I do like to make an impression," Mark wittily responded, looking at their hands reaching across the table, still entwined tightly. "I was thinking next time we could try to set ourselves on fire, just to balance everything out."

"So, there will be a next time?" Erica asked, smiling.

"Yeah, I'm obligated! Don't want you flunking Alan because I didn't call you," Mark said.

"I've been meaning to ask… where is Alan tonight?" Erica asked.

Suddenly, it was as if he had made it to dry land after narrowly escaping some unimaginable sea monster, but it grabbed his foot and began to drag him back toward the water. Tonight had been an escape from the only life he had ever known; he was sitting in the best hotel in Colorado with a fantastic woman, wearing nicer clothes than he had ever owned. He would have never believed it if he saw himself in a mirror.

But it was all make-believe, and it was going to have to come to an end. Tomorrow, he would have to deal with his overly condescending tone of Jenny when Alan was dropped off. Monday, he would return to being a dishwasher and back into the rut, yet…there would be one thing different. Erica had made him feel like a king, like someone of worth, and if he could only keep who he was and the man he wanted to be for her as separate entities for just a few more months, then maybe he and Alan could make their escape.

"He's at the babysitter's," was the only thing he could think to say, and he hoped she could not tell it wasn't exactly the truth. "He won't be back until the morning."

"What just happened?" Erica asked, leaning in close again with a questioning look. "It was like a shadow passed over you for a minute."

Mark, still looking at her hand, simply said, "I'm more content right now than I have been in a long time, but tomorrow is another day and… well, everything that goes with that."

"Well, we don't…" Erica began.

"Mark Soderlind, is that you?"

Looking up from the booth, Mark's heart froze. Standing before him was Tisha Rollins, one of Shannon's friends from school. Mark was caught, and he knew it. This would be when all of the lies and secrets he had been keeping from Erica would be unveiled, like snatching a pristine white sheet of a grotesque, twisted statue.

Mark looked up at the man Tisha was with, and the look on his face told Mark that he had been informed as to what exactly was going on. He looked back at Mark with raised eyebrows, not knowing exactly what Tisha would say.

"How are you?" Tisha asked with a mean glint in her eye, reminiscent of a cat playing with a mouse. Without letting Mark answer, Tisha immediately looked at Erica; the disgust was so apparent that it was palpable. "And who might this be?" Her voice dripped with venomous etiquette.

Erica simply let go of Mark's hand and reached out to shake Tisha's while introducing herself. Mark pulled his hand back across the table and hid it under the table like an injured animal retreating into its hole.

"So. How do you two know each other?" Tisha asked, faking interest while looking back at Mark, silently telling him that she would torture him a little longer before she dropped the bomb.

"We're friends, and I suddenly seem at a disadvantage here. I take it you and Mark work together?" Erica said, looking at Mark, wondering why he had suddenly grown so silent.

"Us?" Tisha laughed. "Oh no. I used to go to school with Shannon." Turning to look at Mark, she lit the fuse and said, "How is Shannon, anyway?"

Like a switch being flipped, Mark suddenly found his spine, and he looked at Tisha with a fire in his eyes, challenging her to say something more.

"I don't know, Tisha. I haven't spoken to Shannon in quite a while," Mark said through the gritted teeth he was trying unsuccessfully to disguise as a smile.

"Yeah, I heard about that," Tisha glared back at him.

So she knew everything. Mark knew he was helpless and that the minute Tisha chose to pull the sheet off and reveal who Mark really was, everything with Erica would be ruined.

Tisha relaxed, and with a slight raise of her eyebrow, she turned away from Mark and addressed Erica directly. "Well, we have to go. It was nice to meet you." Erica was gracious as always and smiled politely again as Tisha, and her date walked away from the table.

After a long silence, Erica said, "You know you're going to have to talk about her sometime." She sat back and looked at Mark, inviting the topic to bloom.

He looked up at the ceiling and bit his lip, furious that this perfect evening had to come to this kind of end. He wanted to tell Erica about Shannon, but he knew when the questions began that they would only lead to more questions, eventually leading to places Mark did not want to talk about with anyone, especially Erica. Yet he knew he had to say something right now. He needed to find the right thing to say so that Tisha's intrusion would not be the last thing they remembered about tonight. He couldn't tell her the truth because that would reveal him to be the monster everyone knew him to be.

"There are things about my life... my past life, with Shannon, that we need to talk about," Mark sighed, giving in to the guilt while knowing he was opening the door to let Erica run far away.

"I've always hated the name Shannon," Erica offered.

"What?"

"The name, Shannon, I've never liked it. My brother's first girlfriend was named Shannon. She'd come over to the house and laugh like a hyena. I remember when they broke up, my brother cried for a week. Never liked the name Shannon since." Erica smiled at Mark, who suddenly felt like laughing when he knew he should be bracing himself for the impact of what he needed to say.

"Look, we don't have to talk about it right now, but when you're ready, I'm here. Okay?" Erica said, putting her hand back on the table again, palm up, inviting Mark to reach out and hold it again.

Mark relaxed and pulled his hand out from under the table, placing it in hers again.

Within minutes, the date was over, and they were standing by the hotel's front door, putting on various scarves and coats, laughing and hoping to make it to the car without freezing to death. Erica was calm and relaxed, but the specter of what had almost happened continued to hang over Mark. Even in a town of almost 400,000, Mark knew enough to know that Tisha was only the first of many that would recognize him. He was running out of time to come clean with Erica.

They made it to Erica's Jeep, turned up the heat, and began returning to Mark's house. The roads were iced over, but the four-wheel drive vehicle made its way along I-25 slowly without incident, even as other cars were sliding around the highway like incompetent ice skaters.

As much as Mark had enjoyed the evening, he could still feel the moment of absolute horror when he first saw Tisha standing there looking at him; the adrenaline had flooded through his veins, and he suddenly was exhausted. Although eternally grateful, he wondered why she did not say anything. Tisha had never been one to keep her mouth shut, but it had been several years since he saw her last...maybe somewhere along the way, she had learned restraint? It didn't matter. Mark was dancing along a razor's edge, and he knew it. The next blast from his past might not be so restrained, and he needed to tell Erica before someone else did. It was that simple.

Yet, as they drove slowly across town, he said absolutely nothing.

"Did I ever tell you that I was engaged before?" Erica asked, concentrating hard on the road but finally breaking the silence in the car.

"No," Mark said, abruptly jerked from his thoughts by both her voice and the topic.

"Yeah. He was the reason why I moved out to Colorado from Cambridge," Erica said.

"So it wasn't that long ago," Mark mused.

"Last summer, as a matter of fact," Erica began. "I'll never forget the night he told me it was over. You hear stories about how women are supposed to have almost a sixth sense about these kinds of things, but I didn't see it coming at all. I was sitting at home, watching television in bed, when he knocked on my door. It was weird because he had the key, but that night he knocked, and I had to let him in. I remember thinking about the old horror movies where vampires had to be given permission to be let inside of a house and that something was wrong." She glanced sideways at Mark and continued. "He started by blaming me. He said that by moving out to Colorado, I was trying to rush into something he didn't know if he was ready for, and that was the one thing he said that really stuck with me. He sat there telling me that he 'wasn't ready for that kind of commitment,' but just before he left, he suddenly revealed the other woman he had been seeing…and how they were now engaged. He wasn't stupid, but he had somehow justified it in his mind that, on the one hand, he wasn't ready to be married, but it was time for him to get married." Erica paused at the memory. Mark wanted to reach across and take her hand but remained silent instead so she could keep her train of thought.

"I remember when that hit me. I could not get that thought out of my mind," Erica made a fist and gently tapped her forehead. "I wandered around my condo, day after day, trying to find the connection that would make the situation make sense to me. I knew the truth that he wasn't ready to get married to me, and yet somehow, the other woman was able to fill whatever void I wasn't, but that wasn't what he said. It drove me crazy for weeks until something dawned on me. If I kept spending all this energy trying so hard to understand why he did what he did, I would be haunted by him for the rest of my life. If I could not let him go, including all of the things that made no sense, then they would be a barrier between me and anyone else I chose to get close to for the rest of my life. Does that make any sense?"

"Sure," Mark said.

"So I guess what I'm getting at is that there is a piece of you that's still hurt from whatever it was that happened to you in your marriage. You clam up and shut down whenever your past life is brought up. Tonight when that woman came to the table, you squeezed my hand so hard it hurt."

"What? I did?" Mark asked, mortified.

"Don't worry about it. The minute I found out that she was somehow connected with your ex-wife, it all made sense," Erica said, turning down the last street leading to Mark's house.

"I don't know what it is, and I'm sure it's a million times more painful than what I went through, but you need to know something," Erica said as she turned into his driveway. "I expect you to tell me everything. Not tonight, but someday. If you keep up that iron barrier you've constructed that shuts out the entire world except for Alan, then you and I will never be what we should be."

Erica turned off the engine to emphasize her point, and the only sound in the car was the heater blowing air, keeping a thin line between them and the night air.

"I will. I promise," Mark said. "You just have to understand something. I don't know how to react to what you do. More than anything, I want to earn your respect because I respect you so much. I know it sounds cliché, but I want to be a better man when I'm around you. But, at the same time, I know that I have all of these walls that keep you at a distance, and I don't know how to tell you what I've been through or to show you what I've experienced without losing your respect. If I tell you the kind of relationship Shannon and I had, you'll either feel sorry for me or disgusted by how I managed to let everything get so bad. How do you tell someone that you want to think the world of you, that you've been nothing but a major disappointment to everyone who ever gave you a chance?" Mark's voice was tight as he stared out the window, purposely avoiding her gaze.

"That's not true though, Mark," Erica pleaded. "Alan thinks the world of you. You're his whole world."

"Okay, so what happens when he learns I'm not the whole world? That I'm not Superman and Einstein and Gandhi rolled up into one man? I've managed to create a safe little world for the two of us, but the time when he sees me as something more than I am is drawing rapidly to a close to an end because we all get older. This world I've created only works when everything stays exactly as it is and the change I dread is waiting for me each day. For us." He sighed heavily.

"Like me?" Erica asked.

Mark could not help but chuckle. "You have no idea."

"I know I have to adapt," he continued. "And I know that I need to be open with you about everything, but that means I have to acknowledge that an entire chapter of my life, the best chapter of my life so far, is over. And how pathetic is it to use that word, 'best,' to describe it? I would not wish upon anyone what Alan and I went through with Shannon, so we've made a silent little world in which we're safe. Stepping beyond that is something I know I need to do, but it's terrifying. I will tell you everything, Erica, but I just need a little time."

Erica leaned over and wrapped herself around him the best she could in the car and then whispered in his ear, "I believe you, Mark, and I'll be waiting for you when you're ready."

Despite their odd position, both of their bodies just seemed to fit together as they sat in the car quietly holding one another. Erica put her hand on the back of Mark's head and let her fingers weave through his hair. They held each other like teenagers, feeling a thousand miles away from their troubles and their respective pasts. For a few minutes, they were truly at peace.

Erica leaned her head back, and Mark knew she wanted to kiss him, but he just couldn't. He had promised to tell her everything, and he would, but somewhere deep inside, he knew he would not be able to cross that final bridge and kiss her until he told her everything that had happened. Yet as they stared at each other, he felt electricity, magnetism, and possibly nuclear fission invisibly pulling on his head towards her mouth. Without touching her, he could feel her lips on his and her warm breath as it entered his mouth. Their faces were close enough that there were no longer any illusions as to what they both wanted, yet Mark found the strength to turn his head, and Erica laid hers on his shoulder.

"I want to kiss you, but..." Mark began.

"Shhhh," Erica said, putting her finger over his mouth. "I know, and it's okay. We'll leave this up to you...when you're ready."

They sat there for a few more minutes until something unspoken between them told them that the night was over. Erica sat up and tried to fix her hair in the mirror. To Mark, she looked more radiant than ever as the small, silent white flakes drifted down all around them in the dim orange light of the streetlamp down the block.

They hugged one more time before Mark got out of the car. Walking through the frigid night air, he stood by the front door of the house and watched as the Jeep pulled out of the driveway and into the night.

Once upstairs, Mark gently took off the suit he had bought earlier, careful not to wrinkle or hurt it in any way. He sure hoped the tailor would come through with his promise. Otherwise, the one suit would be worth more than his entire wardrobe combined. Tonight had surpassed all expectations. Somehow he had started the day with a schoolboy crush and ended it at the starting line of a love affair that was beyond comprehension. He did not sleep right away; he simply closed his eyes and pictured each fantastic event of the evening like he was soaking in a hot bath.

The phone ringing brought Mark out of the peaceful serenity between sleep and consciousness as softly as a car accident. It took a few minutes, but Mark finally reached over to his bedside and pulled the phone to his ear.

"Hey," said the voice on the other end, and just as fast as he was brought out of the peace and tranquility of the evening, a new peace settled back over Mark.

"Hey. I take it you made it home in one piece?" Mark smiled, rubbing his eyes in the dark.

"I did, but I thought of something I wanted to tell you on the way home," Erica spoke in a whisper. "There's a place in Cambridge that I want to take you to. It's called the Gardens at the Cellar."

"Sounds ominous," Mark grinned to himself at the thought.

"They have the best tomato soup with grilled cheese," Erica said, with laughter in her voice.

"You called me to tell me about a great tomato soup?" Mark asked playfully, rolling over on his side and balancing the phone on his head so he would not have to hold it.

"Yeah, I did," Erica said simply.

"Tell me about Boston. Are we going to like it there?" Mark asked. "Tell me everything."

Erica began to speak in his ear, and to Mark, it was as if he was sitting in the center of an auditorium as a symphony played only for him. Her voice was musical. Her laugh was like drinking hot chocolate and feeling it warm him from the inside.

She told him of the house she grew up in and all her favorite places on the east coast. She explained the religion that was the Red

Sox. She talked about how every good Massachusetts citizen openly hated everything to do with New York but still snuck down whenever they could. She spoke of a life that seemed so foreign to Mark that he could hardly form the pictures to match the stories she told. Stories of flying kites with her father or just the simple pleasure of the warm summer months before things turned cold again after the heat was so overwhelming that you just wanted to climb in an air conditioner and die.

As she spoke, Mark found that the words that she was saying and his dreams were beginning to flow into one another as he fought to stay awake and take in every morsel of what she had to say, but he knew that he was going to go to sleep and there was nothing he could do about it.

"You still there?" Mark heard her say.

"Hmmm hmmm," was all Mark managed to mutter, trying to hold on to the peaceful consciousness like a man hanging on a ledge but knowing his fingers were slipping.

"Feel free to go to sleep, I'll keep talking," Erica said softly in his ear.

"We could have a good life in Boston," Erica continued. "I'd get a job teaching, and you could go to school if you wanted or do anything you want. If we get the scholarship, it will allow you to be a part of Alan's life like never before. It would be a brand new start. We could look into getting one of those hundred-year-old homes and spend years fixing it up until it's everything we could ever want."

Mark, in his half-sleep state, could picture it clearly. It was a life full of light and joy, and most of all, it was a life without the anger that had been around him for as long as he could remember. He could picture Erica being the mother that Alan deserved and the wife that he knew he had always needed but never imagined existed. Mark finally fell asleep, mentally roaming through the house he now wanted more than anything to spend the rest of his life in.

*   *   *

The cold dawn was barely breaking through the blinds of his room when he heard Alan say, "...but you have to promise not to look until we get to her house," Then he cannonballed onto the bed, bringing Mark fully and suddenly awake. "Uh, I won't, I promise," Mark said, smiling in anticipation. After showers and breakfast, Mark called Erica with the news that Alan's project was done, and as they spoke excitedly, he could have sworn she pulled up in the driveway before he had even hung up the phone. Erica was waiting outside after folding the seats in the Jeep down, as excited as Mark to see what Alan had spent the last few months in the garage creating. Mark carried Alan's final piece of work out to the Jeep, covered in a bed sheet pulled from his bed.

It had been a month since Mark and Erica's first date, and things were progressing slowly but right on schedule. They saw each other each morning as they drifted back into the comforting habit of Erica standing by the gate with a warm cup of coffee. They had been out a few more times and were more comfortable around each other. They talked about Boston often and the life they would have there. Mark started to keep a mental list of all the places he wanted Erica to show them when they got there; some were full-blown tourist destinations like the Freedom Trail or Old Ironsides, and others were more intimate places only the locals knew about. To Mark, it was as if he had won the lottery, and his prize was to move to an entirely new world. When Alan came to him that morning and said he was finished, it was as if he had been handed his ticket to his new life. He immediately called Erica, who screamed in excitement over the phone and told him she would be right over.

"You can't look, Dad. You promised!" Alan said again as he climbed into the Jeep's front seat, and Mark crawled into the back, holding the large canvas. The only way the painting would fit into the car was if the seats were down, but Mark sat on the floor holding it since they did not want it sliding around.

They returned to the tailor's small shop first; he had been true to his word, but his wife had a counter-proposition when Mark arrived. Instead of a full exchange, she offered that they give him credit in the store for the same amount. With Erica by his side, they picked out more button-down shirts and slacks than he had ever owned while she chipped in and bought him a couple of ties. It was not long before the man he had masqueraded around as on their first date started to be the man he saw himself becoming.

Alan banished them upstairs as they walked into Erica's house until he was ready. Erica gave Mark the tour of the small townhouse, wincing every time they came across something she had left out, like the pile of dirty laundry in front of the washing machine. She snatched two pairs of her thongs off of the drying rack and tried to hide them in her hand, but as she was pointing at various parts of the house she had worked on, Mark could see the pink and green straps making their way free. He would not remember almost anything she said then because all his mind could focus on was the flashes of bright-colored underwear in her hand. She finally came to the bedroom and threw her delicates in a drawer as quickly as she could, trying not to be embarrassed.

Standing in her bedroom, Mark could not help but feel the need to kiss her again. The magnetism that invisibly pulled him to her was stronger than ever before. The desire to kiss her was there on all of their dates, but the fact that he had not told her everything about Shannon still held him back. Mark was under no illusion as to the fact that he wanted another woman more than he had ever wanted Shannon. Shannon became his wife because she was the only one foolish enough to do so, and it was a mistake that they had ended up mutually regretting. Erica was different. Erica had made it clear that even though she had other options, out of her own free will, she chose *him*.

He moved in closer and took her hand, knowing that his will would no longer be strong enough. She turned and looked at him, and seeing the look in his eyes, she knew that this was the moment they had been waiting for. She casually wrapped her arms around his neck and smiled.

"Okay! I'm ready!" Alan yelled from the bottom of the stairs.

Erica and Mark's eyes lit up, and they fell out of the embrace, running downstairs like children on Christmas morning.

Alan had put the canvas in the middle of the room and had Mark and Erica sit down in two chairs he had moved in front of the canvas, still covered by the sheet from his bed.

With huge fanfare, Alan pulled back the sheet.

Painting has a certain emotional quality that photography can never match. First, the lighting the old Italian Master used is unrealistic in that it reveals so much but still keeps so much in complete darkness. With the paintings of the crucifixion of Christ and others where the body of Christ is being held after he died, the light could only have come from God in its ability to highlight the emotional aspects of the event without illuminating anything that was not needed to communicate what the artist was trying to show.

The edges of Alan's canvas were black, but by doing so, he caused the focus of the piece to stand out with powerful clarity.

In the center of the painting was Mark wearing nothing but his pajama bottoms and sitting on the floor with one hand draped over his bended knees while the other covered his mouth. The expression on Mark's face was one of pain mixed with exhaustion as if he had just suffered a significant loss and did not know what to do with himself. Even though the focus of the painting was a man in pain, the use of lighting and its perfection in placement as it flowed over Mark, spilling only slightly onto the wall, still communicated a powerful sense of renewal and hope.

Mark stared, speechless. He saw himself on the canvas and thought of all the times he had felt exactly as the painting conveyed but had never known that Alan had seen it. He had tried so hard to keep it from the boy, but somehow Alan had captured it perfectly. It was alarming in its honesty.

Mark studied each inch of the painting, seeing his bedroom captured so perfectly, but better and more vibrant than in real life. Even though most of the painting was dark, he could see....

Mark's blood turned to ice, and he lost all color in his face as if he had just seen a ghost. In the corner of the room, beyond the sunlight, in the dark shadows beyond where he was sitting on the floor, was a face and then a figure.

Standing above him in the back of the room, captured with just a handful of lines only a degree lighter than the darkness, was Shannon. Like a demonic wraith, the hint of her was terrifying because even the light managed to miss her. Mark could see the look of anger on her face radiating from her eyes, despite being cloaked in the shadows.

Alan came over and stood with his back to Mark. Mark grabbed him and hugged him, leaning down to put his chin on Alan's shoulder, and they looked at the brilliant work together in silence.

Erica was stunned. Looking at the canvas, she felt as if she was looking at a Master's painting in any number of museums she had been in throughout her life, as her father first gave, then nurtured, her appreciation of fine art. The blending of the colors were so smooth that it seemed impossible; the expression was so simple, so subtle, that it reminded her of the Mona Lisa smile. All she knew was that sitting in her living was something that would last longer than any of them. This painting that had been covered by a child's bed sheet would be seen for generations to come. Experts from all over the world would talk about it. She knew instinctively that she was present for something that was not only historic but something that would be history for generations to come.

She turned and saw Mark talking with Alan, his arms wrapped around the boy tightly. Alan was talking quietly, but she could not hear anything. She was looking at the boy, suddenly realizing what a gift it was to know the two of them, to have them in her little home, and to be a part of their lives. She knew the two would be more than either had ever dreamed. Once the world saw this, all the struggle and fighting to keep their heads above water while those around them tried to pull them down would be paid back tenfold. They had no idea of the future they would have and all the joy that would follow.

After all of Mark's talk about being unworthy of her, she knew with a profound certainty that it was *she* who was lucky to be with them.

"Alan, what is it called?" Erica asked, sorry she was interrupting them.

Alan thought for a minute. "I don't know. I didn't know I was supposed to name it. Maybe we can...."

"In the Available Light," Mark said, as if he had always known what it was supposed to be called. He looked at Alan. "Is it all right if we call it that?"

"Can we hang it in my bathroom?" Alan asked.

They spent the next hour photographing the painting until they felt they had captured it effectively. They looked at the pictures individually until they found a shot they liked the best; then, Erica wrote a quick email and uploaded the photo. Holding their collective breath, Erica let Alan hit the send button as if they would receive an answer as soon as the swooshing sound of the email was swept across the computer speakers.

The rest of the day was spent at Erica's. With the painting complete, it felt as if there was a burden lifted off of all three of them. Erica fixed lunches as Alan watched television upstairs in

Erica's bedroom, and Mark sat in front of the painting, still trying to take it in.

Mark laughed to himself as he thought about everything that was happening. All he could think of was the comic books he had read as a kid. They all had a person in the center of the story that had superpowers that enabled them to do things that no other human around them could; where the comics focused on those who were "super", Mark found himself wondering about the others; the brothers and sisters, mothers and fathers of those super-powered folk. How do you deal with the fact that your son is able to do something that is so far beyond your comprehension? How do you guide or give advice to your child when they are better at what they do, far beyond anyone or anything you will ever know? The entire experience was mind-blowing.

"It really is… amazing. The only word that keeps coming to my mind is a masterpiece," Erica said, coming up behind Mark. She put her hands on his shoulders, and her touch still sent a jolt of electricity through his body.

"Did you have any idea? When you were working with him after school?" Mark asked.

"No. Nothing even close to this," she admitted. "It's one thing to have the ability to draw what you see, but it is something else entirely for him to have developed such skill with the brush so quickly. Look at the way he kept everything on the outside of the painting just slightly unfinished, almost as if they were out of focus. Then, as you move closer to the subject, more detail is added until you get to your expression, and then every tiny wrinkle is placed perfectly. It's something called 'creating a focal point' so that no matter who is looking at the painting, they are drawn to the same point in the painting. That's nothing I taught him, and I would bet he doesn't know what it is either; it's just what looks right to him, even though he doesn't know why. It's something that really gifted artists have, not something that can be taught. Some writers can sit down and write a book and know nothing about the structure of character development, yet it is in their books exactly as it should be."

"I'm worried about something, though," Mark said thoughtfully. "I remember I saw somewhere that all great mathematicians, like Einstein, had their breakthrough when they were young. As they got older, they seemed to live in the shadow of what they did when they were young. Can Alan start at this level and still have a lifetime of work before him? Or is he some kind of brilliant flame that's already reached its hottest point, so now it's only going to cool gradually?"

"Look at you talking about the life of Einstein. You're full of surprises, Mark." Erica said, sitting down next to him.

"History Channel," Mark admitted, laughing.

They sat there in silence, looking at the painting as Erica put her arm around him and gently laid her head on his shoulder. It was one of the sweetest moments of their relationship yet. As strong of a woman Erica was, it was surprising how vulnerable she would allow herself to be with Mark at times. Mark was still scared, hoping that the moment that he was in would never end. As brilliant as the painting was, Mark closed his eyes and took a moment to capture everything about Erica in his memory. The smell of her hair, her soft hand on the back of his neck, the way she leaned against him, so trusting of him.

"I think he'll be just fine," Erica said quietly, and Mark murmured in agreement.

The next week became a search for a reply from the school. Before Mark would let the mail sit in the mailbox for a couple of days, as he never received anything of worth, but now it was one of the most exciting parts of the day. Hoping to see a formal reply from Benton Academy was like searching for Willy Wonka's Golden Ticket because they could begin planning the life to come when they received their response about the scholarship.

The late-night talks on the phone had become a habit for Mark and Erica. As soon as Mark was able to get Alan to bed, he would immediately call Erica, and the two of them would talk for hours until they couldn't help but fall asleep. Even with the lack of sleep, Mark found that he had more energy than he had ever known. This was most evident on the long walk home up Fillmore Hill daily. In the past, where the hill seemed to grow in length as he tried to make his way up with Alan each day, Mark now found he was not winded at all by the time he reached the top. Soon, he began to place Alan on his shoulders and tried to run up the hill, which now seemed to be nothing more than a small bump.

The weather had turned once again, the sun was shining each day, and small signs that spring was on its way began to appear across the front range of Colorado. However, it was still winter, and everyone knew that Mother Nature would have at least one or two surprises left in store before the cold days were over. So, each morning began with a quick look out the window to see if the snow had returned or if the warm days would remain one more day. Luckily, even the old mountain that overlooked the Springs was beginning to show signs of spring.

The energy and lightness of the time helped Mark at work. Since Manuel was now needed in Denver and elsewhere in Colorado Springs, he could not spend much time in the restaurant, and he asked Mark to learn how to open the front end of the restaurant and the kitchen. It was great training, and the talk of Mark becoming the next manager was so common that everyone considered it pretty much a done deal. It put Mark in an interesting position. He didn't tell anyone that he was hoping to move to Boston by the time that summer rolled around; if something went wrong, it would be nice to have a backup plan.

With all the newfound attention and respect, Mark felt it was just a taste of the new world he was moving into. He kept thinking to himself that this was kind of like the decompression divers must have to go through when they rise to the surface. He needed to have a moment where he was not totally invisible to those around him, but only on a small scale, because being noticed by people was a brand new experience.

Each day when he picked up Alan from school, Erica would greet him with a smile that was uniquely his. While she would greet other parents and herding her students, she would always take a moment to tell him he was special without saying a word. It was little things, like walking by him and hooking his pinky with hers for only a second, which made him feel like a king.

During those weeks, he never saw Shannon and certainly never thought of her, although it wasn't a conscious decision to shut her out of his mind. He just had better things to think about, so she had been relegated to the depths of his brain like the third-rate passengers crowded into the bowels of the Titanic. Everything about his life was now in a holding pattern, waiting on the decision by the Benton Academy. It was so close that he wanted to tell the world, but just enough out of reach that he knew he needed to keep his mouth shut. It could have been the most nerve-wracking time in his life, but there was no way he could deny that it was the happiest he had ever been. Regardless of what happened, he had finally risen above the waves he had been trapped under his entire life, and all he could do was marvel at the beauty of everything around him.

~ CHAPTER SIXTEEN ~

Erica could not help but smile as she turned under the sheets and reached for her phone. Even though it had only been a couple of minutes since she had hung up with Mark, the fact that he was calling back was a welcome surprise.

"Hey, I thought you were going to sleep," she answered the phone, smiling.

"Hi Erica," the voice said, shocking Erica to the point that she could not move.

"Tom?"

"Yeah. Sorry for calling so late, but I needed to talk."

Erica could not form the words she wanted to say to him. Part of her wished she could reach through the phone and choke him. There was another part of her that reminded her that she was in love with him not too long ago.

"You still there?" Tom asked.

"Yes," Erica said abruptly, feeling her anger accelerate.

"I thought you hung up on me for a second there," he gave a melodramatic sigh.

"Honestly, I am surprised I haven't," her voice was tight.

"Me too. I thought you would have moved back east. I was surprised to find out that you were still in the Springs. I called Nicole, and she told me that she hasn't spoken to you for a while," Tom said hopefully.

And there it was. He wasn't just the guy that ripped her heart out; he was still a part of her life, like a climbing weed cleverly disguised among the roses. Her friends and his friends were intertwined. The mention of Nicole instantly made her ask how her old friend was, and the conversation started flowing as easily as it had when they were a couple.

As they spoke, Erica realized she still had feelings for him. More than that, she had a history with him; she saw him in her mind's eye like he was in the room with her.

After an hour, something stood up inside of her, and she spoke before she could think to stop herself. "Tom, why are you calling me? Aren't you supposed to be married?"

"Yes...but no," he sighed audibly into the phone. "It was a really stupid thing to do, so I called it off."

"You called it off?" Erica asked, shocked at the news.

Tom told her that once his candidate had won, he moved to D.C. and quickly learned that politics is nothing like it was on the campaign trail. When they were trying to get elected, it was energizing and made him feel as if they were really trying to accomplish something. However, when he got to D.C., he quickly learned that what took place in the back rooms was much more critical than what took place in public. Drugs and much worse were rampant through the halls of Congress, and if you did not want to be a part of the soul trading, then it was quickly made clear you were not wanted.

Tom's star had fallen even quicker than it had risen, and he was sent home with nothing. Then, he started thinking about everything he had given up and sacrificed to get to a destination he found repugnant once he arrived.

"With everything that happened, I just woke up and realized what a terrible mistake I had made by letting you go," Tom said. "Erica, I will literally do anything to get you back. Just tell me what to say and do, and I'll do it."

"It's more complicated than that," Erica said slowly.

"Are you seeing anyone?" Tom asked.

Erica told Tom everything. She talked about Alan first and the remarkable talent he had. Tom understood the prestige of the Benton Academy, and it was nice to have someone understand what a big deal it was to be considered. That encouraged her to talk about how the painting was finished, and the board of directors were now considering giving Alan a full-ride scholarship.

"That's great! We can meet when you get back to Boston!" Tom gushed.

Erica paused, then began to explain her relationship with Mark. When talking to Tom, it suddenly seemed as if she had just met Mark an hour ago compared to her history with him. As she talked about Mark, she could not put into words where they were. She confessed that they had not slept with each other, or even kissed for that matter, and when she was done, it sounded as if she had made a close friend, not anyone that could compete with her former fiancée.

"I would love to see you," Tom said finally.

"Wait, where are you? Aren't you in...?" Erica stammered.

"I'm in Colorado Springs. I flew out here as soon as I found out where you were. I'm serious about making amends and getting you back," he said again.

The urge to resist was weaker than she had imagined it would be. The part of her that Tom hurt was strangely quiet as she thought about all the nights after he left when she knew she would do anything to get him back. The time in her life when she was his for the taking seemed to be all that was left, yet a small voice inside told her that she was being as foolish as she had been when she had followed him out here. It was ironic that Nicole had told Tom where she could be found, considering Nicole had been one of the most adamant in believing that Erica was making a huge mistake following him out to Colorado.

"You're here?" Erica said again, barely able to process that knowledge.

"Yeah, I'm staying downtown at the Antlers. I thought we could meet; maybe have dinner?" Tom asked, his pleading tone betraying his otherwise calm demeanor.

"It's late, and I need to work tomorrow. Let's talk tomorrow, and we'll see." Erica finally managed to get the words out.

"Okay, I'll talk to you then," Tom replied, and then the line went dead.

Erica tried to go to sleep, but her eyes stayed wide open as she lay in bed. Within minutes, she walked downstairs to put on a pot of tea and think. Even though it was still pitch black outside, she knew that until she had resolved what she would do, there would be no sleep tonight. When she turned on the kitchen light, she could still see Alan's painting in her living room. Mark was going to come over tomorrow night, and they were going to take it to the fine art museum in town and talk to them about how they could ship the painting without it getting damaged.

She sat down, studied it again, and immediately felt guilty for what she had done to Mark by leaving even a sliver of the door open with Tom. If she chose to try again with Tom, it would have little effect on Alan, but she knew that she had gotten past Mark's defenses, and if she rejected him now, it would profoundly hurt him. She had to admit that even though he still kept her at a physical distance, she had... she felt something for Mark that she had never experienced before. It was certainly something much more profound than what she had with Tom, and the fact of the matter was that Tom would be just fine if she told him she was no longer interested in him.

She breathed deeply and knew that could not be the basis for her decision. She had to take this time to be selfish; she had to think about what would be right for her and her future. Even though she knew she would feel guilty for hurting Mark, she knew she could not allow herself to decide based on guilt. Guilt would make her decision based on whatever would make her feel better in the short term, and she needed to know in her heart that she had made the right decision for the long term.

She never thought it would be like this. She knew that if she got back with Tom, they would get married, and if she followed her path with Mark, they would end up married. As a little girl, no one told her that it would come down to a sleepless night weighing out the pros and cons between two men: one who had already betrayed her and another she hardly knew. A strange thought popped into her head that she had never considered before. Was she ready to be a mother? It would be one thing if she went with Tom and had kids, but the minute she picked Mark, she also chose to be Alan's stepmother. It was one thing to have a room full of kids all day, but emotionally, it was much different to think she would be a mother. Did she want that responsibility just yet? Would Mark want to have any more kids in the future? Even though Tom could be a jerk, he would be starting out at the same place, figuring out what a marriage should be together. He had already been to the show with Mark, and she was still in the parking lot.

She turned out the lights and felt overwhelmed by it all. Regardless of what she decided to do, she made a deal with herself that she would decide before she went to sleep tonight. By the time she saw either Mark or Tom again, she would know what to do; but by the time she got to the top of the stairs, a smile escaped from her lips, and she knew the answer.

~ CHAPTER SEVENTEEN ~

"We're seeking permanent custody of Alan," Jenny said, standing on Mark's porch, holding out the legal documents to back up what she was saying. "After what you did to my sister, you have no right to raise Alan alone, and you certainly won't be taking him out of state," she snorted.

Mark was speechless and took the paperwork out of Jenny's hand. She did not move. She just stood on the porch with her hands on her hips, looking as if this was the most gratifying act she had ever accomplished.

"You should also know that we're making arrangements for Social Services to come around and inspect Alan's living space. If you don't pass, Alan will be taken away immediately," Jenny said smugly. "You can avoid all this if you just let Alan come live with us. Right now."

* * *

Twenty-four hours earlier, Tyler sat in the parking lot of his lawyer's building downtown, making a serious effort not to throw up.

He had told Jenny his idea, and she was, of course, enthusiastically supporting it immediately. He had told her the day after Alan had last spent the night, and every day since then, it was all that Jenny could talk about. The leverage he used was the idea that Mark would have the nerve to move out of state just in case she had any personal reservations against moving forward. She had none and wanted Tyler to immediately get on the phone with his attorney to start the process immediately. After finally convincing her that it was best to wait for the morning so he could go to his attorney's office and take care of the financial aspects of the suit, Jenny immediately switched gears and began talking about how she wanted to redo Alan's room and all the changes she was going to make around the house to get ready for him to finally live with them once and for all.

What bothered Tyler the most about the entire affair was that Jenny never questioned if it was the right thing to do. Yes, they were more financially secure and could provide a better life for Alan than Mark was doing. But there was no question that Mark and Alan had a bond that would not be broken without a price. It was as if Jenny wanted the boy so she could have an excuse to decorate, which would make Alan nothing more than a knick-knack around the house to show off to her equally shallow friends whenever they came over.

Sitting in the parking lot, he realized that he was as furious with Jenny as he had been with himself. He was disappointed with himself for ever thinking of the idea in the first place and even more now that he had pushed the entire scheme into motion. Before, he was just looking down the hill, wondering if he had the nerve to ski down; after telling Jenny, he knew he had made his choice, and he was inexorably sliding towards the natural conclusion, whether he wanted to or not.

He got out of his car and started to make his way across the parking lot. Now that he was in public, he held his head high, knowing that he was a public figure and could run into someone he knew at any moment. Yet every step he took, he regretted.

He remembered an analogy that someone once told him about the difference between premeditated murder and an act of passion that ended in murder: the act of passion was something that happened when the brain simply could not respond to the stimuli presented to it, and it responded by acting without thinking; like a husband finding his wife in bed with someone else shoots them both, and then comes to his senses and calls the police, knowing he is going to go to jail. A premeditated murder was what he was doing right now. It was a series of choices that ended in murder. A killer would buy the gun, drive over to the house, and wait by the house until the person came home; choose to get out of the car and walk to the front door, and knock on the front door. Just a series of choices that were thought about and debated, ending with the death of another human being.

It was all he could think about on the drive over before opening his car door, walking across the parking lot, and finally selecting the floor to his attorney's office in the elevator. At any moment, all he had to do was choose not to do what he was planning, and the chain would be broken, and no one would be hurt.

But he couldn't stop himself. As the elevator rose to the fourteenth floor, he knew there were fewer choices in front of him now, and they were getting easier to make. What kept him going was that Jenny was alive again; selfish and blind but alive. He had become so used to the zombie she had become as she wandered around the house that the fact she was now talking non-stop about everything from what color to paint the walls to how good it would make her feel to be rid of Mark finally, reminded him that there was still hope, even though it came with a price. Nevertheless, as he stood waiting to be met in the law firm's lobby, all he could do was think about the price that would be paid and not the result.

The final boost came when he thought that he would literally throw himself in front of a bus to protect Jenny, and even though the pain wouldn't be the same as having his soul ripped out, how was this any different?

"Tyler, you can come in now," said the attorney's secretary.

* * *

"You can't do this," Mark said, thoroughly stunned.

"Not only can we, but we're going to. I don't care if it takes every penny we have; this will happen," Jenny sneered in the same righteous tone.

"I won't let this happen. There is no way I would ever give up Alan," Mark was starting to literally see red as his fury climbed in his chest. "Alan is mine and Shannon's child…"

She interjected quickly. "Don't you dare speak my sister's name to me after what you did! You and I both know that Shannon would give up Alan almost as quickly as she would give you up if she had any choice in the matter. Besides, I saw Shannon yesterday. When was the last time you saw her?"

"What about Alan? You know that Alan would never choose to go with you." Mark said.

"He is eight years old! It doesn't matter what he thinks. No one person in the world will deny that he'll have a better life with us than he could ever have with you."

"You don't understand. Alan has an opportunity to be…" Mark began, but she cut him off again.

"To leave and move to Boston with you? Don't you think I know all of that? That's why we finally decided to do what we should have done years ago. Part of the court order is that you're not allowed to leave the state until this matter is resolved, and trust me when I say that this will last a long time. Whatever plans you had to sneak away in the middle of the night are gone," Jenny was hissing like an agitated cobra. "Why don't you just not fight us on this? It will be easier in the long run for everyone."

"There is no way in hell I'll ever do this," Mark said in an ominously calm voice. "I will never walk away from my own flesh and blood just to satisfy you...and the fact that you can't have children." Mark knew that was a particularly low blow, but his words had just driven a large stake through this soul-sucking vampire's heart.

"How dare you..." Jenny said, her eyes widening.

"Let's face it, Jenny. You're just a tired, dried-up bitch who's looking to make everyone around you as miserable as you are," Mark said, stepping towards her until she moved off of his porch. "What's the matter? You completed your mission! You made Tyler's life so horrible that you need to move on to me and Alan now, right?" Mark's words made little puffs of steam in the cold, and in the back of his mind, he was reminded of a bull snorting before it lowers its head and charged.

Jenny squared her shoulders and inhaled deeply. "You think this is just me? That I just sat around thinking of the next horrible thing I could do to the man who ruined my sister's life?" she yelled. "This was Tyler's idea! Even the spineless coward I married has finally gotten fed up with the travesty of you raising that boy!" She folded her arms in satisfaction.

"Get out of here right now, and if you think you'll ever see Alan again, you're more delusional than even I thought you were," Mark turned back inside the house and slammed the door as hard as he could.

Outside, he heard her car door slam and the engine roar as she fishtailed the car on the ice and finally sped away. Mark looked at the paperwork and did not know where to begin with the legal documents.

When Jenny first told him what she was planning on doing, he was simply annoyed; but finding out that it was Tyler's idea gave the whole notion legitimacy, and Mark began to get scared that they could actually pull it off. They certainly had more money and connections than he did, and if they pressed long enough, he knew they would win.

Mark's frustration accelerated as he looked over the legal paperwork while leaning against the front door, expecting Jenny to return with a posse and a battering ram to take Alan right this minute. It might as well have been written in another language. Between being generally scared and the adrenaline rush from the confrontation wearing off, all the words on the pages blended together until he couldn't understand any of it. He hated the fact that his hands were shaking as he tried to deep-breathe himself back to something resembling calm.

"Dad?"

Looking up at the top of the stairs, Alan was standing there with his small hand on the railing and wearing a scared expression.

"Alan, it's okay. Go get ready for school, alright?" Mark said dully.

He looked back at the paperwork to find a date or anything that would help him understand what was happening. If only...

"Was that Aunt Jenny? I heard you guys yelling..." Alan was still looking nervous.

"It's okay, Alan, please just go get ready for school. We'll talk about it in a second," Mark said while he massaged his temples.

"Why are you so...?" Alan continued, pressing the subject.

"Alan, PLEASE!" Mark yelled. "Go get ready for school!"

Alan went back up the stairs like a shot, but Mark did not notice that he was gone any more than he noticed the look on the boy's face when he yelled.

Mark finally moved away from the front door and walked into the kitchen. He took the staple out of the paperwork with a butter knife and pressed it down flat on the kitchen island. Searching page after page, Mark finally found that a court date had been scheduled to meet with a judge to go over the report the representative from Social Services would put together. He would be notified when they would show up next week to examine Alan's living conditions. Mark looked around the house, and apart from having no taste when it came to decorating the place, he knew that there would be no cause for them to say his home was unfit; but then a word on the page jumped out at him, and he suddenly knew exactly what it was they were going after.

The Social Services angle was just an excuse to get him before a judge. Tyler was going to use his contacts and influence to say that Mark had violent mood swings and anti-social tendencies; they were going to claim that Alan was not only not being cared for properly but that he was in danger.

Mark repeatedly raked his hands through his hair, at a total loss for what to do. He knew enough to know that even if it was not the truth, the fact that it was brought up would paint Mark in such a manner that he would be put on the defensive and it was all downhill from there.

"Alan?" Seeing the clock, he suddenly realized they were going to be late for school. Mark walked out of the kitchen and looked to the silent second level of the home. The bathroom door was shut, and Alan was nowhere to be seen. Remembering that he had barked at Alan, Mark sighed, walked up the stairs, and opened the bathroom door.

Alan was sitting on the floor crying so hard that the pajamas he was wearing were soaked around the collar. As soon as he saw Mark, he ran and hugged his neck as hard as his little arms would allow him. Mark sat down on the floor with him and just rocked his tiny frame until Alan could breathe again.

"It's all my fault," Alan said, still sniffling.

"What? No, it isn't," Mark said, unsure of what the boy was talking about.

"Aunt Jenny said she wanted to take me away from you because we were going to move away. I told Uncle Tyler about it. It's my fault..." Alan burst into tears again and began to sob.

Mark said nothing and continued to rock the boy back and forth on the bathroom tile until Alan had calmed down again.

"He promised! He promised...he said he wouldn't....say anything." Alan said between deep breaths. "He found me, even though I tried to hide so I could draw, and then he promised."

"It's okay, Alan," Mark said, holding the boy's head against his chest so his heartbeat would calm him. "This is not your fault."

"But it was my fault with Mom," Alan said quietly.

Something snapped within Mark, and he pulled Alan off his lap, grabbing his shoulders and making him stand in front of him as he kneeled on the floor.

"I never want to hear you say that again. Anything that happened with your Mom is not your fault," Mark said sternly. "And this is not your fault either. Want to know what we're going to do? We're going to go to the school and get Erica, and the three of us will get a lawyer, and we'll fight this. Okay? You want to fight this?" Mark asked, smiling and holding his hands like a sparring partner for Alan to box.

Alan smiled slightly and then awkwardly punched Mark's hand. They flexed like the Incredible Hulk, and Mark let Alan punch him in the shoulder.

"Get your clothes on, and we'll run down to the school. It's you and me against the world!" Mark said to the now smiling boy.

Mark got to his feet and watched Alan run to his room to change. He knew it was going to be okay with Erica's help; she was much smarter than him, and with her help, he knew everything was going to be just fine.

"Dad?"

Mark turned around and saw Alan standing in the hallway, struggling with his shirt.

"You called Aunt Jenny a b-i-t-c-h," Alan said, spelling the word to mitigate its impact, looking very disapproving.

"Yeah, I guess I did," Mark tried not to smile.

"Don't do that. It's a bad word."

~ CHAPTER EIGHTEEN ~

Mark had learned that one of the most important aspects of being a parent was that children did not stay in one emotional state nearly as long as adults. After years of training, an adult can remain annoyed, frustrated, angry, or sad for weeks with little effort if they choose to. Children, on the other hand, or at least Alan, would simply respond and adapt to the emotional temperature in the room. If Mark made an effort to be happy or energized, he could quickly pull Alan out of any funk that might have taken over.

Walking down Fillmore Hill that morning, Mark was able to get Alan calmed down and even enthused about the fight that was looming in front of them. As ignorant as Mark knew himself to be, he knew that it would take a superhuman effort on the part of Jenny to get Alan. Natural parents almost always had more rights, and any notion of Mark being unfit would be tossed out before they could take root. He didn't know exactly how he would win, but he knew that he would. His life had made a complete turnaround, and Jenny's horrible treatment of him was the last to go. He would never have to deal with her condescending, hateful attitude towards...

Logically, he knew what he was looking at, but his mind could not process it. It was so foreign to him that he did not have a frame of reference to understand it, yet on a deep level of consciousness, he knew what had happened, and it felt like a knife was slowly being thrust into his chest and twisted unmercifully.

He knew it was her... but it couldn't be. Erica was standing in the parking lot next to the school, and she was holding an impressively huge bunch of bright red roses. She then leaned up and kissed the man in the black overcoat. He reached down and tenderly brushed a windblown strand of Erica's hair from her face, and she smiled.

It took a while for all the hope to drain from him. Blankly staring at the couple, his arms became heavy, and he immediately felt... nothing.

"C'mon, Dad," Alan said, turning around.

Mark did not know he had stopped in his tracks. He looked at Alan and back at the man hugging Erica, then turned around and began to walk away.

"Dad? Where are you going?" Alan called out.

Mark heard Alan, but he might as well have been miles away. Everything just quit. He was numb with the shock of what he saw and what it meant.

He looked down and saw Alan holding his hand again.

"Aren't we going to go fight?" Alan asked, confused and sounding alarmed.

"I'm sorry, Alan. Go to school," Mark said, quietly dropping the boy's hand and walking away. The pain was too much to comprehend, yet he knew that somehow this was the only way it could have ever turned out. The image of the man was seared into Mark's mind even though he closed his eyes so he would stop seeing the tall, dark figure. He was obviously everything Mark wasn't; he was good-looking and looked like he was rich. Of course, she would want to be with someone like that. The pain continued to grow as if his mind was slowly releasing details one at a time so they could all have an equal, separate chance to stab Mark's soul.

He kissed her. The lips I wanted to kiss… He kissed her. Mark said it to himself repeatedly, examining each second of the visions in his mind like twisted instant replay. *He kissed her. I never even got to kiss her.*

The pain in his heart literally spread over his whole body as all the dreams and plans he had been holding onto left him like newspapers scattered by the wind. Everything he had allowed himself to wish for was gone, and the lonely, pathetic, invisible dishwasher remained; except this time, he could not even feel the hopelessness he had before. Everything now was simply gray and numb. He retreated into his mind and was gone.

"Mark!"

He did not turn around.

"Mark, stop! Please!" Erica yelled frantically, and for some reason, he stopped in his tracks but did not turn around to look at her as she caught up to him.

"I know what you think you saw, but… if you'd just listen to me for a minute," she said, walking before him. In the distance somewhere, Mark heard the school bell. "That was my fiancée… well, he used to be…it was Tom. He came by today, out of the blue…" she stammered.

Mark said nothing. He did not know if he was looking at her or not.

"I'm so sorry, Mark….we just have this history…he was in town…I don't know… much thinking… Alan told me…is

everything...I'm sorry...Mark...the bell is...I have to go...call me...?"
She just kept tripping helplessly over her words.

He truly did not know what she said. She moved out of his way, and he started walking again, nothing more than that.

He continued to walk to work feeling nothing, thinking nothing, just moving so that the pain he knew was following close behind could not catch up to him.

Lifting his leg over the curb, he tripped and fell hard, hitting his head on the pavement with a sick crack like a rifle shot.
I never kissed her, was his last thought before the blackness overtook him.

He sat up, not knowing how long he had laid in the gutter of the sidewalk. It could have been an hour or mere seconds. All Mark knew was that the side of his face was warm where it should have been cold from the snow-covered concrete. He sat dazedly in the snow next to the curb until he felt the ice-cold water from the melting snow soaking his pants. He reached up and touched his head where it was warm as it began to sting, and he pulled back a hand covered in blood.

He stood up and began to walk to the restaurant as he had each day for as many years as he could remember. Each step memorized; each step the same as the day before.

Had something happened? Something seemed different than before, almost as if he had forgotten something or left something at home he would need. It was funny because he felt he was missing something important, but he could not remember what it was.

He got to the back door of the restaurant and walked in. A couple of the line cooks were in early and looked at him as if he had snuck up behind them, trying to frighten them. He walked by them and tried to say... something...

They grabbed him by his arms and made him sit down. Did he want to sit down...why? He was missing something. He needed to find it.

Everyone was looking at him with wide, scared eyes. Why was everyone looking at him? He could not think of what he did, but...

Why was he lying on the floor? Did he fall asleep? Why was everyone standing over him? Why did his head hurt? Was he crying?

He felt the darkness begin to close in on him from all sides, but he could not fight it. What was happening? Why was he on the floor? Something warm was in his eyes...

Everyone was standing over, talking to him quietly. He touched his forehead again and looked at his fingers covered in blood.

Two men in uniforms pushed everyone out of the way and put something over his mouth. They touched his forehead, and fireworks shot off in Mark's brain, bringing him back to consciousness for a brief moment longer as he yelled in pain and passed out.

I never kissed her.

Mark woke up, not because of the muffled sound in the hospital hallway or the sounds of trees scraping against the thick glass in his room. It was the slow throbbing pain that brought him back out of the darkness, like the endless crashing of waves on the beach. Each pulse, each wave of pain, woke him a little more until he opened his eyes.

Looking around the room, he saw the white walls of the hospital and wondered why he was there. Another wave of pain came crashing over him, and he was forced to close his eyes until it receded. He found the 'call nurse' button and pressed it. His body hurt, but he felt as if his mind was covered in cotton, almost unable to form a single clear thought. He laid back and almost fell asleep when he heard the door open.

The nurse walked and smiled at him. "You're awake. That's good. We've been worried about you." She patted his hand. "Now you're probably full of questions, so I'll let the doctor know you're awake. He should come by soon."

"Where am I?" Mark sighed, no longer trying to keep his eyes open.

"You're at Penrose Hospital. You were brought in yesterday with that nasty bump on your head. You fell outside Upper Fourth Grill, and the ambulance brought you here." The nurse said, standing by Mark's bed. "I'll let you sleep. Just relax, and the doctor will be in as soon as possible."

Mark almost let himself fall back into the void when he suddenly remembered.

"Wait, nurse! My son. Where is my son?" Mark asked with urgency.

"Don't worry about that. His aunt, I think Jenny was her name, told us to tell you she came and picked him up at school yesterday, and your son is with her." She smiled again and was out the door.

Mark's heart sank. He knew instinctively that they would not give him back. Even though they had no rights to him, Jenny and Tyler would try to keep Mark as far away from his son as possible until they could get a judge to force him to give Alan up.

He needed to get out of the hospital. He tried to get up, but a wave of nausea and vertigo stopped him from being able to even sit up in bed. He needed to get out of bed and get to Alan. They had no right to take him. They had no…

"Mr. Soderlind? Are you awake?" The deep voice rumbled suddenly by Mark's bedside.

Without realizing it, Mark had fallen asleep again. He opened his eyes and found the nurse who had been in his room earlier standing at the foot of the bed, along with a man in a white jacket who could have been the tallest man Mark had ever seen.

"Mr. Soderlind, my name is Dr. Crichton. I was the attending physician when you were brought in. How are you feeling tonight?"

Mark looked out the window and was shocked that it was now dark where the sunlight had been shining through the blinds when he first woke up a second ago. "What time is it?"

"It's just a little after seven o'clock, Mr. Soderlind. Do you mind if I call you Mark?" Dr. Crichton asked.

Mark could sit up a little, and he nodded his head, which caused the room to spin violently. Mark grimaced and raised his hand to his head, feeling the bandages for the first time.

"I'm sorry I wasn't able to make it around earlier, but when I found out that you were sleeping, I thought it best if I let you rest. I'm getting ready to go home for the night, so I wanted to make sure I spoke with you before I left," Dr. Crichton said as he pulled up a chair next to the bed. The nurse quietly excused herself.

"Well, I really have nothing but good news for you. You were very fortunate, actually. You were brought in last night with a pretty severe concussion. We've given you several tests, and it looks like there should be no long-term effects, just a real nasty cut on your forehead where you split it open, I'm assuming, as you fell. You'll have a pretty powerful headache for the next few weeks or so, and don't be alarmed if you have some trouble sleeping because that's common for this kind of head injury. Apart from that, you should be just fine in the long run. I'll leave a prescription for you to help with the headaches, and it looks like you should be out of here tomorrow. Do you have any questions?"

Mark delicately shook his head no but did not say anything. He felt so tired even though he had just woke up, but even through the fog of exhaustion, he could tell he was feeling better than when he had awakened earlier.

"I would also take it very easy for the next couple of days; take some time off of work and get as much rest as you can. This accident could have been much worse, so consider yourself fortunate," Dr. Crichton said as he stood up and left the room.

Mark looked out the window and saw his reflection in the glass. The wind was howling outside, and the trees randomly tapped against the window with each gust. He knew he would go home tomorrow, but he knew that the house would be empty. With Alan gone, it was as if the heart was taken out of the brick, wood, and mortar they called a home; and even though it would look the same, it would be nothing more than a lifeless husk. Mark did not want to go back there. He thought of all the times he walked Alan to school and worked at his terrible job; he did it all because he had to care for Alan. He did not have a choice. He was his father.

Penrose Hospital was nice enough to call Mark a cab the next morning after he had eaten breakfast so that he would not have to walk home. Mark had no other clothes than the ones he was wearing when the ambulance brought him in, so as he sat in the back of the cab that smelled like vinegar and curry, Mark was amazed by the amount of dried blood that was on his jacket and shirt. The cab driver was annoyed when they got to Mark's house at having to wait for Mark to find a few dollars inside, and the fact that Mark moved so slowly did not help his temperament either.

Walking slowly upstairs, Mark collapsed into bed but had enough strength to pick up the phone and dial.

"Dad? Are you okay?" Alan asked, his voice shaky with fear and worry.

Even though Jenny had answered, she showed a small level of compassion by letting him talk to Alan; of course, she had not thought to bring Alan to the hospital or offered to help Mark get home, but she felt Mark talking on the phone to Alan would make up for it.

"I'm fine. I just got home. I was worried about you. Are you okay?" Mark said slowly as if he had the world's largest glob of peanut butter in his mouth. Each sound he made reverberated inside his skull, causing the dull waves of pain to return.

"When are you coming to get me?" Alan asked.

"I'm still pretty hurt, so it might be a few days. Are you going to be okay there?" Mark asked, still feeling weak and not wanting to explain any deeper than that.

"Yeah, I guess so," Alan said reluctantly, but then whispered into the phone, "but I still want to fight them, Dad."

Mark managed a wan smile. "I'm going to get some sleep now, but I'll call you when you get home from school tomorrow, okay?"

"Okay," Alan sighed, clearly disappointed he was staying put.

"I love you, buddy," Mark said quietly.

"I love you too, Dad," Alan replied, and he hung up.

It was almost another full day before hunger got Mark out of bed again. It took him a while to become fully vertical, but once he was out of bed, he looked at himself in the mirror and realized that he looked like he got hit by a truck. He had a large contusion above his right eye with four stitches and butterfly bandages pressing his skin together. Shades of purple covered the side of his face like foul watercolors.

The house was silent and devoid of life. As he walked around slowly, doing his best to keep the dizziness at bay, he finally thought of Erica. Unlike his head, his heart did not hurt as much as before. It was like he suddenly had an empty room in his skull; he still wanted her and definitely missed her, but she had made her choice, so all that was left was a blank space in his mind where she once was. He remembered the story of Icarus. Mark had spent his entire life in dark places and escaped into the sunlight for a brief moment, but it was never meant to be.

He was feeling decent enough at this point to get the mail, and as he walked to the curb and opened the box, he saw a small gold envelope with the Benton Academy logo on it.

Hope stirred, and as he walked inside so fast that he was forced to sit down and literally hold his head for a good ten minutes because he thought it might explode, he finally opened the letter and read:

Dear Mr. Soderlind,

We wanted to thank you for alerting us to your incredibly gifted son, Alan. The kind of talent he has shown at such a young age is exactly the kind of student we seek.

The painting you sent us was, in a word, magnificent. The board of directors described it as "breathtaking" and "the work of a future Master."

We would be honored if you would consider allowing The Benton Academy to be a part of your long-term educational plans for your son. We have already been in contact with several leading artists, not only in the United States, but also in Italy and Paris, who, after seeing your son's remarkable achievement, are very excited about working with Alan.

Additionally, we will provide Alan with one of the finest traditional educations available anywhere. With a classroom size of fewer than four students per teacher for all academic pursuits, we have a ninety percent placement rate in the Ivy League as well as Oxford, the Sorbonne, and the Academy of Fine Arts of Verona, Italy.

We are disappointed, however, to inform you that due to budgetary constraints and lower private donations in the last few years, we are no longer offering any kind of scholarships at this time.

Once again, we thank you for your brilliant submission and look forward to meeting with you soon to plan your son's future with The Benton Academy.

* * *

It was another two days before Mark had enough strength to walk down Fillmore Hill to return to work for the first time since the accident.

Even though the doctor had warned him about the headaches, there was no way to understand how much they hurt without experiencing them firsthand. Mark would find himself moaning, curled up in a ball on the couch, clenching his teeth and hoping that the waves of pain would pass him by. It would sometimes go away on its own, but most of the time, the crashing in his head went away only when he fell asleep, which was almost impossible. The only other way the headaches subsided was by taking one of the pills the doctor had prescribed that made him unable to move because of severe nausea they caused.

Mark had woken up this morning like the darkness finally passing into the dawn, and the headaches were gone. Not entirely; they sat at the back of his head like storm clouds on the horizon, but for the first time since he got home from the hospital, he felt he had the strength to function. Sick and tired of being sick and tired, he decided to walk to work just to be sure he still had a job.

As he walked down Fillmore Hill, he could hear the sounds of children at recess in the distance, and it made his heart ache. He knew that Alan would be there and wanted to see his boy more than anything, but he was worried about how the other kids would react. With the scar down his forehead and the bruises on his face, he did not want to embarrass Alan. He had spoken to Alan every day for short periods; Jenny always pulled him off the phone for one trivial thing or another, but that was about all Mark could handle anyway.

Somewhere inside Mark, he knew that Alan would not care, but he also did not want Alan to see him like this. When he was feeling better, he would see Alan, but he did not know if he was well enough just yet, so instead of turning down the street to the school, Mark simply walked straight to work.

He walked into the back of the kitchen and was greeted by cheers, sad glances, and looks that reflected exactly why he chose not to go to Alan's school. He sat in the kitchen as several waiters came back, all telling the story of what they were doing when Mark had stumbled into the kitchen as a bloody, disoriented mess. When Manuel came in the back, he showed real concern for Mark, so much so that Mark was genuinely touched.

He bought Mark lunch, and the two of them talked in the front as the rest of the staff got the restaurant ready to open for lunch. The warm food prepared properly, rather than his own bad cooking, was exactly what Mark needed.

"After the ambulance left, I looked it up and discovered you have six weeks of vacation time. Have you ever taken a vacation, Mark?" Manuel asked, sitting sideways in the booth so he could keep an eye on what was going on around him.

"I took some time off when Alan was born, but that is about it," Mark said between bites.

"Well, I'll tell you what. You go ahead and take that six weeks and get all healed up. When you get back, the manager's job will be waiting for you, but I'll need you to be ready. I can't have someone running this place who looks like he got stepped on by an elephant," Manuel said with a smile.

Mark left an hour later and began to make his way home. The storm clouds of his headache were moving closer, and even with the recent meal, he was beginning to feel lightheaded. When he got to the bottom of the hill, he looked up, and it seemed to stretch on forever. Mark put his head down and put one foot in front of the other, knowing that he would eventually get home if he found the strength to keep going.

I never kissed her.

The thought escaped into the front of his mind like a prisoner dodging the guard and getting past the fence. He had been so careful to keep it all hidden away; the empty room had been shut, so he did not have to think about it, but with that single thought, he could feel Erica. Her hair. Her hands were on the back of his neck. The way she would whisper on the phone late at night. It rushed at him like one of those mile-wide prairie tornadoes that destroyed entire towns and left nothing but toothpicks in its wake.

Yet, it was more. The day he saw her kissing the man, he could now remember the fragile hope and faith in a life together rushing out of his body, and he was again left with nothing. He was so tired that he finally admitted to himself that amidst the pain, the frustration with Alan being gone, and the exhaustion of just trying to function after his accident; he was deeply and profoundly sad. It was a sadness that covered his entire body like thick tar until he could no longer move. Turning away from the traffic, Mark sat down in the dust next to the sidewalk, defeated. He scratched his stubbled cheek and found it wet from his own tears. The emotions he had been through since seeing Erica kissing the other man began to break through his defenses until he could no longer hold them back.

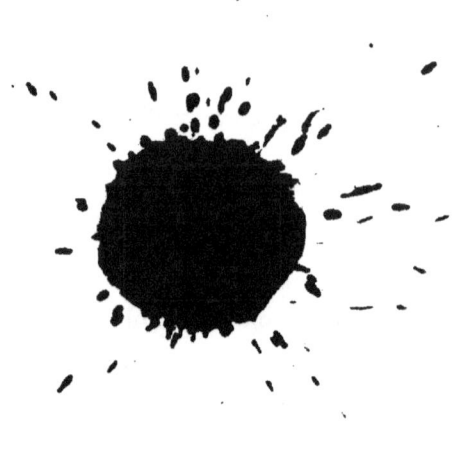

~ CHAPTER NINETEEN ~

Erica had finally reached the end of her rope.

After two weeks, she had not had a single returned phone call from Mark; worst of all, she had just received the paperwork that Alan would be transferring to a new school across town with no explanation whatsoever. There was a feeling that everything had gone full circle. She felt she needed to help Mark remember his priorities as far as Alan was concerned, just like she felt she had to when they first met.

On the personal side, she was upset because Mark had never given her a chance to offer any kind of defense or explanation. He saw her and Tom together and immediately assumed that she was cheating on him, and then disappeared. The fact was that, while she had kissed Tom, it had caught her by surprise. She had decided to be with Mark long before Tom decided to surprise her in the morning; with all of his charm and charisma, Erica had been ready to tell Tom to go away. He handed her the flowers, and before she knew what was happening, he was kissing her. She told him immediately that it was over, and the more Tom pressed, the more Erica's resolve was strengthened...until she felt the tug of a little hand on her skirt. She looked down and was mortified to see Alan looking up at her, but she quickly forgot all about Tom when she saw the look in Alan's eyes. He did not say anything but simply dragged Erica away while pointing at Mark, who was already walking away as fast as he could with his head down.

Erica pulled her Jeep in front of Mark and Alan's house and debated with herself if she would get out of the car. She had already decided that she was going to go back to her family if Mark had really decided to cut ties, but she knew within herself that if she did not see him face to face, she would never know for sure that she had tried everything to make it work with Mark. She owed him that.

She took a deep breath, walked up to the door, and rang the doorbell. As soon as she did, she knew that Mark was home and decided that she was going to knock and ring the doorbell until he came out here and talked to her face to face.

"Erica, please go away. I can't deal with this right now," a tired and muffled voice from inside the house finally broke the silence.

"Mark, just let me in. Please…" Erica said, feeling foolish for talking to the door. "Just let me explain...don't do this. Don't make Alan go to a new school regardless of what you think you saw. He has friends, and I..." She softened her voice. "I want to see you again, Mark."

"What do you mean, a new school?" Mark asked, his voice a little stronger.

Something wasn't right. Erica instantly knew that something was happening that she knew nothing about.

"Mark, Alan hasn't been to school since the other day. I assumed you'd just transferred him..." Erica said.

The silence was as loud as anything Erica had ever heard.

"Mark, is everything all right? What the hell happened?" She was scared, and it was manifesting itself as anger in her voice.

"They've taken Alan," Mark said dully. "His aunt and uncle have filed a custody suit against me, and...they took him." He punched the door in frustration with a muffled thump.

"How can they do that?" Erica was stunned. "Mark, please just open the door. We'll work all of this out...Mark?" She waited, and the cold began to creep in.

She knew that he was still on the other side of the door. She searched for the right words that would let him know he could trust her; if she could just get him to open the door and to look at her in the eyes, she knew that would be all it would take. When the door was unlocked and began to open, Erica sighed in relief and then was shocked to her core by what met her on the other side.

Mark stood there with his hair as much of a mess as it had been when they first met, but something about his entire being made her think of utter helplessness. When she saw the fresh scar on his forehead and the bruises across the right side of his face ranging from yellow to blue, everything she thought she understood was immediately null and void.

"Mark! What happened?" Erica gasped, instinctively reaching up to touch him, but Mark stepped out of her reach, leaving her hand in the air and the uncomfortable silence Erica had thought they'd left behind long ago. Mark mumbled about the concussion, the time he had spent in the hospital, and everything that had been taking place since. He explained his constant pain without looking at her and how he just wanted a chance to heal before he started the fight to get Alan back.

"I just need some time to...heal," Mark sighed and began to shut the door again. Erica put her hand up, stopping him. "Mark, let me help. This has been nothing but a major misunderstanding. I'm here to..." she began to plead her case, but she could tell Mark was not listening. He was there physically, but the door was already shut mentally, doing everything possible to keep her out. She pressed on regardless.

"Mark!" Erica snapped. "You are not going to cast me out like this. What you saw, or what you think you saw, was not important. I'm sorry he dropped by, and I'm sorry he kissed me, but I was just as surprised as you. I picked you, Mark! You are the one I want to be with," she said emphatically.

"I can't," was all Mark could say.

"You can if you choose to, Mark! All you have to do is to let me in again. Just give me a chance to show you that it wasn't what you thought it was!" Erica cajoled.

"I CAN'T!" Mark yelled.

Erica was taken aback, and for the first time, she thought it best to leave. She could tell by looking at him that shouting at her had hurt him physically, as he grabbed his head in his hands and leaned heavily against the wall for support.

"I can't do this," he said in a tight voice. "I don't have the strength to think about you anymore. All I can do is wake up and try not to hurt as much as I did yesterday; until, at some point, I can find enough strength to fight for Alan. I just...I just don't have anything left," Mark said quietly.

"Mark, I can help. If you would just let me in, I can help." Erica said, trying to catch his eyes as he stared at the floor.

Mark sniffed as though he was trying not to cry from sheer exhaustion. "No, you can't. As much as my head hurts, I can't... be with you. I can't allow myself to be hurt like that again. Erica, I don't sleep because all I can think about is you. I miss you more than I have missed anything in my life, but I can't be...I can't be that person right now. I don't have the strength to keep going, get Alan back, miss you constantly, constantly see you kissing that guy, and... I just can't," he said with finality.

"Just let me help you," she wasn't accepting defeat yet. "I can help! You don't need to be alone in all of this." Erica stepped towards Mark, but he stepped back like a scared animal and put his hand on the door.

"So, that's it? You just decided that you miss me so much, but you won't let me back in even though I'm standing right in front of you begging you too?! Everything you saw and feel right now is based on nothing more than a major misunderstanding," Erica said, trying not to genuinely panic. "Mark, I know I hurt you, but it's not what you think! It was nothing. It just happened. There was nothing I could do. Please, Mark, just let me…"

"If I let you in again, you will totally destroy me. Can't you see that?!" Mark pleaded. "Can't you see that if I open up, if I let you in and let you take care of me like my heart is telling me to do, you will destroy me? I let you disarm me, and seeing you with him was like a bomb exploding inside me. All I can do now is try to pick up the pieces. I'm sorry, and I love you more than anything I've ever known, but it's too much for me. I'm sorry," Mark said as he tried to shut the door again, but Erica didn't budge, and he stopped himself from shutting it completely.

"What about Alan? Do you really think it's fair for those people to ruin everything we've been working towards? Everything *Alan* has been working towards? You can't just let them take it all away from him!" Erica said defiantly.

"You just don't understand, Erica," Mark said weakly. Erica noticed how he was beginning to lean on the doorframe a little more and now looked even paler and was beginning to sweat. Whatever had happened to him, it was clear that he had not recovered yet.

"Mark?" Erica said, reaching out for him. He jerked away from her hand as if it would burn him. The strength disappeared before her eyes reemerged, and Mark stood straight once again. Erica could not help but wonder how long he could force himself to hold on.

"You don't understand," Mark said again.

"Then make me understand! I absolutely hate that I'm standing here and apologizing for allowing us to become so close. And then I think I should have never...." her voice trailed off. "I know I'm not sorry about discovering how special and amazing Alan is. He deserves better than this. He deserves..."

"Better than me, right?!" Mark shot back, catching Erica off-guard. "Don't you think I know that? Don't you think I know that Alan deserves so much more than I'll ever be able to give him? Every day, I wake up in fear, knowing that one day Alan will catch on to how useless his father is. And I know that one day, he will look at me exactly how you're looking at me now."

"That is not what I was going to say, and you know it," Erica said defensively.

"Does it really matter?" Mark asked in a sarcastic tone.

"Of course, it matters!" Erica shot back. "Alan needs us...you right now. If you wait any longer, then this opportunity will pass you and Alan by, and there will be no way to recover what you are losing right here, right now. Let me help. Let me do anything. Just don't give up on this, don't give up on Alan."

"I have not given up on my son, and I never will!" Mark yelled again, and it felt like thousands of jagged glass shards rattled around in his skull.

"You could have fooled me," Erica said so quietly he almost didn't hear her.

Erica braced herself for Mark to say something horrible and escalate the argument to the next level where they both would say something they would regret, but at the same time, would make splitting apart in the short term justified and therefore easier to deal with. Mark said nothing, but a strange look came over his face; his strength had given out, and thankfully, Erica saw him swaying a second before he collapsed entirely, and she was able to help him gently to the floor just inside of the door. She laid his head in her lap and hugged him with all her strength, praying secretly to God that He could pass her strength to Mark.

"Why won't you let me help you?" She sobbed repeatedly as she rocked him while his breathing began to calm.

They sat there as the cold breeze from outside blew over the two of them softly. After a few minutes, Mark's body relaxed into Erica's arms, and he began to sleep. Erica twisted herself around, shut the door, and leaned up against it while refusing to let go of him. She stroked his hair, suddenly noticing how the giant bruise on his face extended well past his hairline and across his scalp. She found herself mortified and angry while pitying Mark all at the same time. How had he let everything get so far out of control so quickly? Still, she also knew that he was doing the best he could all by himself.

Thinking of Alan's aunt and uncle using Mark's injury to destroy his world was the most repugnant act she had ever experienced. She finally began to realize why Mark could not ever welcome her back into his life. Alan was his entire world, and Mark had just started to let her into that small existence when she ruined everything. The butterfly effect took over in a room like that, and even the smallest transgression could only have disastrous effects. She had not fought hard enough to help him, offended by what she thought had happened, and now it was too late. She could blame Alan's relatives for their actions, but had she been any better?

Maybe the difference was that she could do something to help Mark, even if he did not want her to. Considering the shape he was in, there was not much he could do to stop her anyway.

She woke Mark up just enough to get him up and over to the couch, and she then set about trying to make things right. She knew that she had blown it, but the least she could do was to go out with a bang so that one day when he thought back on her, he would remember she had at least tried to make up for what she had done. Or failed to do. Once Mark was on the couch, she looked around the house and saw he must have stopped cleaning since

Alan was no longer there. Even though there was so much to get started on, a little cleaning to tidy up and help Mark would not be a bad thing.

During the third load of laundry, she found the pictures. She had always wondered what Alan's mother looked like, and stared at the picture of the baby Alan in his mother's arms. She could see that Alan had inherited many of her features. Even though they had talked about it (hadn't they?), Erica had always wondered what had happened to her. How a woman could ever abandon her only child without so much as an email now and then was a complete mystery to Erica. Walking downstairs to check on Mark, she wondered if she could be capable of doing the same thing. If she had a child, could she ever walk away? *No*, she firmly said to herself. Apart from losing Mark, not getting to see Alan or work with him on his art was heartbreaking. Not knowing what would happen to Alan in the coming years would be a constant source of frustration to her; she was in awe of his talent, in awe of his spirit. Erica knew she could make these two misfits into her family... but they would never have her.

She sat on the floor in front of Mark and listened to him breathe. The guilt that Alan and Mark had gone through so much pain, both physically and mentally, in the last few weeks while she pouted in her comfortable life was almost unbearable. But there was still a significant puzzle piece missing. Why had the aunt and uncle been able to get Alan so easily? Where did Alan's mother fit into all of this? Where was she? Mark never talked about her, but surely she would want a say in all this. It just didn't make any sense, and it frustrated Erica even more, knowing there was still so much she did not know.

~ CHAPTER TWENTY ~

It was the moment that Mark had been dreading for years, and he knew that there was no way to escape its inevitable arrival. Mark had just hoped he would have had more time.

It was the moment that Alan looked at him with profound disappointment in his father. The same look everyone else in his life had eventually arrived at. It was the beginning of the more profound realization that his father was a failure and nothing more than a dishwasher, unable to provide him anything he deserved in life. Just like Shannon had realized. Just like his mother had realized, Mark now saw the same look in his son's eyes.

"I can't go to the school?" Alan asked, looking at his father, hoping that he had heard him wrong, pleading silently to explain to him what was happening.

Earlier that week, Mark had been forced to convey to Erica the news that all of the hopes and dreams of the last few months had been destroyed against the rocks of the financial reality that Mark and Alan lived in.

When he woke up on the couch and found Erica waiting for him, he showed her the letter from the Benton Academy, and she understood instantly; her disappointment was the final nail in the coffin that had been their relationship. They sat in the living room for an hour in strained silence before she left Mark and Alan's life. Mark wanted to reach out to her and wanted her to stay, but there was no justifiable reason for her to tie herself to the sinking anchor that was Mark's life. With all hope of Alan going to the Benton Academy gone, there was no hope of a new life; just the one that Mark knew all too well, and he would never want that for Erica. It was better that she just leave him behind while there was still enough clarity of thought and lack of obligations to do so.

"But, you said we were going to fight," Alan said, just above a whisper.

Only now, looking into Alan's disappointed eyes, did Mark understand the overwhelming tragedy of the situation. Alan began to cry in bitter disappointment, silently holding onto Mark for dear life. Still small enough to crawl into Mark's lap, Alan did not have the walls around his emotions to keep them suppressed like any adult; his emotions were pure, and they flowed out of him unhindered. Alan cried because he was beginning to understand that sometimes in life, when genies appear, they have to be put back into the bottle unused, leaving you with nothing but the distant taste and memory of what could have been.

They sat silently on the porch of Jenny's and Tyler's home in the fading warmth of the afternoon as the hope and joy of the last several months floated away.

Even in Jenny's anger and bitterness, she could not deny that Alan needed to see his father, even while she dedicated her substantial time and wealth to ripping the two apart. She had agreed to let Mark come over and see Alan, and even though his head still felt as if it was cracking open every time he moved, Mark immediately got on a bus to see his son.

Mark did his best to keep rocking Alan back and forth long after he sensed the boy was no longer crying. Alan did not move, taking comfort in being wrapped in the arms of his father while he was still small enough to do so.

"How's your head?" Alan asked, sitting up quickly as if he suddenly remembered the injury. He reached his small hand up and touched Mark's face, where the bruising had calmed a little and was now only a sickly yellowish green.

"It's better. I think I'm going to try to go to work tomorrow," Mark said, trying his best to put on the best face he could. He knew he could not show weakness here, but the pain was still constant and unrelenting. He had hardly taken the six weeks off he had been ordered to by Manuel, but he had no choice.

"Good, because I want to come home. Aunt Jenny said I couldn't until you felt better." Alan's voice was muffled against Mark's chest.

"I want you to come home soon too. I miss you," Mark said. "It's weird not having you around the house, stinking up the bathroom."

Without looking, Mark could feel his son smile.

"Aunt Jenny also told me that I didn't have to go home if I didn't want to. She says she's going to talk to some people who will make it all right if I want to live here all the time," Alan said.

"Yeah, she told me that too," Mark sighed.

He knew that he needed to get better physically to fight for his son, but the headaches and dizziness kept him from thinking clearly most of the time. He thought about returning to Dr. Crichton again, but the last time he went, they just told him that head injuries like his just took time to heal and offered him more medication that made him feel less in control than the raw pain did, so he refused.

"I don't want to stay here. I want to come home and keep painting if that's okay. I really had fun doing that." Alan said, climbing out of Mark's lap and sitting on the porch next to Mark.

"You want to keep painting?" Mark asked.

Alan shrugged and then responded, "Yeah, it was really fun. I liked it."

"Okay then, when I feel better, I will buy you gallons and gallons of paint, and we will paint every wall in the house. I've been reading about artists, and did you know that all the really great painters did that? They were paid boatloads of money for painting on walls and ceilings." Mark said, trying to sound upbeat.

"Really? So I can paint on my walls anything I want?" Alan asked, cheering up instantly.

"Anything you want." Mark smiled.

"Then, when you feel better, I will paint a giant Darth Vader over my bed. Oh! Then I'll make him step on a space alien octopus kangaroo!" Alan laughed at his own idea.

"It's time to get ready for dinner, Alan," Jenny said, standing in the doorway disapprovingly.

Alan's brief moment of levity disappeared in an instant, and he immediately hugged Mark and did not let go. Mark hugged him back and then slowly peeled Alan off of him, seeing that Alan was on the verge of tears again.

"Listen, Alan. Eat dinner, and I'll call you later. I have to go to the doctor so they can drain my brain and make me feel better." Mark said, making googly eyes and sticking out his tongue.

"Drain your brain?" Alan asked, smiling a little at the joke but unsure if his father was kidding.

"Yeah, they suck out stuff that looks like creamed corn!" Mark said, tickling Alan.

"Eeeeuuuuwwww!" Alan yelled, laughing.

"I'll call you later," Mark yelled after Alan as he ran past Jenny and into the house.

Mark caught Jenny's eye accidentally.

"I hope you feel better," were her words, but her eyes made it clear she hoped Mark died silently in a ditch on the way home.

"No matter what you do, you will never know the bond a parent shares with their child," Mark said as he turned to leave. "In time, you'll be nothing but a distant memory to Alan, and you'll be forgotten because it's not like he loves you now or ever did. On the other hand, no matter what you do, I will ALWAYS be his father." Mark said before walking away, leaving Jenny furious on her porch. The DMZ had been breached, and as Mark walked to the bus stop, he set his will against her. War had been declared, and it would not end until he got his son back.

* * *

It seemed he had been away from The Cage for years instead of a few weeks. Even though he was supposed to begin his management training, he had returned unannounced, so Manuel was still in Denver. Mark decided to do what he knew best and headed into the kitchen and to The Cage.

He now understood the looks of fear and horror on the faces of those who had passed through the restaurant over the years when they were first told they would be working there. The humidity and heat cast off by the industrial-strength dishwasher were overwhelming, and the stench of the giant gray buckets full of discarded food and wine was putrid. This was an awful way to make a living. Just being removed for a short time made Mark wonder how he was ever capable of working in such a horrible environment for as long as he had.

Standing outside of The Cage, Mark had the realization that the weeks he had spent away from this place was the longest he had ever been gone since the day that he started.

He had done a sufficient job of fooling everyone that he was feeling up to working again. The scars and the swelling were small enough now that everyone believed him when he said he was ready to return to work. What he was careful to avoid talking about was the constant pain and dizziness. He needed to get back to work and show that he could care for Alan. Whatever discomfort he was experiencing had to be set aside until he had Alan back. Once that was accomplished, Mark had already decided that he was going to sell the house and get as far away as he could from Tyler and Jenny as possible. One of the advantages of working in a franchise was that he could move and pick up where he had started in just about any city he chose. Now that he was being groomed for a management position, he would even start making more money than ever before. It would be a hard transition for Alan, but Mark would ensure he found a city with an art college so Alan could keep training. It may not be the Benton Academy, but it certainly would be better than nothing.

Both he and Alan had prepared themselves to leave Shannon behind when planning to go to Boston. It was a hard and terrible choice, but if Shannon ever woke up to find her family gone, Mark seriously doubted she would care.

He stepped into The Cage with a sigh and began his day. Small things were different simply because other people had moved things around while he was gone; but within a matter of minutes, it was as if the time he was gone had been no longer than a lunch break. Dishes and silverware began to flow from into The Cage, and Mark began to try to stay ahead of the tsunami as best he could. It was a series of tasks he had done thousands of times, over and over, for twenty years and...

Mark stared at the gray tray full of dishes and did not know what to do with it. He knew he should know what to do, but in a split second, that part of his brain had closed down, and he could not access it. There was no pain or strange sensations, and that was when Mark knew something serious was happening. The pain had been constant, and suddenly, in a single heartbeat, it was gone... but he could not remember what he was supposed to do. He reached over to grab a bottle of water, but his right hand did not move. Fear was beginning to rise inside him, as he knew something was really wrong with him, but his mind refused to cooperate. He was thinking clearly, but his body was not responding. Standing in the middle of The Cage, he suddenly understood that he was trapped inside his own body.

He watched the kitchen and the wait staff run around, trying to take care of the chores in front of them. He tried to call out but found that the only sounds coming out of his mouth were not words but grunts and groans that made no sense and were so quiet they were lost under the sounds of the kitchen.

More gray buckets of dishes were tossed on the rack before him as he stood there helplessly. Each bucket put into the rack in front of him at eye level made Mark feel he was being sealed away in a tomb. He knew he had to get someone to notice him before they put enough bins on the rack so that no one could see him.

Mark found he could move his left arm but not his right. He did not test to see if his legs were working, fearful of collapsing in the kitchen for a second time. Slowly, he reached over to a wine glass near the sink, trying to only move his left arm in fear of losing his balance. With his fingers reaching into the glass, Mark was able to grasp it firmly in his hand.

Mark braced himself and threw the glass across the room where one of the line cooks was cutting vegetables. The glass shattered at his feet.

"Hey! What the hell?" the line cook shouted, jumping back in surprise. "That's not funny, you jackasses!" Seeing no obviously guilty parties, he threw a dirty look to the kitchen over his shoulder and returned to cutting carrots, swearing under his breath.

Mark waited, then tried to look around to see if there was anything else to throw within his reach. Done with his carrots, the prep cook got out a broom and began cleaning up the glass on the floor when he happened to look over at The Cage.

Catching his eye, Mark did his best to wave and make a sound, but all that came out again was another grunt. The prep cook finished sweeping up the glass, then headed over to Mark to give him the much-needed ass-kicking for throwing the glass. Thankfully, the waitress that had been spying on Mark and Erica saw what was happening and was able to get to Mark first.

"Hey, are you okay?" She asked, standing at the opening of The Cage.

Marked looked at her from behind, terrified eyes not knowing what to do, still unable to move.

"What's wrong with your face?"

~ CHAPTER TWENTY-ONE ~

It had been Terri Evens' idea for Erica to take a long lunch with her in the teacher's lounge. Erica made it clear that she was not interested, but Terri reminded Erica that she was her boss and that you should never refuse when your boss invites you to lunch.

It had been several weeks since Erica had spent any time with Terri, and Erica wasn't sure if she was in trouble for her job performance lately or because she had essentially dropped off the face of the planet in regard to their friendship.

They sat through the entire lunch without a word of any substance passing between them. Terri had brought in a salad for the two of them, and when the bell rang, causing the few remaining teachers in the lounge to leave, Erica knew that whatever the real reason for the lunch was about to be made clear. Terri had made arrangements for Erica's class to be watched by another teacher so they had the rest of the afternoon in the most secluded place of the building for Terri to say whatever it was she needed to say.

"So, when are you moving back to the east coast?" Terri wasn't going to beat around the bush.

"How did you know?" Erica asked, surprised. She had made her final decision only a few days ago and had told no one.

"Well, for one, you haven't been here in weeks. I mean, truly been here one hundred percent, going back to ever since you and Mark broke up and Alan was transferred," Terri said gently.

"I've been doing my job," Erica tried not to sound defensive but failed miserably.

"Honey, your worst day as a teacher is better than most people I got around here. I'm not talking about your job. I am talking about you. You've checked out, and I can't think of anything keeping you here. Add heartbreak to the mix, and it seems like the most logical step is to retreat back home." Terri said, looking at Erica intently.

"I miss him... I miss both of them," Erica sighed heavily. "I know it's stupid, but for a brief moment, it was...miraculous. Alan is just amazing, and it breaks my heart knowing I will never know anyone with this little boy's talent. The chance to teach, the chance to be a part of all he is and all he will become, is the opportunity of a lifetime. And on top of all that, I just loved him as a kid, you know? With all the children we deal with, he's the only one that makes me want to stop what I'm doing just to hear what he has to say. If I had to pick what my child would be, it would be as close to Alan as possible." Erica felt tears rising and fought them back.

"So you miss Alan? You miss the boy?" Terri asked with a raised eyebrow, knowing Erica was still missing the bull's eye.

"Yes... and no," Erica said, sitting back from the table. "I miss Mark too, but that's harder to put my finger on."

"Do you love him?" Terri asked.

"I would, if there...if I knew what he was keeping from me. Not that it matters anymore, but it's driving me crazy." Erica said, running her hands through her hair. "The entire time we were seeing each other, there was a wall between us. He never kissed me;

not a single time. He never let himself go. He stayed behind that wall of his. We were so close to being something really great, but, in the end, he couldn't...." Erica dropped her arms and sat back again.

"That shouldn't be too surprising considering everything they've been through," Terri said carefully.

"What do you mean?" Erica said, genuinely confused.

"With the trial and what happened to Alan's mother. You can't expect someone to go through all of that and..."

"Wait, what trial?" Erica asked incredulously, interrupting Terri.

Terri was taken aback, and looked at Erica the same way she might look at a student when they answered one plus one equals five.

"You don't know?" Terri asked, leaning forward.

* * *

Mark knew it had been a mistake to leave Alan with Shannon the minute he walked in the door. He immediately sensed the frustration that filled the air like a putrid smell, and he began taking off his jacket quickly while hoping to find Alan as quickly as possible.

Earlier that morning, Mark was surprised to be awakened by the smell of bacon and the sound of Alan's laughter. Still rubbing the sleep out of his eyes, he was shocked to find that Shannon and Alan were in the kitchen, laughing and playing while fixing breakfast.

"Dad!" Alan ran to Mark, giving him his morning hug. "Mom's going to fix breakfast!" Alan sounded like an excited puppy. "Do you have to work today?"

"Yeah, I do," Mark said, trying not to look as confused as he really was. He couldn't remember the last time Shannon had eaten with them, much less in such a jovial manner. Not really knowing how to handle the situation, Mark stood in the living room looking into the kitchen and waiting on Shannon to confirm the news.

"I thought I'd stay down in the Springs for the weekend. I haven't had much time with Alan lately, so you can go to work, and I'll take care of him today," Shannon said to Mark, doing her best to put on a pleasant face. He wasn't sure, but for an instant, he saw something in her eyes that told him something bad had happened. She was apparently serious about being around for a while, but if Mark had to guess, she was not doing it for Alan.

Cautiously, Mark stepped away from the kitchen and returned up the stairs to shower as quickly as he could without saying anything. Shannon being in the house was one thing, but her coming home wounded, for whatever reason, was something that Mark knew would not end well. But what could he do? She was Alan's mother, and regardless of her mental state, the idea that she was actually making an effort with Alan for the first time since she had given birth to him was something Mark did not want to stand in the way of, but he at least wanted to watch for a while.

He got dressed quickly and went back downstairs, knowing that he had a full hour before he had to leave for work to make an assessment of how things were going. In the worst-case scenario, he *could always take Alan to work; it was frowned upon, but if he needed to do it, he would not hesitate. By the time he made it back downstairs, Alan was sitting on the couch with Shannon watching one of his many cartoons and doing his best to explain it to Shannon. She was relaxed and smiling, something Mark had not seen in a long time, which made the whole scene even more surreal. As much as he knew she was his wife, the casual Shannon put him on his guard more than the stressed Shannon because it was such an unknown entity. Without interrupting them, Mark scooped some of the breakfast leftovers out of the pan, sat at the kitchen island, and did his best to watch the two of them without appearing he was watching them.*

Shannon asked questions about the ridiculous show, laughing with Alan as he tried to explain the chaos of sounds and colors.

By the time he was ready to walk out of the house to go to work, Mark was cautiously optimistic. Shannon had stayed calm and relaxed as if a tremendous burden had been lifted off of her shoulders that she had been carrying around for the last several years. Somehow the weight was gone, and the Shannon Mark had known long ago had mysteriously reappeared.

He was not foolish enough to think that their problems were over, but he hoped as he walked to work that maybe they were leaving the dark place they had been parked in for so long.

Mark called home three times that day and talked to Alan, who seemed to be having the time of his life while finally getting to spend time with his absentee mother. Whatever had happened to Shannon, she had been able to keep it up all day, and for the first time in as long as he could remember, Mark was looking forward to seeing Shannon when he got home.

But when he opened the door, and the house was ominously silent, Mark knew that all he had hoped for was for naught.

He was halfway up the stairs, headed to Alan's room when he saw Shannon sitting on the couch with the wine glass in hand. Mark instantly knew what was happening and froze.

"I don't know how you do it," Shannon said without looking over her shoulder toward Mark. "I... wasn't cut out for this. I tried, Mark. I really tried." She took a long swallow of wine and looked out the window blankly.

"Shannon... where is Alan?" Mark asked, holding his breath.

"Is that all you care about?" Shannon asked with increasing venom. "Where is Alan? Where is Alan? Don't you want to know why I'm here? Why I've been stuck inside this....hellhole all day?"

Mark looked towards Alan's room at the top of the stairs and saw that his bedroom door was closed. The house felt palpably strange, as if every object in the house was also holding its breath, waiting for the inevitable explosion. Mark took two more steps up the stairs and Shannon turned around with her eyes on fire.

"What do you think, Mark? That I would hurt Alan? Do you really think that I'm such a monster? I put him to bed because he wouldn't shut *up. All day long, just talking and talking! I couldn't take it anymore, so I told him to go to bed an hour ago," Shannon said flatly.*

"Let me just check on him and I'll be right back," Mark offered.

"I was having an affair with my boss, and he not only dumped me yesterday, but he also fired me," Shannon said in a defeated tone, downing the last mouthful of wine from her glass before throwing it with all her might against the wall.

* * *

"What?!" Erica exclaimed, then putting a hand over her mouth in embarrassment at her shocked outburst.

Terri looked at her, trying to reconcile the situation in her mind. The confusion visibly soon gave way to pity, and Terri sat back in her chair while giving a long hard look at Erica, as if she was assessing if Erica was putting her on. Then she began to pack up her lunch without saying a word.

"I don't think that I should be the one to tell you the rest. If Mark thought it best to keep it from you, then it's not my place to spread gossip. I can at least do that much for him," Terri said.

Erica sensed that the missing puzzle to all she had been through was in front of her and reached over and grabbed Terri's hand. "Please, you have to tell me! You don't know... I've been going crazy trying to understand what I have been missing. Terri, if we're friends, then... please."

"I can't," Terri sighed. "Haven't you noticed the way that the other parents act around Mark, how they avoid him? To their credit, they let their kids play with Alan, but I'm sure you've noticed he isn't part of any group like the other kids. All because of this, and all I know is what the news said, which I believe is highly suspect at best."

"The news?"

"Yes, the news!" Terri said, pulling her hand away. "You really don't know, do you?"

Erica sat back in her chair, knowing she could not force Terri to tell her anything she did not want to. Hearing that Mark and Alan had been on the news regarding something that caused them to become social outcasts was so shocking to Erica that it felt to her that her world had just been turned upside down and shaken.

Watching her friend's pained expression, Terri took pity on Erica and, with a deep sigh, pulled her chair around next to Erica and, with cautious tones, began to speak.

"It happened last year when Alan was just finishing up first grade. To Mark's credit, Alan has adjusted to everything beautifully, all things considered. When you discovered Alan's talent, I thought it was a way the universe balanced it all out, to be honest. After all, they'd been through, the idea that Alan would have such a wonderful gift seemed to almost make up for everything... almost. I also thought you were part of that puzzle. To have a woman as impressive as you are, Erica...to find Mark and to help him... it was as if everything was finally being healed, and all the crap those two had to put up with was being paid back tenfold," Terri said, more to herself than to Erica.

"I still don't understand..." Erica said, feeling deflated.

"Of course, you don't," Terri said with a tight smile, finally telling Erica the full story she knew she should have long ago.

"We know the signs of child abuse and what to look for in a child. We also know what to do if a child's mother shows up with a bruise. We have been taught and trained to look for these signs, but when was the last time you even thought to look for those same signs in a father? I saw Mark every day. I saw the bruises, and I saw all the signs. If it had been a woman, I would have done...

something, but in this case, I never even thought twice about it."
Teri said sadly.

"Mark was..." Erica said, stopping short and trying to grasp the idea.

Terri leaned over and put her hand on Erica's arm. "He hid it well. I don't even think Alan knew what was happening until the incident...and regardless of what the newspapers and people around here say, I don't think Mark had much of a choice."

Erica braced herself, knowing the answers she had been searching for were in front of her.

* * *

The sound of the shattering wine glass hung in the air long after the pieces landed and scattered on the floor as tiny, razor-sharp land mines.

All Mark could think about was Alan upstairs asleep. When Shannon got in these moods, she would lose control, and it was all Mark could do at times to keep her anger and hatred focused on him until she would eventually collapse into a ball of sobs and self-pity. Mark knew that he would definitely be her punching bag tonight, and he knew he would not fight back because if he did, she would take Alan away just to spite him; and then the next time she got like this, there would not be anyone there to stand in the way of her getting to Alan.

Mark knew he would have the strength to get through tonight, just as he had every other night. Even if he woke up battered and bruised, it was worth it for Alan to wake up innocent and unscathed.

"Can you believe that?" Shannon asked, petulantly wiping her tears. "After all this time, he calls me into his office and tells me that I'm fired and that he never wants to see me again." Shannon was pacing back and forth in the living room like a caged tiger. "I was stunned, but you know what he told me? He had the nerve to look at me and tell me, 'Go see your kid,' like he was the father of the year or something. He was cheating on his wife with me and has the nerve to call me a bad parent. The funny thing is, I drove straight home to do exactly what he said! Can you believe that?" Mark silently watched her rage building and began to make his way down the stairs again. If Shannon was going to lose control tonight, Mark hoped he could get her as far away from Alan's bedroom as possible. She was crying again, sitting on the couch with her arms between her legs.

Mark gave her a wide berth and began cleaning up the glass, keeping an eye on her.

"I just told you I've been cheating on you, and you don't say anything?" She sounded weak and defeated, but Mark knew better.

Shannon, at least in her own mind, was the perpetual victim. Her pattern was consistent: find even the flimsiest reason that Mark was treating her badly and then blow the situation so far out of context that, at least in her own mind, she was justified in her actions. Mark winced and braced himself for the beginning of the verbal attack that always followed, but this time, he misjudged the situation, and she attacked before he had a chance to turn around.

The first blow landed just behind his right ear and made the entire room disappear for a split second, leaving behind only a high pitch tone that was as painful as it was deafening. She was all over him in the next second, screaming and hurling every foul and disgusting word she could think at him while hitting him as hard as she could with her fists. She kicked and scratched at him, not caring where her blows landed as long as they made contact.

Tonight was different and worse than ever before, and after only a few seconds, Mark realized that she was so far out of control that if he did not defend himself this time, she would kill him. Without thinking, he struck back and knocked her to the floor with a blow to her face, just above her left eye.

"Stop, just stop!" were the only words he could get out.

Shannon stood up again quickly, her eyes narrow and looking as if the devil himself had possessed her. In her right hand was the broken stem of the wine glass, its edges gleaming in the dull light of the room. He had a strange moment of slow-motion clarity as he saw blood dripping from the hand closed around the glass stem, but Shannon was obviously so far gone that she hadn't noticed she had probably cut herself badly when she grabbed the weapon. Mark braced himself for her attack as she rushed at him, screaming incoherently and brandishing the glass.

As he held up his arms to protect his face, he felt her repeatedly slash his forearms; for the first time, he began to realize how much stronger he was than her, and he easily disarmed her by twisting her wrist just short of breaking it.

"Stop!" Mark yelled, but this time with power and authority behind it.

Shannon took more half-hearted swings at him, but he had her under his power, and she quickly gave up.

But just as he relaxed his grip on her, she gave him one final look and bolted upstairs toward Alan's room. Mark chased her, but she reached the door first, and as he arrived at the top of the stairs, he saw the single, most evil moment any parent could ever witness. Even as Alan was still half asleep, Shannon picked him up out of his small bed and began to punch the helpless child in the face as hard as she could. Mark moved towards them and cried out, but everything moved in slow motion. Each step took an eternity as he helplessly lunged forward, unable to stop her fist from connecting with his son's angelic face. The way Alan's shoulder was bent wrong from when she had jerked him helplessly from sleeping in his bed, and the sounds of her assault, were all instantly branded forever into Mark's mind.

Mark did reach Alan, but somehow it was not Mark. A monster within Mark was unleashed, and this new person did not think about what he was doing; he simply reacted. He punched Shannon between her wild eyes with a blow so powerful it broke two of his knuckles.

She dropped Alan and stood dazed as her knees began to quiver and give out underneath her. Alan was now screaming helplessly at their feet, and Mark grabbed Shannon by her throat while dragging her out of the room as she choked and tried to breathe.

The monster stood there with no expression, no thought to what he was doing, simply resigned to nothing more than killing his wife. The monster would not stop, despite the pain in his hand screaming out to him or the blood flowing freely from the cuts on his forearms mingling with the blood flowing from Shannon's split face. Yet somehow, the monster heard the cry of the boy. The monster felt the hand tugging at his shirt, trying his best to pull him away from his prey.

The real world came crashing back down in an instant, and Mark let go of Shannon, who collapsed in the hallway just outside of Alan's door and only a few feet away from the stairs. She coughed and choked as the air began to rush back into her lungs through her bruised trachea. Mark held onto Alan, crying hysterically in pain and sheer terror. Mark bent down and began to pick him up when he saw Shannon standing once again. He pushed Alan behind himself as he stood up and prepared for another onslaught...

The end of Shannon began with a simple slip of her foot on the top stair, causing her to lose her balance and fall backwards down the staircase towards the front door. Mark was suddenly aware that, once again, time had slowed to a crawl as he watched the look of surprise come over her face as her hands reached for nothing but thin air.

Her body rolled over, pinching her neck unnaturally, as she fell down the stairs and slammed into the front door. Her clothes were twisted and bent *around her, and she did not move. Mark stood at the top of the stairs and did nothing, frozen. All he could think was that she must have blacked out before her head hit the tile at the bottom of the stairs because she never tried to stop or brace herself; she just rolled down the stairs like a rag doll.*

She lay there, and the sound of the cracking and snapping bones as she fell seemed to echo off the house's walls.

Mark knew he should do something, yet he stayed on top of the stairs and looked down as she lay on the floor against the front door, and she still hadn't moved. He kept waiting for her to get up at any moment and come racing back up the stairs in a murderous rampage, but she simply lay there in a gruesome heap. Blood started to pool and spread slowly, first under her head and then across the white tiles with the consistency of syrup and darker than any blood he had ever seen.

Turning around, Mark picked up Alan and walked him into his bedroom. The small boy sometimes cried until he threw up, so Mark held him close for several minutes and walked around the small room in a circle until Alan was calm enough to lay down.

When he was finally able to get Alan to sleep, Mark walked out of the room, half expecting her body to be gone, but it was not, and the blood continued to flow.

* * *

"What was clear was that Mark was defending Alan and that he went a little temporarily insane," Terri mused. "But the prosecutor went after Mark for two reasons. First, was the bruises on her neck from where Mark had choked her."

Erica had stood up and was leaning against the wall, unable to process what she was hearing. "He choked her?" she asked in a small voice.

"As Mark described it in court, he lost control when he saw her hitting Alan. He felt guilty and mortified that he had choked her, but considering the circumstances, that part was understood," Terri explained.

"But Mark doesn't have a violent bone in his body!" pleaded Erica. "He ... I just can't imagine what it would take to get him to..." she said, rubbing her hands through her hair.

"I think seeing your child beaten before you would do that to almost anyone. That part of the story, just about everyone understood. If it had only been that, I think they wouldn't have charged Mark at all," Terri said.

Erica sat down on the floor and just looked at Terri. She had been completely unaware of all these sordid details, yet as much as it sounded impossible to believe, it explained so much. It explained why Mark clearly wanted to be with Erica but never let himself be vulnerable around her. It explained why when she hurt him, he shut down and completely cast her out. After being in a tragedy on this scale, would she have acted any differently?

"What really made the news was that even though it was easily proven that Mark reacted impulsively to protect his child, it was the blood stains on the back of his pants that made the DA think something more sinister had happened," Terri began.

* * *

Mark could hear Alan crying in his bed as he looked down the stairs at Shannon's body again. He knew somewhere in the back of his mind that he should be doing something and trying to help, yet he did nothing until he saw that Shannon was still alive.

Her ring and pinky fingers twitched and then he saw that her eyes were open and looking around the room. Instinctively, he moved back towards Alan's room, but he stopped when he saw clearly for the first time that she was looking at him. It was not a look of panic or of pleading, it was the same look Shannon always had when she looked at him: deep, undying hatred. Mark stopped, and before he knew it, he was simply sitting on the stairs, looking down at her quizzically as she silently watched him.

If I help her, all she'll do is hurt Alan again, was the single moment of clarity passed through Mark's mind. At that moment, he knew what he was going to do, but for some unknown reason, he got up, walked to her body, and sat down next to her, feeling the sticky warm blood quickly soak through his jeans.

"I'm sorry I couldn't be better or more for you, Shannon." Mark began as he took her cold, limp hand while her eyes looked up at him with hatred and horror. Mark knew that if she could move, she would have by now, but her eyes told him that her brain was still functioning...at least for now. At the current rate, she was hemorrhaging; it was only a matter of time. When she was gone, he would call the police and suffer the consequences, but the most important thing was that Alan would be safe.

Mark sat calmly and watched Shannon's eyes dart frantically, and then she surprisingly began to cry as her fate dawned upon her silently. No help was coming or any quick release from the pain; she was dying in the home she despised while the man she threw her life away on did his pathetic best to soothe her passing. Her hateful tears could have burned acidic holes through the floor.

He silently waited for her eyes to close finally, and once he knew they would never open again, he slowly picked himself up and walked over to the phone to dial 911. They asked him to stay on the phone, but after answering their questions, Mark climbed the stairs again and looked in on Alan, who had drifted off to a fitful sleep.

Mark slumped down in the boy's doorway, exhausted. He looked at his caked and bloody forearms and vaguely wondered how many stitches he'd need this time. By the time the paramedics burst in through the door and found him, he had joined Alan in sleep.

* * *

"She didn't die?" Erica asked, not knowing what to think about anything any longer. The entire story of Mark's past was like small shards of glass cutting into her emotions. How could she have spent so much time with Mark, and considered making all the sacrifices in the world to be with him, yet be so utterly clueless about who he was? It seemed impossible, but the pain in Terri's eyes told her that every horrible part of the story was true.

"Because Mark sat by her and did nothing to help her, the DA tried to charge Mark with second-degree murder and then negligent homicide. However, Mark's attorney made it public that Mark had been abused for years and that Mark had only defended himself and Alan, and sitting next to her was simply the act of a man in shock. Needless to say, Mark got off, but it didn't stop the public debate about spousal abuse. While some tried to make Mark a hero, others made disparaging remarks about his manhood and cowardice, just awful things. The only thing he wanted was to be left alone." Terri went on, "Eventually, the news of the trial went away, and the entire city moved on to the next big story, but I always wondered how being exposed the way he was affected him. As long as I've known him, Mark has kept to himself, and the idea that something so personal was broadcast across the entire city must have been devastating."

"He never said anything. Not a single word about it." Erica said, now sitting on the floor across the room from Terri.

They sat in silence for several long minutes.

"I don't know what to do with this." Erica finally said quietly.

"Part of me wants to go to him and tell him that I know everything and that it just doesn't matter to me," Erica said, stretching her legs out while looking at the floor as if she was unaware that she was speaking out loud. "But I can't. Worst of all, even if I could justify what he did in my mind, he still won't have anything to do with me."

Terri picked up the remains of her lunch, tossed it in the garbage, and then sat on the floor next to Erica.

"I don't know how I managed to be on the wrong side of every problem with Mark," Erica sighed as she stared blankly across the room. "Each time I think I know exactly who he is, he turns out to be the opposite. At first, I thought he didn't care for Alan because he wouldn't send him to Boston. I thought he was selfish, and then he turns out to be this great guy who loves his son more than anything. So then I relax, thinking that maybe there could be something between us, only to find out he tried to kill his wife." Erica laughed in disbelief. "What the hell is wrong with me?"

"Don't be so hard on yourself," Terri offered. "Or on him. What would you do if a man charged into your classroom with a gun? You'd fight to the death to protect those children. You know Mark; would he do anything less for Alan? I've always thought that if Mark was simply responding to being hit by Shannon that this would have happened a long time ago, but it was only after that woman turned on Alan did Mark react. Even with what happened, I have difficulty condemning him for fighting back."

Erica could not argue the point, but she could also not reconcile that Mark had kept all this from her the entire time they had been together. She sat there, with Terri as a comforting presence, and stared blankly at the floor, hoping that a sign from God Himself would point her the way.

She did not have to wait long.

The door opened, and the school secretary poked her head inside. She was not flustered or surprised that Terri and Erica were sitting on the floor in the teachers' lounge; she just motioned for Terri and stepped out of the room.

Terri patted Erica reassuringly on the knee and then stood up and walked out the door, straightening her clothes as she went. Erica watched her leave without saying anything.

As she sat there, Erica realized she wanted out of Colorado as quickly as possible. With all that Terri had just told her, she felt betrayed by the entire city. Why hadn't anyone told her? Then she thought of the woman that approached the table at the Broadmoor who seemed to be keeping a secret about Mark but, for some reason, held her tongue at the last minute. Erica finally stood up, frustrated that everyone around her had known all of this, leaving her to stumble along in the dark, only to find out when it was too late to ask any questions and too late for it to matter.

She knew it would take more time than she would have alone in the teachers' lounge to figure all of this out, but it was behind her, and as soon as she got back to Boston, she would figure it all out. She knew she was going to walk away, try to get up to Denver tonight, and get on the first flight back home. It was, without question, time to move on and put all of this behind her.

She went back into the hallway and saw Terri and the school secretary speaking just a little down the hall. Terri held up a hand for Erica to wait for her. Something about the look in Terri's eyes made Erica stop.

Terri approached Erica and then simply said, "Come with me."

Erica followed her as she stopped by her office to grab her coat before heading into the parking lot.

"Terri?" Erica finally said when she realized Terri was walking faster and faster to her green Honda Passport.

"Trust me. Please. You need to come with me; I'll explain on the way." Terri said forcefully while unlocking the car door to the car with her keychain remote.

Erica was puzzled but climbed into the passenger's side.

Terri did not say anything until they were out of the parking lot.

"I just want you to know that I'm here for you," Terri began, and Erica tightened her throat. Emotionally, she already felt like Swiss cheese, but she knew from the expression on her friend's face that whatever strength she thought she had left was about to be torn away. "It's Mark.... he... Erica, he's dying. He's in the hospital, and he's dying, and he's asking for you."

Suddenly, all the churning gray clouds in her mind turned black, but Erica knew that none mattered. All she wanted was to get to the man that she loved.

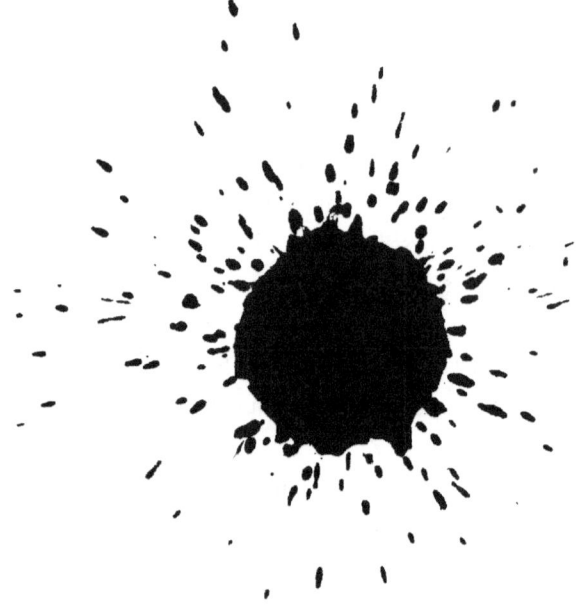

~ CHAPTER TWENTY-TWO ~

The operation had been a failure. It was explained to Erica that when Mark had fallen, he had suffered a subarachnoid hemorrhage, which meant that ever since the accident, a part of his brain had been bleeding. It had been so small at the time of the accident that the hospital did not detect it, so they had sent him home to suffer unimaginable headaches. The doctors said it had been a miracle that Mark had been functioning for as long as he had been, but all Erica could think was that he had been in pain and scared, but worst of all, alone.

It had been two days since Terri had brought her to the hospital, and Erica had not left his side since. Erica had slept in the bed next to Mark and ate every meal next to him. The nurses on the floor had been instructed to help her in any way; maybe it was because they knew they would have to take her out of the room kicking and screaming, or maybe because they knew they had missed the problem when Mark had been in the hospital originally. The best they could do now was to make him as comfortable as possible in his last days. After all, it would not be long now.

Mark had been asleep almost the entire time she had been there, but a few times, he woke up and smiled weakly, seeing Erica's exhausted and tear-stained face. He would reach out and hold her hand for a few minutes and then fall back asleep.

Since the operation last night, Mark had not woken up, and they were not sure he ever would. The damage had been severe; Mark had hemorrhaged at work, had caused extra damage to his brain, and if he did wake up, the doctors had warned her that he might not ever be the same. What he would remember and what would be forgotten was impossible to tell, but they encouraged her to simply wait and see, which was quite possibly the hardest prognosis of any she could have received.

Erica looked outside and saw the bright blue sky through the trees. Puffy white clouds were high in the sky, and all Erica could think about was how winter was finally over. It was a perfect 65 degrees outside, yet Erica could feel nothing but a chill in the air.

She had never been around death other than her father, but that had been nothing more than a phone call. When she saw him, he was resting peacefully in a coffin at the front of a church. She had been able to say goodbye to him then, but it was like bidding someone farewell at an airport: impersonal and in public. Yet laying in the bed next to her was a man whose pulse she could feel gently beating in the limp hand she held onto. She watched him breathe slowly in and out. She could feel his presence in the room far beyond the broken shell he was still trapped within. Her soul reached out to his on an invisible level, and she hoped that even in the darkness, he would know she was with him. Even as he lay there with tubes in him and machines monitoring every detail of the mechanism they still called a body, Erica could not wrap her mind around the fact that Mark would no longer be. Mark would no longer exist at any moment, and as she sat there, the anger and futility of the entire situation began to overwhelm her.

What was the point in bringing someone into the world only to torture him for forty years? Erica thought of the stories he told her on the way to seeing his mother and all the horrible things he had to endure as a child. Somehow Mark had managed to escape that demon, only to be tracked down by another and tortured anew. Then, the one time Mark lost control and fought back, he was brought out into the open like a criminal and humiliated publicly.

Finally, a miracle happens, and a light at the end of the tunnel comes out of nowhere; a chance to go to Boston with a woman who loved him and a child who could make Mark rich and content for the rest of his life, yet God could not allow even that happiness. No, Mark had to see Tom kiss her, and then as he fled, he slipped on ice and set off a time bomb in his head that was now doing its best to kill him as slowly and painfully as possible.

It was futile. It was pointless, yet through it all, Mark had carried himself with a quiet dignity. His wife abused him, and Mark did not complain or tell sob stories; he simply kept moving forward. What was the point of it all? What was the point of God creating a man in these days where everyone believes themselves to be a victim of anything that causes mild discomfort? After heroically enduring this torture, he sees no reward but simply dies anyway at the end.

Erica turned and looked at Mark, moving her chair so she could rest her head on his shoulder. There was an intimacy about this time, she realized. Where a man like this deserved to have multiple generations surrounding him on his deathbed, he got Erica. She would be the one holding his hand when his spirit left his body. She wondered if, like an electrical current, she would feel it when he was gone.

She wanted to be closer to him than just sitting beside his bed. She slipped off her shoes and, being careful of the machines, slowly climbed up in the bed with Mark, curling her body around his. She felt his peaceful warmth and his heartbeat over his entire body as the tears began to flow unrestrained. She pulled the blanket back over herself and lay quietly with him until, for the first time in days, she fell into a deep sleep with her head on his chest, listening to his heartbeat. As she drifted off, all she could think was that she should have done this a long time ago.

~ CHAPTER TWENTY-THREE ~

Tyler stood at the door of Mark's room and watched as Erica quietly lay next to Mark. Without her knowing, he had watched the two of them from a distance the last few days but never like this, never witnessed anything so intimate. She silently stroked his hair and looked down at his face, taking in every inch of who he was, knowing their time was growing short. The moment was not lost on him, and he immediately felt as if he would be sick.

Tyler walked away from the room and frantically searched for fresh air. There were no open windows on the hospital's fourth floor, so he quickly walked to the elevators, feeling that he would suffocate if he did not get outside. He jabbed the down button as fast as he could, knowing full well that it would not cause the metal doors in front of him to open any quicker. When they finally slid open, he prayed that no one would get inside the white mirrored box with him. The man he was, or, rather, the man he used to be, was beginning to wake up inside, and the reality of what he had been planning to do to Mark was slowly revealing itself to be the horrendous act that it was, and Tyler had to suppress the urge to scream.

How had he let it get this far? As each floor passed with a small ding, he hoped that he could make it outside before he threw up.

The doors finally opened, and Tyler did not hide his haste. By the time he reached the massive glass outer doors, he was ripping off his tie and breathing deeply, trying to calm his stomach and nerves. He bent over near the bushes, not knowing if his remorse would cause him to vomit, wishing it was as easy as purging his stomach to get rid of this crushing guilt.

There had been something about the way the woman had been looking at Mark that had brought everything back into perspective, and in that sweet moment, he knew Mark had been right all along. All the small little justifications regarding having Alan around the house and how it would save his marriage seemed to blow apart like charred pieces of paper caught on the wind. His defenses and faulty rationalizations were exposed like raw nerves under broken teeth. The horror of what he had been doing to please a woman who could never be pleased was suddenly obvious.

Standing up, he finally felt that his stomach would cooperate, so he walked over to a cement bench overlooking the vast parking lot. Taking off his coat, he wiped his sweaty temples and realized that his life would never be the same when he finally stood up to Jenny.

He played the last couple of days out again in his mind, and he knew when he must do. Tyler reached for his phone and began making the calls Mark had asked him to when he saw him a few days earlier. As he did, he could only think that Mark, with all his faults, had been right about everything and stronger than them all.

Tyler was getting ready for a City Council meeting a few days earlier when he got the initial call from the hospital. Even though he and Mark had never been close, they were still family, even if the women in their lives loathed the idea. Tyler immediately canceled his meetings and rushed to see what help he could provide.

Mark was in bed and looked as if he had been hit by a bus. The doctors went over his condition with Tyler, telling him that Mark would need surgery quickly but that they had postponed it until they could speak with him. They informed Tyler that there was not much time left and quietly left the room.

Mark could only talk in whispers at that point, but his intensity was powerful. He asked if Tyler would accept his power of attorney, just in case something happened and he did not wake up after the operation. Tyler agreed, telling Mark that he would contact an attorney friend to have the paperwork drawn up and set over immediately. Mark seemed to find a little comfort in knowing that at least that small part was taken care of. But there was one more thing; Mark motioned for Tyler to lean in closer and made his last request. When Tyler left Mark's room a few minutes later, he had no intention of completing that request. He would assume a power of attorney to ensure that all of Mark's affairs were handled, but his request was so impossible that Tyler never seriously considered it. As horrible as it sounded, Mark would be gone soon anyway, and no one would be the wiser if he chose not to honor it.

Over the next few days, as they waited on any news regarding Mark's condition, Tyler did not tell Jenny or Alan anything that was happening other than that Mark was going to be at the hospital again, so he would not be able to call. The news seemed to drain some of the life out of Alan, who was still obedient and a shell of his former self. He had looked forward to the call from his father each day, even if it had only been for a few minutes. Alan still functioned with the loss of the connection with Mark, but his joy was visibly gone.

Maybe it was the shadow of the boy, or maybe it was the look of love on Erica's face as she lay with Mark that snapped Tyler's soul awake again. As he made phone call after phone call outside of the hospital, he finally felt like the man he had always wanted to be for the first time since all of this began. He knew what he was doing was right; there was no question about it.

After an hour, he finally hung up his phone, knowing that everything would be set right with a single signature. Tyler was finally able to breathe in deeply. When he finally stood up, Tyler knew he was back on course, even though Jenny would never forgive him for what he had just done. She would not leave him because she wasn't strong enough to function on her own, but she would retreat even farther into her bitter, ghostly existence. It didn't matter though; he had enough love for both of them. He would remain steadfast and strong because it was the only thing he knew how to do anymore.

The one badge of honor he would walk away with after the entire ordeal was that he had been able to pull himself back from the brink of his own destruction. Knowing the whole situation was over, only now did he clearly see that the act would have cost him everything if he had not awakened before stealing Alan from Mark. Instead of Jenny becoming the silent and resentful wraith, it would have been him. Alan would have been raised in a house where both adults were damaged beyond repair, and, eventually, the boy would grow up damaged himself. At least now, Alan would be allowed to become everything he was supposed to be.

Tyler had a smile on his face as he walked back into the hospital. As the elevators opened again, Tyler promised that Alan would be cared for no matter what. His nephew was the closest thing he would ever have to a son, but he would do this on Mark's terms and not Jenny's, which would be enough.

Walking into the room, he did not immediately call attention to himself. He looked at Erica as she lay with her head on Mark's chest, silently resting, hoping she would understand how important the next ten minutes of their lives would be.

He cleared his throat and waited.

Erica sat up and saw Tyler standing in the doorway. His hair was a mess, and he was holding his wrinkled jacket in his hands. His tie was loose, and the top button on his shirt was unbuttoned, revealing the collar of his t-shirt underneath. He looked like a stockbroker after the market had crashed.

Erica did her best to sit up, but she was careful not to disturb Mark.

Tyler waited patiently as Erica slowly climbed out of bed. She looked tired but was still strikingly beautiful. *Good for you, Mark.* Tyler thought to himself.

Erica walked over to Tyler with her arms wrapped around her even though the room wasn't cold. Tyler held out his hand to her. "Ma'am, my name is Tyler Parker. I'm Mark's brother-in-law."

Erica had been reaching for his hand, but with the revelation of who he was, she stopped short, and a scowl covered her face as the look of sleep left her eyes and was quickly replaced with hatred.

"You shouldn't be here," Erica said as she backed away from Tyler. He said nothing but watched as she fixed the covers around Mark.

"I understand why you would feel that way, but there is an important piece of business that we need to discuss," Tyler said, putting his coat down on the back of the chair across the room before sitting down to let her know he was not going to be so easily dismissed.

Erica sat silently next to Mark and did her best to ignore Tyler.

He decided to try again and cleared his throat tactfully. "I don't know if you knew this, but Mark asked that I be given his power of attorney while he... is... unable to make any decisions," Tyler said, leaning forward with his elbows on his knees. "So it is my legal duty to inform you of Mark's last request should he not... wake up..."

Even though the words were delivered as lightly as possible, they still carried the weight of a fist. Sitting by his side had been one thing, but the idea that there were those who were making plans, assuming Mark would be gone soon, brought the entire experience to another depth. A single tear escaped her eye and burned down her cheek. As much as it hurt to hear the words coming out of Tyler's mouth, she would not give him the satisfaction of seeing her any more distraught than she already was.

"Erica, his last request was for me to take care of all the legal requirements so that you could adopt Alan," Tyler said simply, not knowing how else to put it.

The words hung in the air for an eternity before they could finally sink into Erica's consciousness. Her defenses were shattered, and she looked at Tyler, helpless to stop herself from feeling the enormity of the request.

"What?" was all she managed to whisper.

"Before he asked them to send for you, he made sure that I understood that he wanted Alan to be with you. For you to be Alan's legal guardian. His...uh...mom," Tyler stammered. "It was his last request."

"I can't..." Erica said, looking down at Mark's sleeping body. "I can't... it's too much."

For the first time since she arrived at the hospital to care for Mark, Erica felt as if she wanted to run out of the room, into the fresh air, and all the way to Boston.

"Erica, it was his last request," Tyler said gently but urgently.

"But he isn't dead yet! Why would he do this?" Erica cried, looking at Tyler, terrified.

"You're the only one who really understands what Alan can be," Tyler said, standing up and touching her shoulder.

"I can't!" Erica blurted out, just below a shout. "I... I... don't even have my life together. I was going to leave for Boston to try and figure out what I'm supposed to do." She looked out the window as though she was contemplating jumping.

Tyler slowly turned Erica around on her feet until she looked into his eyes. He gripped her shoulders gently but firmly and said, "You know Mark, and you know that Alan was his entire world. He would not have made this decision lightly, and He. Chose. You." Tyler squeezed her to emphasize his point. "He must have loved and trusted you very much, but this is not a request you can just refuse. If you ever cared for him, you must do this."

Erica looked at Tyler and wondered how a man who looked so genuine and honest could have been responsible for turning the last weeks of Mark's life into such a living hell.

"I thought you were trying to take Alan from Mark," Erica said, stepping back, feeling her hostility rise again.

"Yeah," sighed Tyler, visibly deflated. "Thankfully, I've put a stop to all of that." He turned around and sat back down.

"There is a thing about love that people who haven't been together for decades don't understand. I would do anything for my wife because she is as much a part of me sometimes as I am." Tyler said with his head in his hands.

"You tried to take Alan away! So while..." Erica began hotly, feeling the anger of the situation rise in her again. Tyler simply raised his hand in a signal to let him finish, and Erica stopped.

"What I did was... wrong. It was wrong beyond anything I have ever dreamed I was capable of doing, and there is no way of making up for it. I can, however, make sure Alan is taken care of for the rest of his life the way Mark would have wanted, and that begins with you." Tyler said. "The only way I could ever make up for what I've done is to ensure his last request is carried out. I hope you understand that it's the only way I can regain my honor as a man and basically be able to live at peace with myself," he explained.

Erica did not answer but simply sat down in her seat and looked at Mark silently. After a few minutes, she reached out and retook his hand.

Tyler watched her, letting her sort out the enormity of the situation inside her head. They sat in silence for a long while, secretly wishing that Mark would wake up and end the tension.

"Tell me about his wife. About Alan's mother," Erica said finally.

It was an unexpected question. Tyler thought about it momentarily but could not suppress a small chuckle.

"She was... beyond horrible." Tyler began. "My wife, who is without question cut from the same cloth, always said that Shannon was on a constant search for the next train wreck throughout her entire life. She was always looking for problems where there were none so that she could take on the weight of the problem and, therefore, be its next victim."

"Where is she now, I mean?" Erica quietly insisted.

"She's across town in a private care facility. It's nice, actually." Tyler said quietly.

"Why did he never mention her to me? Why didn't he tell me what happened?" Erica asked.

"I don't know," Tyler said, shaking his head slowly. "Jenny made a point of telling Mark he was not allowed to see her ever again. She even got a restraining order and forced Mark to sign the divorce papers. I imagine that he was doing his best to move on. Honestly, I didn't know about you until he called me the other day and told me about the adoption request. I guess he was trying to rebuild his life and leave the accident and all the rest of it behind him. I doubt I would have done any different."

"I didn't know about any of it. I had just moved to town and... I didn't know anything." Erica said.

"Does it make any difference?" Tyler asked.

"I just feel that Mark never got the chance not to be anything but alone," Erica said with pain in her eyes. "I am so angry at him that he didn't trust me enough to tell me the truth. Even if it had been for just a few short moments, Mark never gave me a chance to show him that none of it mattered. I wanted to show him that he didn't have to fight for everything all alone."

"What about Alan?" Tyler said. "Alan is going to need you."

"I don't know. How do I take him away from his family?" she asked.

Tyler was silent for a few moments, choosing his next words carefully.

"If Alan stays here, my wife will suck the life out of him," Tyler said firmly. "Jenny and I can't have kids of our own, so she's built up this make-believe situation in her head that tells her that everything will be all right if she could only have a child. But the fact is, she is nothing more than a child wanting a puppy. She wants it, but once the responsibility and the day-to-day tasks become her daily life, she won't be able to handle it. Jenny is incapable of caring for more than one person at a time, and many times, that's even a stretch for her. I wish I could sit here and tell you that Jenny is nothing like Shannon, but she is her sister right down to the fact that she may think she loves Alan, but she will only grow to resent him. At that point, I cannot say she will be any different than Shannon. I thought, like an idiot, that I could shield Alan from it, but I now know that's what Mark was doing this whole time. Jenny thinks she can't have children because God wants to punish her for some reason, but if I'm honest with myself, I think Jenny can't have children because no child deserves to have a grown woman's entire self-worth placed upon their shoulders."

"Do you think your wife might hurt Alan?" Erica asked, finally looking at Tyler.

"Not if I can help it, but what sort of life is that? If she doesn't hurt him physically, she'll slowly drain his life and happiness. Slowly but surely, she'll bury all of her fears and depression inside of him because, let's face it, misery loves company, right? I saw Alan's notebook. I saw how special, how incredibly talented he really is. If he stays here, the first thing Jenny will take from him is his art because she won't understand it. He will never rise to anything greater than her or her way of thinking because she simply will not allow it. She may not hurt him, but she will make him pay dearly for her own inadequacies and insecurities."

"So I'm just supposed to take Alan and run?" Erica asked.

"Yes," Tyler nodded. "Take Alan to that school of yours and ensure he gets everything he deserves in life. It's nothing more complicated than that."

"I can't," Erica said in a strange voice.

"Erica, we don't have time to keep..." Tyler said before he noticed that Erica was laughing.

"The first time I met Mark, I was furious with him because he told me he couldn't send Alan to the school. I got mad because I thought he didn't care about Alan enough to do what was right, but it was just that he didn't have the money," Erica said, wiping her eyes. "So now, *I'm* supposed to do it, and I can't because I don't have the money. How ironic is that?"

Tyler was silent for a few moments, watching as Erica held Mark's hand once again.

"I'll pay for everything," he said, letting her know he wasn't bluffing.

"What? Can you do that?" Erica looked up at Tyler, suddenly not finding the situation funny.

"Actually, Mark will, if you want to be specific. Before the accident, Shannon used to complain that Mark wanted to leave his job all the time. She used to tell Jenny that Mark's only worth was his insurance. Well, not only did Mark's company provide health insurance, but he has been paying into a life insurance program for almost twenty years without fail. I looked into it, and he has over $900,000 payable upon his..." The words stuck in Tyler throat. "From what I can tell, apart from the house, he has no debts. So, after expenses, I think you and Alan will have more than enough to provide Alan with any education available. If you ever need anything over and above that, I would happily give you whatever you need."

"Really?" Erica said, smiling wide and looking back at Mark, wishing he heard the good news.

"I may have acted like a monster, but I just want what is best for Alan. If Mark trusted you enough to want Alan to be with you, then who am I to stand in the way?" Tyler said, standing up and collecting his things while putting on his jacket.

Erica stood up and held out her hand.

"I'm really sorry I was so rude, Mr. Parker," Erica said shyly.

Tyler smiled at her and gave her a hug, which she gladly received and returned.

"When he wakes up, tell him everything is taken care of, would you? I'll be over in the next couple of days with some paperwork for you to sign," Tyler said after letting Erica go. He began to walk out of the door but stopped and turned around.

"I know my actions were inexcusable, but I'd like you to consider letting Alan call us now and then. After all, he is family, and I'm going to miss him more than you know," Tyler said with a small hitch in his voice.

"Of course," Erica said.

The room was strangely silent after Tyler left. Erica walked back to her seat and took Mark's hand. Leaning close, she whispered in his ear as she finally let herself cry. After all the pain and suffering she had been wrestling with, the news that Alan would go to the Benton Academy was the small crack that allowed her emotions to explode.

"You did it, Mark! You did it!" were the only words she could whisper as she held on to him tightly and sobbed uncontrollably as her emotions finally washed over her.

~ CHAPTER TWENTY-FOUR ~

Mark knew that time had been passing by him, but he did not know how to escape the blackness all around him, so he floated within the darkness like a man relaxing on a summer's day on a smooth as glass lake. He was not in pain or scared, he just... was.

He could feel her presence. He could not think of her name (or his own), but he knew she was there, and somehow, just knowing that brought him joy. He heard her talking to him now and then in quiet, muffled tones that he could not quite make out; at times, she sounded happy, and at other times she sounded sad and alone.

He floated along for a while more, but her presence seemed to grow as he allowed himself to be aware of it. He knew he would drift away into the blackness forever if he chose to ignore her. It was nothing to be scared of, just another place to exist, but her presence caused him to stay where he was.

It was when he felt her hand that he suddenly remembered her. Erica. Her name was Erica. She had loved him, and he had loved her. Remembering her name caused him to feel even more joy than before, but something was wrong; something had happened that made Erica sad, and she was trying to reach him.

It was not panic he felt because, in this place, there was nothing but peace, but he suddenly just knew that he needed to be somewhere else, that he should not be where she was.

He tried to think about how he might be able to move from where he was to where Erica was, but he simply did not know how. Mark tried to move, but there was nothing but darkness to hold on to.

"Please, let me see her one more time," Mark prayed.

The light flooded over him, and he was suddenly aware that Erica was sleeping next to him with her head on his chest. Of all the things he wanted to notice about her, all he could process in those first few moments was how her hair had the faintly delicious smell of fruit.

His eyes continued to adjust to being open for the first time in days as he looked out the window and realized that it was night. The room that was bright when he first opened his eyes was actually dark, with only the light from a small lamp on the nightstand next to the bed that seemed to cast more shadows than light.

"Erica?" he said softly.

She stirred and faintly purred like a cat as she tried to speak from her deep sleep.

It didn't matter; he would wait. He moved his arm, even though it caused his head pain, and wrapped it around her the best he could. He lay with her as she moved closer to him... then suddenly sat up and looked into his eyes.

"Mark?" she asked incredulously.

"Hi," his voice was raspy from underuse.

She hugged him so hard that it hurt, but it didn't matter. He did not know how or why, but whatever troubles they had had before had disappeared while he had been asleep. She was here, and that was all that mattered.

If only the pain in his head would go away.

"Let me call the nurse," Erica said, smiling and carefully climbing out of bed.

He heard her bare feet slap the floor as she ran out of the room and into the hallway. A few minutes later, shards of glass were shoved in his eyes as the nurse turned on the overhead lights to examine him. Erica saw him wince and quickly ordered them to turn off the lights.

She sat down beside his bed and held his hand while the nurse talked to Mark about how he was feeling. They found that Mark only had partial movement in his right hand and leg, but other than that, everyone seemed to be cheerful that he was at least awake. The nurse said she would call the doctor at home and get him to come in as quickly as possible. After giving a wide smile to Erica, the nurse left, shutting the door quietly behind her.

"Hi," Erica said softly, touching Mark's face. "Mark?"

Mark realized that the pain had caused him to close his eyes. He opened them up again and smiled at her the best he could.

"How long have I been...?" he began.

"Just a few days," Erica said.

"Where is Alan?" Mark furrowed his brows and closed his eyes again.

"He's with Tyler and Jenny," Erica said confidently.

Mark was taken aback by the way Erica seemed to be so familiar with his horrible in-laws.

"Tyler has been here a few times. It's nothing to worry about," Erica said reassuringly.

Suddenly, the truth of the situation dawned on Mark. She knows...she knows everything.

"It's okay, Mark. Everything is going to be okay. Tyler told me that they were not going to take Alan away. We're going to get you better. And then, even if you don't like it, I'm going to take care of you," Erica smiled.

"I need to tell you something," Mark said.

"It's okay. I know about Shannon and what happened. I'm not going to leave you. I'm going to stay and help you get better, okay? All you have to worry about is getting better," Erica smiled at him again through eyes swimming in tears of joy.

Mark looked into her eyes and knew that it would be.

"I'm so tired," Mark breathed. "There's so much I want...I need to tell you."

"Just rest. We'll have plenty of time. Just take it easy. Everything is going to be all right." Erica stroked his hair and couldn't help but keep smiling at him.

Mark looked at her and relaxed into the peace of what was to come. Just as he sensed her presence in the darkness, he could now sense the darkness around him. Even though he was no longer lost in it as before, he could feel the darkness that once cradled him was now pulling on him as if he was caught in an ever-growing rip current.

"Erica...I have to go now," Mark said in a matter-of-fact tone that was devoid of fear.

The look that crossed Erica's face was how he imagined he must have looked when they had turned on the lights. "No... Mark, please..." she held her hands to her face.

"I'm so sorry," was all he could manage to say.

"It's okay," Erica said, no longer looking in Mark's eyes. Her soft hand patted Mark's chest softly.

"I'm so sorry," Mark said again, pleading.

"Please stop. It's not your fault. It's just life. It isn't fair," Erica touched Mark's face so gently he could barely feel the warmth of her hand. "It's just not fair."

"Did you talk to Tyler? About Alan?" Mark whispered.

"Yes. He's taking care of everything. I'm going to take Alan to Boston this summer, and he's going to go to the Benton Academy in the fall. It's going to be... perfect," Erica said, wiping her eyes and refusing to look at Mark.

"Good," Mark said, smiling the best that he could. "Alan is going to be so happy."

"Why me, Mark?" Erica asked suddenly.

Mark reached up with his left hand and lifted Erica's chin. "My entire life, I have never known beauty. Then suddenly, you were in my life, and all I could see was how wonderful the world really was. You made my tired, pathetic little world alive and beautiful. I want Alan to know the beauty you see in the world, not the misery and ugliness I've known." His eyes were clear as he looked at her.

"How can you say that now, Mark? I hurt you; I let you down when you needed me the most." Erica sighed, fighting back the tears.

"Erica, I need you now more than ever. I need to know that Alan will have the life I've always dreamed of for him. His entire life, I have wanted nothing but for him to feel safe and at peace. Don't you see that the only way for Alan to get beyond everything he has endured in his short life is to see life for what it is and not be tainted by my sadness?" Mark said. "Do you remember that day in the Garden Of The Gods when you told Alan that when he needed to see what he was painting, he should see what was there rather than what he believed to be there? You told him to look for all the small shapes that made up the larger shape? I want you to teach him to see all the little things in life that are good. I want you to teach him to see the beauty all around him so that he will finally forget everything that's happened to him here." Mark felt the fatigue and that weird pulling sensation again but fought to stay in the present.

"He will never forget you, Mark." Erica gulped as she fought through her tears and the rising urge to grab him as if she could physically hold off the inevitability that was on its way to claim him.

"I can't go with you because I can't see beyond the pain anymore," Mark was fighting to keep his eyes open. "I saw Shannon around the house every day after she was gone. The pain Shannon caused has haunted me. I could still hear her in my head, still felt her when she was out of control. I could never see beyond the darkness or the pain of life, Erica. I tried so hard when you came into my life; I would see you and think that maybe the fragments I'm in could be put together again, but I could never see beyond her. I could never get Shannon out of my head."

Mark winced in pain as he grew in frustration. Erica held him closer, stroking his hair slowly. When she looked at him again, he was crying, unashamed.

"Alan is so much more than me... more than I could ever become. I wish I could see him...all he is going to be someday," Mark felt the darkness begin to close in all around him.

"Mark, please don't go. Please..." Erica said as loud as the lump in her throat would allow.

Mark opened his eyes and breathed in deeply.

"You can't go, Mark. I can't do this alone," Erica begged.

"You can, and you will," Mark said. "Erica, I have never loved anything as much as I have loved Alan until I met you. Thank you for that. Thank you for letting me love you."

Erica finally gave in and smiled at Mark. She, too, could sense the current that was pulling him away, and without knowing why, she straightened his blankets, trying to make him as comfortable as possible.

"I love you too, Mark. I will never forget you." Erica said, looking into his eyes.

"I'm sorry I never kissed you," Mark said with a faint smile.

Erica laughed and wiped her eyes. She sat up and gently put her hands on both sides of his face, leaned in, feeling the heat from his mouth, and pressed her lips against his.

The feeling of her lips on his was the single greatest pleasure in Mark's life. He could feel every part of her mouth and smelled her as he slowly finally let go, still feeling her lips on his, and fell forever into the blackness.

Erica felt Mark's spirit leave as she kissed him. His final breath filled her with peace and joy, as if Mark had passed right through her, leaving his love inside her. She sat back down and looked at him with one hand on her mouth, still feeling his last moments on earth.

~ CHAPTER TWENTY-FIVE ~

To Alan, Denver International Airport looked like a giant circus tent. Walking on the polished tile floors, all he could do was look up at the tent structure above him and try to avoid being run over by one of the many travelers rushing to make their flights. It was one of the most marvelous places he had ever been. He looked around for Erica, who was now a few steps ahead of him and watching him with her "serious" face.

Ever since she came to Tyler and Jenny's house to pick him up, she had not smiled once. She had arrived in a cab that smelled like cabbage and burritos, told him she had sold her Jeep, and that they would get whatever car he wanted when they got to Boston.

Aunt Jenny glared at Erica but said nothing before walking back into the house without saying goodbye, just like she had always done with his dad. Tyler helped them with Alan's luggage and hugged Erica after Alan was in the cab. Still, Erica did not smile.

Erica silently sat the entire hour and a half to Denver from Colorado Springs. Alan did not say anything because he could tell Erica was still sad because his dad had died. He did not know how to talk about that, so he found it was better just to be quiet.

Alan was sad, too, and had spent the days that had followed his father's death crying in his room. Erica came over every day before the date of the funeral and took Alan out for ice cream or to see a movie. Tyler seemed to go out of his way to help her, and when she left, Tyler and Jenny fought a lot. Jenny stopped smiling as well, and Alan noticed that whenever he walked into the room, she would leave.

When the funeral was over, Erica took Alan out to the Garden Of The Gods and they walked along the paths without saying anything.

They sat on the same bench where his dad had sat while Alan had painted earlier that year. "There is something I need to talk to you about, Alan," Erica said, still wearing her pretty black dress. "Your dad told me before he died that he wanted for me to adopt you and to take you to Boston so you could go to that school we always talked about."

Alan did not remember much after that because he was so excited to be able to go to the school. During the following week, he and Erica would spend all day planning where they would live and talking to Erica's family about Alan and getting him registered at the school. Even after talking to her family, Alan never saw Erica smile.

He could not help but notice that Erica acted like she did not know what to do with him. When she was his teacher, she seemed happy and always had ideas about what to do, but now she just sat quietly and looked out the window. Alan did not understand why one kid was harder to care for than an entire classroom.

When he asked, Tyler told him to give her some time. Adults sometimes need more time than kids to heal, and Erica was having a "rough time of it," Tyler said.

Alan watched her all the way up to the airport, wondering what their life would be like when they got to Boston. He missed his father, but he realized the night that he learned his father had died that there was something of his father in every one of the pictures he drew in his notebook. He could not explain it, but whenever he finished a drawing, he would lift it up and say out loud, "How's this one, Dad?"

Alan knew that Mark was dead, but no one in the world would ever convince him that his father was gone. He was still with him and always would be; Alan didn't understand why none of the grownups could understand that.

They were walking toward security when Erica stumbled in her heels. Wincing in pain, Erica sat down in one of the many grey seats that were all over the airport. She closed her eyes and held onto her foot.

"Don't worry. I just twisted my ankle," Erica said to Alan as she tried not to grimace in discomfort.

Alan reacted instinctively, climbing into the chair next to Erica and began to stroke her hair like his dad had always done when Alan had hurt himself. "It's all right, you're going to be okay," Alan said softly over and over to Erica, then leaned over and hugged her, wishing that the pain would go away which always seemed to work with his Dad.

Erica looked at Alan; shocked and taken aback by his tenderness.

"Are we going to be okay, Alan?" Erica asked while looking at the boy intently.

"Yeah, I'll take care of us," Alan said confidently.

Whatever trappings of sadness Erica had been covered in fell away at that moment, and she smiled at Alan with her perfect smile for the first time in what seemed like forever.

She grabbed Alan, hugged him, and kissed him on his cheek, to which Alan squirmed and giggled in mock horror.

"One thing you're going to have to get used to is that I will never forget to kiss you and tickle you as long as you live," Erica said, wrestling with the boy as he shouted in the throes of pure joy.

As they got up from the seat, Erica held the straps of her heels in one hand and Alan's small hand in the other, and they walked to the plane in a quiet, peaceful silence.

The End

www.ingramcontent.com/pod-product-compliance
Lightning Source LLC
Chambersburg PA
CBHW070445030726
47503CB00004B/905